SEARCH
AND
DESTROY

Also available from James Hilton and Titan Books

Fight or Die (June 2017)

SEARCH AND DESTROY

A Gunn Brothers Thriller

JAMES HILTON

TITAN BOOKS

Search and Destroy
Print edition ISBN: 9781783294862
E-book edition ISBN: 9781783294879

Published by Titan Books
A division of Titan Publishing Group Ltd
144 Southwark Street, London SE1 0UP

First edition: June 2016
10 9 8 7 6 5 4 3 2 1

A CIP catalogue record for this title is available from the British Library.

Printed in the USA.

This is for my Wendy, the centre of my universe.

PROLOGUE

Jeremy Seeber huddled in the doorway of the mini-mart, his raised jacket collar proving little protection against the chilling rain that beat down without pause. He glanced back over his shoulder, half expecting the man to be behind him. He'd spotted the same man four times that day, twice on foot and twice in a car. A small, nondescript guy, really, but it was his eyes that had caught Jeremy's attention. Unblinking ovals with the colour and compassion of slate.

There was no one behind him. The breath that he hadn't realised he was holding escaped in a soft *whoosh* of relief.

The London Eye, usually a looming presence, was all but invisible in the downpour. He cast another furtive glance up and down the street, then began a waddling run, half crouched as if that would protect him from the rain. Something that felt almost alive coiled in his stomach, threatening to bring back his lunch. Damn, what had he gotten himself into?

He was already pulling the padded envelope from under his coat as he approached the FedEx depot. Soon he was back on the street, empty-handed. Ten minutes later, he slipped his key into the lock of his front door. A glance each way along his road satisfied him that he was not being followed after all. He allowed himself a brief smile. He knew he was probably overreacting, but the events of the last few days had shaken him to the core.

Better safe than sorry, he thought, as he shook off his waterlogged overcoat. "Tess, I'm home."

There was no answer. He called out again. All he could hear was the steady timpani of the rain lashing against the door. There was none of the usual bustle of his wife's presence—no smells of cooking, no music playing softly. Just the damned rain.

"Tess..." The coiling sensation gripped his abdomen again.

The floor beneath him seemed to give way as he stepped into the kitchen. Tess was on her knees, surrounded by four men. Her hands had been secured behind her back and the gag that encircled her face stretched the corners of her mouth into a taut grimace.

Jeremy lunged forward, reaching for his wife. He heard the distinctive sound of the revolver being cocked. The gun was pressed against the back of Tess's head.

Jeremy managed an impotent, "Please, don't—"

The man with the slate-coloured eyes put a finger to his lips in warning.

The others closed in on him.

Outside, the rain continued to fall.

1

Andrea Chambers watched the desert pass by through half-closed eyelids, her arm resting against the cool glass of the car window. She hadn't stirred since they left the outskirts of Las Vegas earlier that afternoon, drifting in and out of sleep. The excesses of the previous night were really taking their toll. Her gaze slid to her brother Greg sitting up front, lounging in the passenger seat, a large map spread over his lap. His partner Bruce was at the wheel, hands in the textbook ten-two position.

"Where the hell are we?" asked Greg. The late-afternoon sun glowed as twin reflections in his mirrored sunglasses.

"You know where we are," snapped Bruce. He shot him a scathing look, then returned his gaze to the road, endless grey asphalt stretching into the distance. Greg scowled back theatrically. Andrea smiled and closed her eyes. *Best to leave them to it.*

"If I knew where we were I wouldn't be asking, butt-head."

"Why did we come to Nevada, Greg?"

"I know *why* we're here, I just don't know where *here* is."

"You're the one reading the map."

Andrea heard the sound of paper crumpling, then Greg's mischievous laugh.

"How's Sleeping Beauty?" asked Bruce.

Another laugh. "Three-quarters legs with a set of boobs and a head on top. And not much of a drinker!"

There was the sound of a cap being unscrewed.

"She'll kick your arse," warned Bruce.

"Maybe."

"It's your funeral."

Andrea's eyes opened, but too late. She let out a howl as ice-cold water soaked the front of her white T-shirt. Greg was twisted round in his seat, clutching a now-empty water bottle in one hand. She sat up, gasping, then slapped at her brother's head with both hands.

"Greg, you idiot! You could have given me a heart attack!"

Greg giggled as he ducked to avoid his sister's assault.

"For a so-called serious journalist, you're very prone to exaggeration."

Andrea felt a sudden surge of panic and her eyes snapped to her MacBook on the seat beside her. It was safe in its padded carrycase, only a few drops of water on the material. Relief. She wiped it with the back of her hand, then took a calming breath. "Where are we?" she asked, brushing yet more water from her torso.

"Ask Davy Crockett, he's the only one who knows," said Greg.

Bruce took his hands off the wheel long enough to spread

them wide. "We're in the great Tikaboo Valley on Highway 375... The famous Extraterrestrial Highway."

To illustrate the point, he slowed the car as they approached a yellow diamond-shaped road sign. On it a UFO hovered over a cow, beneath which were the words OPEN RANGE. Bruce pointed at the sign. "Shouldn't that read 'open season'?"

"Holy crap, this is gonna be great." Greg laughed again, and turned in his seat. Andrea rolled her eyes at him, but she shared his excitement.

She'd struggled to pick up jobs as a freelance journalist over the last year. It seemed London was saturated with freelancers, with an ever-increasing number of them clamouring for the few precious assignments each week. The competition was cut-throat and Andrea had only scored this job thanks to her friendship with the editor of the newly launched travel magazine, *World of Adventure*. A week-long trip to Nevada, all expenses paid, to report on the growing UFO-spotting subculture that buzzed around the outskirts of the legendary Area 51. The story was to be a double-page spread. That would pay the mortgage on her apartment for the next two months.

Andrea had told her younger brother about the trip, and Greg had promptly invited himself and Bruce along. The expenses didn't cover Greg and his partner Bruce, but Bruce made a healthy living at a big music company and had paid for their travel without hesitation. She was glad of the company and Bruce had offered to drive. Mr Dependable loved the open road while she hated driving abroad.

She felt a pang of envy as Greg rested a hand on Bruce's

knee. They looked good together, comfortable. Greg was tall and a bit on the skinny side while Bruce was a little portly around the middle. The contrast seemed to suit them. She often warned Greg not to mess things up. Good men were hard to find, a fact she could personally attest to.

She peered into the sky. The sun was a dark orange and the distant mountains were reduced to a ridged silhouette. No houses, buildings or shopping malls to blemish the landscape and no mysterious lights in the sky—yet.

"Just remember I'm here to work. So keep quiet if I'm interviewing anybody."

"Andrea, I'm just here for the hot dogs, beer and cowboys." Greg waggled his eyebrows.

Bruce shot him a look.

"Relax those green eyes; you know I'm a one-cowboy guy."

"Maybe *he'll* take you out," said Bruce, pointing to a bearded man at the side of the road. He was busy relieving himself against the rear wheel of his Toyota pickup.

He gave a casual wave as they passed but didn't stop urinating.

"GBA," said Greg.

"Huh?"

"God Bless America."

"Hey, slow down." Andrea pointed to a mailbox standing at the side of the road. "That's the black mailbox. I read about it on the plane. That's where a lot of the sky-watchers meet up. It's the only landmark for miles."

"Black mailbox? But it's painted white..." Bruce noted.

"Yeah, there's a story behind that," Andrea waved her

copy of *The UFO Handbook* at him. "The mailbox used to be black but one of the secret experiments over in Area 51 made it change places with its opposite in an alternative dimension."

She saw Bruce raise an eyebrow in the rear-view mirror. "What a lot of crap. Somebody just painted it white; probably because the tin-foil-hat brigade kept hanging around."

Andrea laughed, nodding. "I just said it was in the book. I don't believe everything I read."

"This from a journalist."

"Shut up, Greg." She pointed at a cluster of vehicles at the side of the road. "Hey, that looks promising." A dozen or so shadows moved in the fading light and someone had lit a campfire. "Pull over."

Bruce did as requested. Andrea was out of the rental car before the wheels stopped turning. She quickly brushed the front of her wet T-shirt and Greg laughed as she checked that her breasts weren't too visible through the cotton.

The group definitely belonged to the UFO community. A young man sporting the traditional I WANT TO BELIEVE T-shirt waved as Andrea approached.

"To boldly go where no man has gone before."

Andrea turned and frowned, all business. "Greg, you'd better zip it. I don't want you getting clever with any of these guys out here. Just remember, we're in the middle of nowhere, so if anything bad happens…"

Greg opened his eyes wide with innocence.

Bruce leaned over and gently kissed him on the cheek. "Behave."

* * *

Two hours and a few beers later, the three returned to the rental Jeep. Greg was feeling buzzed and it was only partly the beer. Andrea was smiling to herself, reading through her notes. It was good to see her happy. Not that he'd say so out loud.

"You get anything good?" he asked.

She grinned at him and waved her notebook. "I got some great material, I can't wait to write it up. A lot of urban-legend stuff, but that's part of the appeal. I'm working the 'what people are *willing* to believe' angle. They were a friendly bunch. Most of their information is unusable—'a friend of a friend saw something in the sky' stuff. Nothing I can substantiate, just colour." She pulled out her phone. "Damn. No reception."

"Twitter addict. Guess your army of followers will have to survive without constant updates."

Andrea punched him on the arm. "Right, like you're any better? Your photo essays on the changing face of breakfast hardly set the Internet alight."

Bruce flapped his arms placatingly. "Okay, children, let's just agree that you're both the cream of the Twitterati. Now. Where next? Back to Vegas?"

Andrea grinned and tossed her useless phone on the Jeep's back seat. "I got a tip from one of the older sky-watchers. According to 'Darrell from Seattle, aged forty-six', the Power-lines Overlook is nearby. It's high up; you can see right into Area 51." She turned to Bruce. "It's up a pretty steep hill, rough terrain. Think the Jeep can handle it?"

Bruce puffed out his chest. "Point the way."

The vehicle didn't disappoint them, but the going was slow as darkness fell. The pitted track up the hill made the

Jeep rock violently. Andrea clutched her laptop close.

The overlook was formed of a natural plateau some thirty feet in circumference on the summit of a wide peak. Rows of power lines stretched into the distance, each connecting pylon weathered to a dull grey. The ground was rock strewn and hard underfoot. Surrounding Joshua trees cast eerie shadows as the Jeep's headlamps illuminated their spiny boughs, pointing toward the sprawling Air Force base at Groom Lake—Area 51. Stepping from the Jeep, Greg stared at the lights below, and wondered how many of the tales were true. Did the highly classified area really hold crashed UFOs, the Spear of Destiny, or the Ark of the Covenant? He wasn't convinced, but they were still great stories.

He watched as Andrea walked to the edge of the plateau, her laptop bag swinging at her side. He held Bruce back, sensing that she would want a moment to herself. The constellations were bright above their heads, much brighter than back home in London. But he wasn't really one for stargazing. He pulled his iPod from his pocket. This view needed some accompaniment.

"Would you look at that," said Bruce.

"Yeah, it's really something." Greg didn't raise his eyes from the player.

Bruce swatted the iPod. "Would you put that away! We're supposed to be enjoying our quality time together and you'd rather listen to Miley friggin' Cyrus."

The player slipped from Greg's hands. "Hey, you'll break it!" He bent over to pick it up. "And it's Beyoncé, if you must know..." He glanced up at his partner.

Bruce was looking at the centre of his shirt, his hands

held in angry claws. The look on his face was something Greg had never seen before, a mixture of agony and shock. Like one of those weird Japanese Kabuki masks.

What was his problem? Greg opened his mouth to speak, then stopped. A dark crimson butterfly was spreading across his shirt. "Bruce?"

Bruce took one step forward, then collapsed face down.

"Bruce?" Greg's voice jumped an octave.

Greg fell back against the side of the Jeep, his head whipping round desperately towards Andrea. She was staring out over the valley below, her back to him, hands on hips.

He tried to shout her name.

2

Danny Gunn opened one eye. The view was much the same as when he'd fallen asleep; dark hills and a straight highway that stretched into the distance. He glanced at his watch. He'd only been asleep for twenty minutes. He stretched his shoulder, which emitted an audible pop, and sat up fully in the passenger seat. The windscreen of the Winnebago was huge, and the dashboard console below had more dials and digital displays than most aircraft.

"Wakey, wakey, eggs and bakey."

"I haven't heard that in a long time." Danny grinned over at his older brother, who was driving. "I would kill for some real eggs and bakey, though."

"I'll pull over in a couple of minutes. There's an abandoned casino up ahead. We can stop there for the night."

"Abandoned casino?"

"Yeah, it looks kinda spooky but there's plenty of parking space."

"Is there a diner nearby?"

"No, but I've got a month's worth of food in the back.

You'll just have to put up with my cooking tonight. I've got enough steak and eggs to feed a football team."

"Sounds good to me."

A few minutes later, Clay Gunn steered the large Winnebago off the main highway and allowed it to roll to a gentle stop. Danny peered out. The jagged silhouettes formed by the buildings appeared somehow medieval in the failing light.

"Is that the casino?"

"Yeah. It's been empty as long as I can remember."

Danny shook his head. He'd never heard of a gambling joint going out of business before.

Clay leaned forward on the steering wheel. "I guess it couldn't compete, with Vegas just an hour away."

"Suppose." Danny opened the passenger door and stepped down. "Nature calls."

"Don't be pissin' on my wheels, y'hear?"

Danny thumbed his nose in mock annoyance and headed towards the derelict building. He recalled something his drill sergeant used to say: "If you want to find a man or a dog just look for the nearest tree and they'll be pissing on it." And, sure enough, his feet gravitated towards the wall. When nature had run its course, he scooped up a handful of rough sand and rubbed his palms together; an old trick he'd learned in his army days when water was in short supply. He smiled and clapped his hands to disperse the dust. There was a top-of-the-range RV a few metres away that offered better amenities than his house back in England, yet here he was pissing in the sand. Old habits died hard.

He closed his eyes and listened to the sounds of the

evening. Almost no noise, save for the soft *tink-tink-tink* of the RV's massive engine as it cooled. It provided a welcome change from gunfire. He pushed the thought from his mind. This was time to relax, no muss, no fuss. Some quality rest and relaxation with his older brother. He smiled as he caught the smell of fried potatoes on the night air, and returned to the Winnebago to look for them.

Clay was already busy in the kitchen area as Danny entered. He looked oddly at home surrounded by the beech panelling and the brass swan-shaped cupboard handles. A single photograph was fixed to the side of one of the cupboards: a woman, caught mid-turn. Her smile was spontaneous and her brown eyes crinkled at the edges with undisguised mischief. Danny watched as Clay paused, eyes on the picture. He touched a finger to her nose as he often did when reminiscing, a delicate gesture for a man topping six foot.

A Jace Everett CD was playing but not at the ear-wrecking decibel level that Danny usually had to endure. He didn't mind country music but enjoyed a variety of styles, unlike his brother. At least Jace was modern country with a rock-guitar twang to it.

"Need a hand with anything?"

"Nah, I've got it covered," replied Clay brandishing a spatula coated with some dark and sticky sauce. Danny knew better than to question his culinary skills. "Wanna beer?"

"Sounds good."

Clay pointed to the curved refrigerator door. Danny pulled it open and lifted out two chilled Coronas. A sheen of condensation coated the glass. "Got any lime?"

Clay clicked his tongue.

"I guess we can rough it."

"Yeah, they made you tough in the British Army, all right," laughed Clay.

"Hey, I once went two weeks without toilet paper." Danny winked and took a long pull on the beer.

"Did you get a Scouts badge for that?"

"What, the chapped-arse merit badge? No, I never did."

"Harsh."

"Indeed…"

Ten minutes later Danny accepted a plateful of steaming food. Both men moved to the dining area at the rear of the RV and chewed through two of the best rib-eye steaks money could buy. With thick-sliced potatoes and fried eggs on the side, the meal was simple but perfectly cooked.

"You could make a fortune selling these," said Danny between bites. He wiped Budweiser barbecue sauce from his chin. He saw Clay's eyes flick to the photograph. His voice dropped.

"I hardly cooked anything while Diana was alive."

Danny smiled in sympathy. "I don't think she married you on the promise of your short-order cooking skills."

"I guess not."

Danny raised his beer. "To fallen friends and lost loved ones."

"Ay-men to that."

The brothers lapsed into an easy silence as another track began. The country guitar twanged a sorrowful melody.

"Got any Duran Duran?"

Clay scowled. "I'd rather stick cactus spines in my ears than listen to that noise."

Danny started to sing. "Her name is Rio and she dances on the sand…"

"Please stop."

"Just like that river twisting through that dusty land…"

"I can see I'm going to have to put a bullet in you to shut you up."

Danny paused. "You can't shoot for shit. I'm surprised the Rangers ever let you near a rifle."

Clay narrowed his eyes, sighting along two fingers. "At this range even I couldn't miss."

"Ah, you Yanks are all the same; spray and pray. You couldn't hit a bull's arse with a blunderbuss." Danny knew the mock insult of calling a Texan a Yankee would do the trick of lightening Clay's sombre mood.

"And you Brits are so stiff-assed that you don't need a gun. Just shove a round up there and let one off."

Both brothers grinned. It was a routine that never seemed to get old. They clinked their bottles together in mutual respect.

Danny turned in his seat, favouring his right hip. The web of recent scar tissue on his left side was still tender.

3

Andrea stood at the edge of the outlook, taking in the view. The evening air smelled and tasted so different from the city air back in London. So clear, fresh and somehow raw. And it was so quiet. No blaring taxi horns or wailing sirens. She hugged herself against the evening chill, enjoying the moment. It was good to see Greg happy. He and Bruce were the real deal.

A noise—a strange, unfamiliar sound she couldn't identify—made her turn towards the Jeep. The towering pylons stood sentient; their only contribution to the night was a low and constant hum. The twin beams of the Jeep's headlights cut into the twilight, the glare ruining her already meagre night vision. Her brother was huddled over something, something dark and still. His mouth was working like a fish out of water. His eyes met hers.

A low metallic *whoomph* sounded through the evening air. The middle three fingers on Greg's right hand detached themselves in a spray of crimson. His arm jerked, folding at an unnatural angle behind his shoulder. As the ruined limb flopped back into view, Greg screeched—an unearthly howl.

"Greg!" Her brother staggered towards her, clutching what remained of his hand. Streaks of crimson had transformed his freckled face into a terrifying visage. His eyes stood out in stark terror, bright dots amidst so much blood. An old photo taken in Iraq flashed into Andrea's mind; a grief-stricken mother looking up from her dismembered child, her eyes and hands imploring assistance. She was horrified to recognise that same expression on Greg's face.

Fighting her own shock, she ran towards her brother, her laptop satchel slapping painfully against her hip. Jesus Christ, his fingers were gone! "Greg, what's happened? Where's Bruce?"

Two savage impacts caught Greg in his right side. A sound like the slap of wet washing against a rock and Greg's jaw all but detached itself from his skull. Then a chunk of muscle and a thin line of blood erupted from just above his heart. He tumbled sideways.

Andrea fell on top of her brother's body, repeating his name over and over. She looked around frantically. "Bruce!" Then louder, "Bruce, help us!" Her screams went unanswered, echoing in the barren landscape.

Greg had been shot. The ragged fist-sized hole in his chest left little doubt. She gagged, ashamed at her reaction as the contents of Greg's bowels escaped. A fierce trembling began in her hands as if a live current were passing through them. She tried to stand but her legs folded weakly beneath her.

Who did this?

Then a strange but familiar sound cut into the night.

Cssssht.

"Help me…" The words were like shards of broken glass in her throat.

Cssssht.

Andrea crawled on all fours towards the Jeep. Her hands were slick with Greg's blood. As she grabbed the door to pull herself upright, both of the Jeep's halogen headlights exploded in turn. Andrea screamed.

She hesitated, her mind momentarily frozen by indecision as a shadow detached itself from the base of one of the nearby trees. Andrea squinted, her eyes struggling to adapt to the sudden blackout. The figure was a mottled grey with a misshapen head. It moved towards the Jeep, hunched forward, in a short scuttling walk. As it drew closer she saw huge black eyes staring down at her, unblinking, alien.

A staccato voice whispered.

"'Fermative. Got eyes on her."

Andrea scuttled backwards, crablike, as survival instincts began to nip at the nerves in her cerebrum. Run! Run! RUN!

Her legs pumped into action, spitting up loose gravel and shale as she threw herself bodily in the opposite direction.

A rattle of automatic gunfire sent up a cloud of sand and stones as the rounds impacted around her feet. Then a horrendous pain seared up her left thigh. Andrea screamed, but kept running full tilt. Her laptop case bounced awkwardly as she sprinted, slapping against her back and rebounding high into the air.

A second figure burst into view twenty yards to her left. He had some kind of short-barrelled machine gun carried at waist level. As Andrea veered away from him, she reached the edge of the overlook. She had two options: give up and suffer whatever fate the attackers had planned for her, or risk breaking her neck by going over the edge. An unseen rock decided for her as her ankle slammed into the unyielding obstacle. There was a moment of terror. Then she fell into darkness.

4

The gunman known as "Mark" watched as his target tumbled out of view with a screech in an uncoordinated somersault. Another man joined him, looking over the drop. The night-vision goggles they wore turned the vista an unearthly green. They watched as the woman bounced and tumbled down the steep incline. Even from their elevated position they heard a resounding crack as she hit a rocky outcrop. Then she disappeared from view.

He sucked air between his front teeth. "She'll be a bag o' bones at the bottom."

"You were supposed to shoot her in the leg, and only if absolutely necessary. She's valuable until we have the package."

"I did. Well, I clipped her, anyway."

"You'd better shape up, Mark. Topcat will tear you a new one if we don't deliver on this. You'd better not have killed her."

Mark shrugged, trying to feign nonchalance.

"And your radio lead must be loose. I could hear static bursts all the way over from my position."

Mark tapped the walkie-talkie unit at his waist. The resulting *csssht* made him wince.

The other man raised his own walkie-talkie. "This is Matthew. Bring up the ATVs. The target went over the edge. We need to get to the base of the hill and collect the package." He turned to Mark. "Search the vehicle."

As Mark started going through the Jeep's contents, he heard a low growl of engines. Thirty seconds later, two Kawasaki All Terrain Vehicles rolled to a stop behind the Jeep.

Matthew spoke. "The two males are down. The girl took a swan dive over there."

The two men driving the quad bikes were dressed in almost identical clothing to Mark's: dark-grey camouflage trousers and jackets. The webbing packs they wore held numerous pouches and a compact sub-machine gun lay slung across each man's back. Their night-vision goggles were pushed back high on their heads. They both nodded without speaking.

Mark gestured to the Jeep. "There's nothing in here."

Matthew gave him a hard stare. "Look again, just to be sure."

Mark clenched his jaw muscles but he did as he was told. As he carefully rechecked each bag in the Jeep he tossed them out into the dirt. He swept his hands under the seats, rifled the glove compartment and checked behind the sun visors.

"Nothing."

"Come on then. We better get down and finish this. Find her, get her to talk, terminate her."

Mark looked over at the man he knew as "John". All four of them had been assigned tags by their employer, who himself used an alias. Topcat was one of those people that seemed to have been created in a military test tube. Every other word out of his mouth was delivered in grunt-speak. It was all military acronyms, abbreviations and warrior philosophy. But as long as he paid as well as he did, Mark would endure his staccato Patton-esque speeches. Plus, the guy knew his stuff.

The ATVs rumbled as the two men designated as "Luke" and "John" revved the powerful engines. Matthew clambered onto the back of John's Kawasaki, pushing his stubby Heckler & Koch MP5K firmly against his hip to stop it bouncing. Mark rode pillion with Luke, his eyes searching for any sign of movement that would indicate the woman's location.

The rugged treads of the ATVs kicked up a cascade of dust as the four-man team powered down the hillside.

5

The dregs of his fourth beer had formed a small, damp Rorschach pattern on the chest of his grey T-shirt. Danny paid it no attention. He was enjoying the down time with his brother way too much to let spilled beer bother him.

Clay grinned and continued his story, "So then the guy comes back into the bar with a six shooter and starts getting all Clint Eastwood on us."

"What… just because he got a slap from a bouncer?"

"Yeah." Clay took another long pull on his beer.

"So what happened to quick-draw McGraw?"

"Well, Patty makes a chilli that you can grease an axle with. So when he passed by Buffalo Joe, he got a face full of it. I grabbed the gun and Joe landed the hammer on him. That was pretty much the end of him. The sheriff rolled by ten minutes later and hauled his ass off to jail."

"You still keep in touch with Joe?"

"I see him now and again on the rodeo circuit."

"I liked him. Plus he's the only Indian I've ever really talked to."

"We say 'Native American' these days."

"Whatever, I remember he had hands as big as a gorilla."

"Yeah, he's a tough one, all right. He took a lot of crap in the army on his way up. Good in the field though. For a big guy he never made a sound when he was on duty. He'd just turn up out of the darkness like a ghost."

"Well, Casper he ain't," Danny mimicked Clay's southern drawl perfectly.

"You got that right."

Danny drummed his fingers on the neck of the bottle. "Talking of things that go bump in the night, what do you reckon about Area 51?"

"What, about the UFOs?"

Danny nodded.

"Well it's an Air Force base and testing range, one of the biggest in the world. People are bound to see lights in the sky. You know how people are. I don't doubt there's some secret shit going on in there, but little green men? I don't think so."

"We say 'Alien Americans' these days," Danny smirked.

"Wiseass."

"Still, I'm looking forward to seeing the alien café tomorrow."

Clay stretched out his long legs, sliding lower in his seat. "They do a good burger. And the folks of Rachel are friendly enough. Probably sick to the back teeth of sky-watchers, though."

"You want another?"

Clay emptied his bottle and nodded. Seconds later another cold one was in his calloused hand.

As Danny sat down he again favoured his right side.

Clay looked on, his face impassive, only his eyes displaying concern for his younger brother. "How you feeling now?"

"It hurts like a son of a bitch. But I'm still alive and kickin'… and still got all of my pieces. That's more than I can say for some of the boys over there."

"Why don't you end that shit an' come and live with me? I thought that when you left the army, you were done. Yet here you are, still yomping around with the private sector."

Danny looked down at his hands; they were clean but not too long ago they hadn't been. *His left hand closing over the sentry's mouth as his knife slipped deep into his kidney. Once, twice, three times to be sure. The body stiffening, high on tiptoes; then falling as a loose pile of limbs.*

"Ground Control to Major Dan…"

Danny gave a weak smile. "I'm not ready to settle down yet. But I do appreciate the offer."

"Consider it an open invitation. I can get you as much work as you want. The studios are always looking for ex-servicemen to act as extras and I'm good friends with Harry H. He knows good men when he sees them and he uses them in all the movies he works on. The pay is good, and there'll be no more of these to contend with." Clay traced the jagged scar that ran from his hairline down to his left eyebrow.

Danny's mouth twitched as he remembered.

He is sixteen—just a few weeks away from joining the army—and using his last days as a civvy in the Scottish town of Dumfries to try to get into Cindy Howard's pants.

Cindy is a great-looking girl and rumoured to be free with her favours to the right boys. But she also has an on-off boyfriend, Steve Grayson. Steve is two years older and fifty pounds heavier than Danny.

The couple happen upon Steve and five of his friends at a local shopping arcade. It is early evening and the cold night air has just started to turn their breath to mist.

"Wha' the fuck's goin' on here, eh?"

Cindy backs up a couple of steps. "It's no' wha' it looks like — this is Danny. We went to school together for a while."

"Why's he got his arm 'round you?"

Danny quickly takes his arm from Cindy's shoulder. "Steve, we're just friends, just larkin' around. Cindy tol' me she had a boyfriend, I wa' just teasing her, that's all."

"Well, she's got a fuckin' boyfriend!" Then Steve plants a head-butt full into Danny's face, sending him tumbling to the ground. He's on the verge of blacking out. When he manages to struggle to his feet, he sees Steve laughing, leading Cindy away.

"You bastard." He wipes blood from his face.

"Want some more, eh?" Steve cocks a fist back level with his shoulder. He charges.

Danny tries a kick to the groin but Steve's fist crashes into his already bloody nose, knocking him down again. He plants kick after kick into Danny's kidneys. Then his friends get in on the action. Within seconds, kicks are raining down from all sides.

Danny has taken karate lessons for almost a year, but it's no help once he's down. He's outnumbered and outclassed. The gang leave him in the street. He can't open his right eye and every breath sends shards of pain lancing into his ribs.

He lies curled in the foetal position for long minutes, then walks home. It usually takes ten minutes; tonight it takes over an hour. He hides his face in primitive boyish embarrassment. Being beaten is bad enough, but being pointed at is somehow even worse.

He reaches home and sees Clay parking up his motorbike at the kerb. His older brother is swinging his leg free from his motorbike as he turns and sees Danny, sees Danny's face covered in dried blood, his jacket torn.

"What the hell happened to you?" His voice a Texan drawl.

Danny just shakes his head and goes into his uncle's house. Clay is staying there while on leave in the UK and Danny is there for a month, rather than following his parents to Germany again. One last attempt at reconciling their marriage would only be hampered by having Danny under their feet. Clay follows him in.

"Danny, what happened?"

Danny doesn't want to look at him; tears well up in his eyes, shame plucking at him.

"Hey, it's all right, little brother. Come on, let's get you cleaned up."

Danny lets himself be led to the bathroom. Clay washes the blood from his face.

Clay is six years older and has been a US Army Ranger for two years. To Danny he seems like the toughest man in the world.

"At least your nose isn't broken. Mind you, it's swollen pretty bad. You'll feel like death tomorrow."

"Thanks for that." Danny tries to smile but his teeth hurt too much.

"Now, who did this?"

"Steve Grayson, Cindy's boyfriend."

Clay frowns. "He's a big fucker for you to tackle. What happened?"

Danny hangs his head. "He saw me trying it on with Cindy

and put the head on me." Danny's pronunciation of "head" comes out "heed" in his broad Scottish accent.

"And…?"

"When I tried to go back at him, he put me down and then his friends joined in…" Danny sweeps his hands down his face and body to indicate the results.

"So it wasn't one on one."

"No' for long," Danny spits a glob of congealed blood into the sink. "Truth is, Steve had already fucked me over before they joined in."

"That makes it worse, not better, in my book. Anybody can get beaten in a straight fight. But spineless pricks who put the boot in afterwards, they're the ones that really get me riled."

"I just want to go to bed."

"You can't, not yet." Clay stares deep into his brother's eyes. "We're going to go and sort these fuckers out."

"Clay, I feel like shite."

"You'll feel ten times worse in the morning. Every muscle will be as tight as Uncle Adrian's ass and your face will feel like it's been run over by a truck."

"You're not helping."

"If we don't go tonight, you won't want to go tomorrow. Then you'll regret it for years to come."

"It's all right for you. You're bigger than me, tougher than me…"

"None of that matters. It don't matter how big or strong you or your opponent are; it's how you handle him that makes the difference."

"How?"

"By not doing what he expects you to do."

"How d'you mean?"

Clay sighs. "Danny, you know this already. You don't go toe-to-toe with a big lump like Grayson, you outflank him; hit him when he's least expecting it. The only time a fight is fair is in the ring. Outside, anything goes."

"So what are we gonna do?"

"Go get changed. Put on your boots. Where do these boys normally hang out?"

"Down at the car park by the river."

They leave the house, Danny's legs unsteady.

"If they're there, just wade into Grayson as hard and fast as you can. Aim for his eyes and his balls. Don't worry, I'll be watching your back this time."

"He'll just kick my arse again."

Clay stops dead, holds Danny's injured face in his big shovel hands. "That's not going to happen. He was in charge last time. This time you're in charge. When we get close I'll slap your back. That's your signal to attack, and you don't stop until it's done."

Danny sighs, but with a newfound resolve. Butterflies dance the rumba in his stomach and he feels bile in the back of his throat. As they walk at a brisk pace, Clay repeats his simple instructions several times.

Ten minutes later, Danny sees them, nearly twenty young men, clustered together. Some are drinking beer from cans while others are just loitering and jostling. One of the gang seems intent on giving every passing motorist the finger.

Danny spots Grayson in the crowd. He's sitting on a bench eating chips from a takeaway carton, laughing and gesticulating. Cindy is nowhere to be seen.

Danny begins to walk faster. Takes a deep breath and holds it.

Grayson glances up but doesn't register the young man stalking towards him.

He doesn't wait to feel Clay's hand on his back—the signal. Danny has already exploded forward.

Grayson looks up again, just in time to take a boot in the face.

Danny watches his own foot slam into Grayson's face with a strange detachment. An alien sensation takes hold, a cyclone of channelled rage possessing his limbs. They start to rocket into Grayson with a vengeful will of their own.

The heavier man struggles to rise but can't cope with the sudden onslaught of savage punches and kicks. Danny lets out a guttural roar with each blow.

The gang scatters, surprised by the sudden violence. Then some return, circling Danny.

Clay fells the first comer with a right hook to the side of his jaw. Then a second tumbles away, holding his nose, unable to contain the fountain of blood. The third grabs at Clay's throat. The two men each lock grips upon the other's neck. Clay twists and throws the man to the ground.

Then a beer bottle is pitched from the crowd and smashes into Clay's head. The glass fragments into a welter of countless shards. The older Gunn brother keeps fighting. Seeing blood, more of the gang run at Clay. Danny knows they don't really want to fight; they just want to punch or kick an easy mark.

Grayson tries to push Danny away but his legs are kicked out from under him. His mouth is open and slack, his eyes glassy.

"You had enough?" yells Danny, his fist raised for another blow.

Grayson struggles to answer. "Aye. I've had enough."

Danny steps back, his breath ragged and angry. Grayson

springs, his fingers clawing at Danny's eyes. But this time he is ready. He smashes an elbow full into Grayson's face. The big man goes down. Flat on his back, he paws the air. Danny looks down at him, then looks for Clay.

Four men lie at Clay's feet. Another hobbles away clutching his groin. The rest have retreated to a safe distance. A few shout promises of retribution but Clay ignores them. His face is a crimson mask, blood streaming from a deep gash on his forehead. His eyes warn of more violence.

"You all right?" asks Danny.

"Better than these fuckers." Clay grins, showing bloodstained teeth. "Come on, time to vamoose."

The brothers walk home. None of the gang follow. Danny stops to vomit but Clay pays him no heed; just everyday business for the Ranger, new business for his brother.

Danny Gunn became untouchable. One month later he was wearing the uniform of a British soldier.

Danny smiled at his recollections and held his beer aloft. "Here's to easy livin' and big-titted women."

"A big Ay-men to that."

Both men jumped as a bloody hand slapped against the window.

6

Andrea's hand slid down the window, leaving a smudge of crimson. She could hear curses from the occupants of the RV, then silence. As she drew level with the side door, it flew open with force. She tripped over her own feet as she tried to avoid getting a face full of aluminium. As she sprawled in the dirt, a man's silhouette filled the doorway—a large man. A huge, silver-plated revolver reflected the light from within as it was pointed directly at her.

Andrea, her voice barely audible, managed only a weak "Help..."

The man stepped out into the cool night air, bulging arm muscles tensed. Over six foot, he had close-cropped blond hair over a deeply tanned and weathered face. Andrea watched, frozen, as he dropped into a slight crouch. He took his eyes from her, sweeping the gun slowly over her head, eyes darting, as if he was straining to see into the darkness, to find a threat. After nearly ten seconds he once again dropped his eyes to her, then lowered his weapon towards the ground at an oblique angle.

"What the hell happened to you, gal?"

The only response she could give was to point into the darkness.

The man slipped the revolver into the waistband of his jeans and scooped her up as if she weighed no more than a child. As he turned to the Winnebago, another man appeared from the shadows to the rear of the vehicle. He was far shorter and leaner, and held a knife in one hand.

The first man spoke. "What have you got there?"

"Steak knife. Snagged it from the kitchen and came out the side window. Done a sweep—seems clean. Didn't want us falling for the 'damsel-in-distress-turns-hijack' ploy."

The first man grunted with what sounded like approval, then carried Andrea into the Winnebago, putting her gently down on a plush seat alongside a dining table. She looked up at her rescuer. Dark-blue eyes, intense but not unkind, stared back at her from a deeply weathered face. The man towered over her, his head nearly touching the ceiling of the motorhome. The smaller but equally intense-looking man stood behind him, dark-haired and lean, a first-aid box open in his hands.

The larger man brushed hair slicked with drying blood from her face. "What's your name? Can you tell me what happened to you?"

She tried to talk but the only sound that escaped was a high-pitched whine. Her throat felt like it was filled with gravel and broken glass.

"Here, drink some of this," the smaller man pushed a tumbler of water towards her. Andrea gulped down the liquid, spilling a large quantity down her chin.

The big man spoke again. "I'm Clay. This is my brother, Danny. Now I need to lift your shirt to check where all of this blood is coming from. Okay?"

Andrea nodded, her face a mix of fear, shock and confusion.

He peeled back the fabric of her shirt. The material was crusted with blood and dirt and clung to her skin like an old Band-Aid. Andrea winced as a sliver of pain shot across her ribs. She looked down at countless scrapes and bruises that decorated her midsection. A deep laceration covered a four-inch patch below her right breast. Splinters of wood were embedded in the flesh from the tree she'd encountered halfway down the hill. The big man gently removed her laptop bag from around her neck and lowered it to the floor.

"Damn, girl, you've been banged up real good. I'd better call 911 and get you to a hospital." He gave her the once-over again, his eyes stopping when he saw the gash in her jeans over her right thigh, the blood seeping from a long graze beneath. He gently pulled back the torn denim. "This looks like a bullet wound... not deep..." His eyes narrowed. "What happened out there?"

"My brother and his boyfriend... somebody killed them..."

She saw the brothers exchange a quick glance.

"We need to leave," croaked Andrea. "Those men might still be after me!"

"Which men? Why are they after you?" asked Clay.

"I don't know who they are. They just appeared out of nowhere. They...they shot Greg and Bruce."

"Did you see these men? What they looked like?" Clay's

deep voice rumbled like desert thunder in her ears.

"Not really, just one of them. With a machine gun. He had some kind of headset on. Like a…" She cupped both hands in front of her eyes.

"Night-vision goggles?"

Andrea nodded. "I think so. He looked like a giant bug in the dark."

"Where were you when this happened?"

Again she motioned vaguely towards the hills. "Up by the Power-lines Overlook."

Danny looked at his brother, a quizzical expression on his face.

"A few miles up into the hills," Clay responded.

"What were you doing up there?"

Andrea looked at Danny. She suddenly realised that his accent was Scottish. He was as far away from home as she was.

"My name's Andrea Chambers, I'm a journalist. I'm doing a story on the saucer community." She almost laughed at how ridiculously inane it sounded.

"Have you been trying to sneak into Area 51?" asked Clay.

Andrea winced as she shook her head. "No, we were just on the tourist trail. I talked to a few of the sky-watchers this afternoon, that's all."

"You're talking about someone with military kit. The only military out here are the camo-dudes. They guard the perimeter of Groom Lake and Area 51. Those guys just shoo you off the land. The most anyone has suffered at their hands is a trip to the sheriff's office and a hefty fine."

Danny moved in and began wiping dried blood from Andrea's face with a wet dishcloth. "What if it wasn't military? There are plenty of whackos out there. What if they came to the desert to off a few of the saucer-heads for fun?"

Clay shrugged, noncommittal. "Back home in Texas you hear about locals killing Mexican border jumpers. Maybe this was the same thing—Nevada-style. But…"

"What?"

Clay turned to Andrea. "They shot the men you were with? I'm sorry to ask, but was it professionally done?"

Andrea swallowed. "It was quick, if that's what you mean."

"And they only winged your leg? Sounds like maybe they didn't want you out, just down."

"You thinking collection team?" Danny grimaced.

"Whatever they were after, we'd best be moving on. Just in case. We can make the town of Rachel in about forty minutes. We can call the police from there."

"What about your cell phone? We can call from here…"

"There's hardly any reception, but I'll give it a go." Clay tapped in the three digits, then shook his head, turning the phone so Andrea could see the NO SERVICE error message.

"It was worth a shot. You drive and I'll keep trying with the phone," said Danny.

Clay nodded. Andrea watched as he slipped his bulk into the driver's seat and started the engine. The diesel motor rumbled like an agricultural machine but moved out smoothly onto the blacktop.

Danny came and sat beside her, and began cleaning her wounds. "Tell me what happened. From the beginning, in detail." His eyes were not unkind, and there was a palpable strength in his demeanour that made her feel suddenly safe.

She sobbed as she recounted the night's events.

"I know it's hard, but the more we know, the more we can help you." Danny continued to wipe detritus from her face. He checked the large gauze pad he'd placed below her chest. Crimson dots now decorated the bandage, but the bleeding had definitely slowed.

"The man came at me, I ran, he shot me in the leg. But I fell backwards over the edge of the outcrop. I must have fallen about twenty or thirty feet down the hill. I ended up wedged under the trunk of an old tree. I don't think they could see me from the top."

A thought barraged its way to the front of her mind. "We need to go back there. Maybe Greg or Bruce is still alive!"

Danny shook his head sadly. "Andrea, if those men were as professional as you're saying, there isn't much chance that they're still alive up there."

Andrea curled up into a ball, sobs racking her frame. She felt Danny place a light blanket over her. She closed her eyes.

Clay turned his head from the road as Danny slipped into the passenger seat beside him. The two-lane blacktop stretched out into the darkness ahead of them. Clay held the large RV at a steady fifty miles per hour. He could have coaxed more speed from the vehicle but saw no sense in the risk involved. The large Winnebago, his "road-blocker", was built for slow and steady transit, definitely not for speed. On most trips he enjoyed the looks of other frustrated drivers as they finally passed the bulk of his bus, usually ready to give him the finger. Then they would see the battle-scarred face staring back at them, grinning; the finger usually went back to their steering wheel as they sped away.

Tonight there were no other motorists as far as the eye could see.

"How far to the next town?" Danny asked, tapping keys on Clay's cell phone. After the fourth unsuccessful attempt he let the handset drop into the inset cup-holder in the arm of his seat.

Clay shrugged. "About thirty miles, I reckon."

An occasional sob issued from the rear of the RV, but Andrea's grief was muted by the rumble of the engine and the echo of the tyres on the asphalt.

The two brothers glanced again at one another. Neither smiled, but Clay felt something akin to a ripple of excitement. "I guess we're on the roller-coaster again, little bro."

Danny nodded. "And I didn't even buy a ticket."

7

The Iridium 9600 satellite phone buzzed on the mahogany desk only once before the deeply tanned hand snatched it up. "Is it done?" No preamble, no pleasantries.

"Two targets down."

"Two?"

"Yes sir, one of the targets is still in play."

"Which one?"

"The woman."

"Are you telling me that the main target is still out there?"

"Sir—"

"Tell me that you at least recovered the package!" The anger in the voice was not reduced by distance.

A deep breath sounded over the airways. "No sir, the package is still in play at this time."

"I was assured that your team could handle this, no sweat."

"They can sir, it's just a matter of time. The woman is injured. One of my men tagged her, but she fell over the edge of a steep incline and—"

"Well get your lazy arse down the *steep incline* and make sure she's taken. Make her talk. We need that package secure. Now get it done."

"As I say, it's only a matter of time. I've got operators sweeping the area as we speak."

"Good, call me as soon as it's confirmed."

The man known to his team as "Matthew" folded down the stubby aerial of his satellite phone and slipped it into a pouch on his chest webbing. Under his breath he muttered, "Limey asshole."

The four-man team had only been together for the past seven weeks, but in that short time Matthew had realised that the less he told them and the more he barked, the better they operated.

"All report," he grunted into the walkie-talkie affixed to the front of his chest webbing.

"Mark… nuttin' yet."

"Luke, negative."

"John… I've got a dead dog and a bike wheel but no female."

Matthew shook his head in frustration. This was the first operation Topcat had given him to lead. He knew he'd suffer if it wasn't a success. "Stick with it. We need to be out of here before sun-up."

"'Fermative." Mark's thick Georgia accent grated on Matthew as much as the man's lack of attention to detail. Mark seemed to think it was enough to just fire multiple rounds in the required direction. No finesse and no apparent desire to learn higher skills either. As soon as he was in charge of his own fire-team, Matthew would be free of shit-kickers like Mark. They were good for shooting squirrels and not much else.

The other two, Luke and John, were better. They had both been around the block enough to get the job done. Luke sported an odd accent, maybe French-Canadian, maybe Creole. None of the team were too forthcoming with their pedigree and Matthew wasn't exactly the prying kind. John was unmistakably an Afrikaner. The militant-sounding accent was curious yet familiar to Matthew's ear. He'd heard plenty of it when he'd worked in the shithole known as Jo'burg. South Africa was one place he'd dotted on his map and had no burning desire to ever see again.

A buzz of static from his radio made him refocus.

"Luke… Nothing down here, she's gone."

Swearing again under his breath, Matthew pressed the most prominent button on the handset. "Regroup at the bikes."

"Wait, I've found something…" Luke again.

"Report." Matthew waited a few seconds.

"Blood smear on a rock."

"Any sign of the woman?"

"No. She may have climbed back up as we were coming down…"

"Shit. You and Mark get back up top and see if she's there." Matthew again found himself shaking his head in frustration. How much trouble could one woman be?

Within ten minutes Matthew was watching as the operative known as Luke followed an intermittent blood trail from one spatter to the next. The distance between each smear varied. Some were only a few inches apart, others separated by a good many feet. But they were constant. Luke's compact flashlight bobbed in the darkness as he moved from one to the next. The remaining three men moved the quad bikes in a wide loop to intercept his path. Luke pointed out a path that ran on a rough parallel course with the rutted main track.

"She went this way. She's got a good half-hour lead on us now."

Matthew rubbed his chin as he calculated possibilities. He swung one leg over the seat of the ATV so he was sitting side-saddle. The average walking speed for a healthy adult was around three miles per hour. So with a thirty-minute lead the woman could be a mile and a half away. If she had been running, which she would have been, if fearing for her life... if she had averaged seven or eight miles per hour... Shit; she could be up to four miles away. How badly was she injured? He considered the blood she'd left behind on the rocky slope. She'd been shot. Even just a flesh wound would slow her down. Then she'd taken the tumble down the hillside. Maybe picked up a concussion. Too many possibilities. Time to move and end this.

"Come on, back down the trail. Stop when we get to the main turn-off. Luke, when we get down there, do your thing again."

Luke tapped two fingers to his head in acquiescence. Again, the Kawasaki quad bikes sped down the hillside. Mark and Luke reversed positions so now Mark steered the vehicle while Luke rode pillion. As soon as they reached the T-junction, Luke dismounted and began searching the nearby ground. By tracing a slow loop fifty metres wide, it took him less than four minutes to pick up her trail.

"She came this way, sure enough. She was fairly movin' as well. Long strides. She was running with a steady gait." He pointed to regular depressions in the loose dirt spaced roughly thirty inches apart. The rest of the team looked into the arcs of light provided by the bike headlamps. The depressions they saw told them none of the details that Luke seemed to intuit. "She joined the road here. She probably followed it back toward the main 375."

"Good work. Let's see if we can manage to catch up with an injured woman on foot, seeing as we have the small advantage of these motherfucking monster quad bikes."

The men looked at Matthew, unaccustomed to hearing him curse. Usually he was Mr Cool. John gave a minuscule nod, then revved his bike and sped along the road at full speed.

Luke vaulted onto the back of the other ATV and Mark sent the vehicle rocketing after the vanishing taillights.

Five minutes later, the two ATVs pulled over. Almost immediately Luke pointed out another series of scuffs and depressions in the sand at the side of the road where the asphalt met dirt. "Looks like she fell down here." He pointed further along the road. "There's an old building just another few minutes down there. She might be hiding."

"Let's go," barked Matthew. The bitch wasn't free and clear just yet. He would personally add the final bullet in return for the trouble she'd caused him. Once they had the package.

John powered the vehicle forward, the rapid acceleration making the tyres spin momentarily on the cracked road surface. As they reached their destination, John applied the brakes and pointed to a large recreational vehicle that was pulling away from the ramshackle structure.

"What do you think?" asked John over his shoulder.

"She could be in there, all right."

The second ATV parked level with Matthew's.

Matthew stabbed the air with his finger twice. "You two search the building, we'll follow the Winnebago."

"What are the chances of her still being in there? She'd be stupid not to have made a beeline for that camper van," asked Mark. Matthew could tell that he would much rather be chasing down the RV.

"Just do it. We'd look even more stupid if we scooted off after some pensioners in their crusty bus and she was sitting in there watching us."

Mark clicked his tongue in annoyance but set to his allotted task. As he and Luke moved towards the remains of the casino, John and Matthew began their pursuit.

8

Andrea awoke with a start. A deep stinging throb had taken up residence in her thigh. When she looked down, a tight bandage encircled her leg. Spots of blood had seeped through in a number of places. A raw burning sensation also nipped at her ribs. Damn, she hurt all over.

"How long have I been out?"

The man called Danny emerged from the front of the vehicle. "Just a couple of minutes. We're heading for a town called Rachel. We'll get you some help there."

She nodded. She'd read about the town in the UFO guidebook. The alien café was there. A lot of the sky-watchers had mentioned it earlier. Was that just today? Time seemed distended, unreal.

"Are you up to talking a bit more?" asked Danny. "How are you feeling? You looked kind of dizzy as you sat up."

The vehicle slowed slightly as Clay looked back from the driver's seat.

"I feel sick," replied Andrea, holding her stomach. "Can

I have another drink?" Seconds later, a glass of orange juice was in her hands.

"Take your time. Try to take small sips. How did you find us? The overlook is quite a few miles from the old casino car park."

"Pure luck, really. I fell down the hill and banged my head really hard on the way down. I didn't know where I was going but I heard engines—motorbikes, I think—coming after me. They must have assumed I'd fallen all the way down to the bottom, but I probably only went down twenty or thirty feet. When I stopped rolling I couldn't see the top of the hill, so I don't think they could see me either."

"Go on."

"As I heard the engines, I climbed halfway back up and then found a narrow track. I just kept running as fast as I could. I'm not sure how long I was out there. I thought I was going to die." Harrowing images of Greg and Bruce flashed before her eyes. She took a breath. "I just ended up crashing into your van by accident."

"It's a good thing you did. There's a lot of barren ground out here. If you'd taken another direction you'd be just another statistic."

"My brother and his partner are dead, they're not statistics!"

"That's not what I meant." Danny spread his hands in an open, placating gesture.

"I know, I know. It's just so hard to believe. Why would anyone want to harm us? We've never done anything…"

Danny steepled his fingers, his chin resting on the uppermost digits. "Well, I think that whoever was responsible did it for a definite reason. The guys you described don't sound like yahoos out looking for random victims. Whoever they are, they probably came after your party specifically or they were under orders to kill anyone on the overlook."

"That doesn't make sense," said Clay. "The overlook is a popular place with the sky-watchers. There're people up there all the time. And besides, the Area 51 guards don't go anywhere near there. That's public land, unrestricted. The guards are there to keep trespassers from government land. There's never been a fatality—you'd have to be a clear and present threat to the base for them to challenge you."

"Governments are good at not talking about their dirty laundry, especially where the forces are concerned," said Danny raising an eyebrow. "Remember what happened in Belize."

Clay considered a moment then shrugged. "This is different. This is America."

They had not been driving long when Clay saw vivid blue and red flashing lights ahead from a stationary vehicle parked across the road. Cop cars the world over were more similar than different and the programmed response was also the same. Clay applied the brakes. He heard Danny coming up from the back of the RV and spoke under his breath. "Cops. We can report it all to the state trooper up ahead." He raised his voice to reach Andrea. "It's going to be all right now, hon."

As the RV came to a halt, a man's silhouette approached, casting a long, distorted shadow as he cut through the halogen beams of his dark-blue squad car. The state trooper wore his hat low on his head and walked with a confident swagger. His right hand rested lightly on the butt of his service weapon; his left balanced a flashlight on his shoulder.

Clay pressed one of the many buttons on the driver's door console and the window slid down with a muted whirr. Cold night air invaded the cabin. The hairs on Clay's arm prickled with the sudden temperature change.

The trooper leant an arm against the door panel. His badge read RYBACK and his face was deeply lined, telling of long hours spent in the harsh Nevada sun. A neat, bristling moustache remained static even while he spoke. "Sorry fella, the road ahead is closed. Tourist in an RV managed to crash into a cow half a mile up ahead." He shook his head as if he'd delivered this message many times before. "You need to turn yourselves around and head on back the way you came."

Clay leant out of the window. "Officer, we need your help. We picked up a woman at the old casino—says she's been attacked in the hills. Her brother and friend were killed."

The cop gave Clay the flat eye. Then he spoke again, in a different tone. "Sir, how many people are in your vehicle?"

"Three. Me, my brother and the woman."

"Sir, licence and registration please." Officer Ryback held out his hand. To Clay, the cop didn't look like he would be the sort to underestimate any potential threat.

Clay fished out the documents from a utility pouch on the side of his seat. He did so slow and easy, so as not to spook Ryback. He knew the trooper's instincts would be buzzing at the mention of murder.

Ryback took the documents and took a step backwards. He directed the beam from his flashlight into the RV, studying the interior for long seconds, then turned on his heel and began to walk back to his patrol car.

The distance between the vehicles was roughly thirty feet and illuminated by both sets of headlights. All was pitch darkness beyond the meagre radius of the beams. Clay's eyes followed the cop back towards his patrol car. He knew that Officer Ryback would perform a quick check for any outstanding violations or warrants in his name. Clay wasn't worried. It was a long time since he'd tangled with the law, and never in Nevada. Once Ryback had called it in and was satisfied, he would listen to Andrea's story in detail.

Suddenly the trooper pitched forward, his legs giving way, his body crumpling as it fell. A spray of crimson surrounded his head as his hat was snatched off as if by an invisible hand.

"Jesus H. Christ!" Ice water rippled down Clay's spine. "Danny!"

9

The Kawasaki quad bike was much faster and infinitely more agile than any RV, but Matthew knew that the big road-blocker wouldn't be easy to stop. Just like a pride of lions trying to bring down a wildebeest, they'd need to pick their moment carefully.

The RV turned right onto the main highway. John steered the quad into the big vehicle's slipstream. He flicked a toggle switch and the main light changed from full beam to a much reduced glow, just enough to provide illumination but less noticeable.

"Just follow them until Mark and Luke catch up. If the woman isn't in the building we'll overtake the crusty bus a couple of miles down the way, flag it down and search it."

"What do we do with the occupants of the vehicle?"

"You know our brief: terminate anyone who has had contact with the package." Matthew gave his reply matter-of-factly and without emotion.

John nodded. Matthew knew that his subordinate had no problem with killing. He had killed on contract in more countries than he had fingers. It was a little unusual to be doing so in the continental US, but a job was a job.

A rattle of static sounded in both men's ears simultaneously, then Mark's southern drawl announced, "Negative on the building. The target is not here."

Matthew tapped his send button. "Get your butts up here and we'll take the bus down."

"Roger that." Mark's voice conveyed unhidden pleasure at the command.

John opened up the throttle and let the Kawasaki do its thing. Both men hunched low against the wind that whipped at their faces.

The Winnebago wasn't the fastest thing on wheels but it was moving at a decent clip. The taillights shone through the darkness like a pair of demonic eyes.

"Boss, we could have trouble ahead."

Matthew peered around John's head and saw the flashing lights. *Cops!*

"What do we do now?"

Matthew scowled in the dark; then he repeated the mission brief out loud like a mantra. "Proceed as planned. We need to recover the package and terminate anyone who has come into contact with it."

"That include cops?"

"That includes the goddamned Pope if he gets in our way."

Five hundred yards ahead, the RV slowed to a halt. The flashing lights of the police cruiser were obscured by the bulk of the bus.

John killed the headlights and slipped the engine into a

lower gear and the bike crept slowly forward in the darkness. He placed the quad on a path that kept the bulk of the RV between them and the patrol car.

Two hundred yards…

"There's a cop talking to the driver."

One hundred yards…

Fifty…

Matthew calculated the odds. If the target, that tricky bitch, wasn't in the RV then he'd be in a deep pile with Topcat. Killing a cop was not a thing that any operator would consider lightly. He drummed his fingers against the barrel of his Heckler & Koch MP5K sub-machine gun. Then fate decided for him. The woman sat up and looked out of the rear window. The ambient light inside the vehicle framed her face perfectly.

"Got her. She's inside the RV. Move up quickly and quietly."

John gently braked as Matthew tapped his shoulder twice. Matthew clambered off the bike and darted towards the driver's side window.

The cop turned and walked back toward his cruiser, with what looked like documents in his hand.

Matthew dropped to one knee, brought up the stubby weapon to his shoulder and squeezed off a short burst. The cylindrical sound suppressor fitted to the barrel reduced the gun's retort to an angry rattle. The cop went down in an untidy heap.

Inside the RV, the driver yelled something unintelligible. A yell of distress or warning? The driver was just an indistinct shape from Matthew's vantage point, no way of telling age or appearance. No matter; a quick burst from the MP5K would take care of him.

Matthew scuttled along the side of the RV, his back barely touching the amber and tan aluminium skin of the bus. He measured two steps then sprang out smartly, level with the driver's door. Seventeen 9mm rounds from his MP5K ripped through the door like it didn't exist. But where seconds earlier a human silhouette had been framed, now there was only shattered glass and bullet holes.

Matthew moved cautiously to the front of the vehicle, weapon held high and ready. He tapped his radio control button and hissed, "John, move up."

10

As Officer Ryback slumped to the ground, six things happened within the space of as many heartbeats.

Beat one: Clay shouted a warning to Danny. Basic and guttural.

Beat two: Danny pushed Andrea flat to the floor and yelled for her to stay down.

Beat three: Clay snatched up his bulky Colt Python revolver from under his seat. As he leaned down, bullets ripped through the door over his head.

Beat four: a gunman stepped in front of the RV's windscreen, weapon raised.

Beat five: Danny grabbed a steak knife and launched himself out of the side passenger door.

Beat six: Clay put two bullets through the windscreen into the gunman's face.

Matthew squeezed the trigger of his MP5K as the pair of lethal .357 rounds ripped through his face and exited through the rear of his skull. A stream of hot lead stitched countless holes in the windscreen and roof of the RV. Clay Gunn ducked instinctively as fragments of glass exploded around him. As the gunman fell away from view, he turned to check on Danny and Andrea, his ears ringing from the gunfire. The woman was curled tight into the foetal position, her hands clamped over her ears.

Danny was gone.

John had lost sight of Matthew for no more than ten seconds. Yet in a combat situation he knew that ten seconds could last a lifetime. There was an intense burst of fire then silence. With his own MP5K trained on the Winnebago he crept forward at an oblique angle. Within a few feet he saw Matthew's prostrate form spread-eagled on the blacktop. His boots reflected the red and blue lights that still pulsated from the stationary police cruiser. Wisps of steam drifted into the air from the bloody ruin where his face had been. Fury erupted in John's mind. Matthew had been a good man, a good leader; he didn't deserve to die like this. With a roar he pulled back on the trigger and sprayed the Winnebago from back to front several times. He could hear the 9mm rounds rip through the near side skin of the vehicle and apart from the occasional ricochet, exit through the other side. The thirty-round magazine was depleted in seconds and he ejected the empty and slapped in a fresh one with a practised hand. As he moved cautiously to the front of the RV, he scanned the windows for any signs of life and more importantly, danger.

A descending blur caught his eye as something primeval flew at him from above.

As he heard his brother loose off two shots, Danny Gunn flung himself bodily out of the RV, pivoted without pause and climbed up the utility ladder bolted to the rear corner of the vehicle. Crawling on hands and knees, he traversed the roof like a cat, freezing as the second gunman sprayed the RV with bullets.

As the man stalked forward, Danny launched himself over the edge. The serrated blade of the steak knife sliced down the side of the man's face and glanced off his collarbone before burying itself to the hilt in his neck. Both men slammed into the ground with a bone-jarring impact. Ignoring the gouts of dark crimson that flowed from the wound, the gunman rolled to his left and forced the muzzle of his sub-machine gun ever closer to Danny's chest. They struggled, both men striving for the advantage. A burst of automatic fire ripped through the air so close to Danny that it singed his skin through his shirt.

His opponent pulled the trigger in several short bursts but Danny blasted him in the head with an elbow and used the momentum to scoot around onto his back. He clamped his left hand around the stock of the weapon and used his right to rip the knife free from the man's throat. Danny plunged the knife repeatedly back into the unprotected neck until the gunman's body went limp. An ugly, vicious death, but that was all a soldier could expect.

Danny stood upright, kicking the slack body away as

Clay emerged from the front of the RV, his huge revolver held before him, ready to split the night if required.

"These boys are packing some real heat. Top-notch stuff."

Clay nodded, his eyes flicking to the man at Danny's feet, who looked like he'd been savaged by a wild animal.

"This is bad. We're caught up in the murder of a cop; we've just killed two men; and don't forget the bodies on the overlook. This shitstorm is going to take our lawyers years to sort out."

Danny Gunn rolled his shoulders and wiped his face with the back of his hand. The dead man's blood was smeared across his features like war paint. He snatched up the man's discarded gun, inspecting it in the moonlight. The MP5K was a very fine weapon: the firearm of choice for many military forces, armed police units and independent operators. Originally German-built, the *Maschinenpistole* 5 was now produced across the world and had many variants. The model he held was the MP5K; the "K" designated the short (*kurz*) barrel. He examined the three-burst selector switch, the choice of the more precise and better-trained soldier. When the MP5K was switched to full auto, the standard thirty-round magazine could be emptied in two seconds. Devastating but short-lived.

He walked to the front of the RV, dropped to one knee beside the first dead gunman and began to methodically search the corpse's chest webbing. When he was finished the haul consisted of two spare magazines for the MP5K, a short-range radio cum walkie-talkie, a heavy satellite phone, a black SOG-issue knife, two Hershey bars and an angular Glock 37 pistol with a full clip. No wallet, no identification.

Danny slung the MP5K across his back and stuck the Glock in his waistband.

He raised his head to see that Andrea had appeared from the RV and was surveying the carnage, half hidden by Clay's bulk. It didn't take a genius to realise that these were the same men who'd murdered her brother and his partner. Although she appeared momentarily horrified by the two dead bodies she was also clearly elated. "See how you fuckers like it!"

Clay looked down at her and gave her a perfunctory nod. "Ay-men to that." He walked over to the body and scooped up the Hershey bars and the knife. "What do you wanna do with the comms stuff?"

Danny straightened up, the cartilage in his knees popping loudly, holding the dead man's walkie-talkie and satellite phone. "Radio should warn us if there are more coming." He hooked it onto his belt then examined the satellite phone. "This thing's off. Shouldn't be able to get a fix on us from it. Keep it in case we need to make an emergency call out of cell-phone reception. Then dump it." He pocketed the sat-phone and looked straight up into the night sky. Countless pinpricks of light, too many to count, dotted the firmament above. He stood immobile for long seconds, puffed breath out of his cheeks then turned to Clay and Andrea. "These guys won't be alone. If there's a kill squad on your tail there will be at least four to six men assigned. We'd better get to high ground because the rest of the team won't be far away."

Clay patted Andrea on the shoulder, pushing her gently towards Danny. "Stay by him."

* * *

Clay walked over to the body of Officer Ryback. A pool of dark sticky liquid had formed around his head. Clay bowed his head for a moment in silent tribute. He wondered about Ryback's family. Did he have a wife sitting at home, blissfully unaware of her husband's demise? Children, maybe? He knew only too well the grief that the news would bring.

He picked up his licence and registration from the blacktop, where the officer had dropped them. Then he stalked over to the squad car and slid into the driver's seat. Reaching for the microphone mounted on the dashboard, he keyed the mike and found his voice, "Officer down, repeat officer down. I'm reporting the death of Officer Ryback. We're out on the 375. Twenty miles south of Rachel."

A brief burst of static preceded a local Nevada accent. "Who is this?" A second's pause then, "Please identify yourself and repeat your last message."

"My name is Clay Gunn. Officer Ryback has been shot and killed. When you see the video playback from the car camera you will see that I was not responsible. There are two more dead bodies out here as well. You'll see what happened on the tape."

"This is dispatch… Is Bobby really dead?" The timbre in the voice turned from impartial controller to a scared young woman in an instant.

"I'm sorry, but he is." Clay pictured the woman sitting in the radio-control room of a squat brick and breezeblock building that was so typical of rural police stations. She would probably know all the serving officers as well as her own family. A death like this affected everyone in the community. He gritted his teeth as the radio remained silent for long seconds. Then the woman spoke again. The professional air had returned to her voice.

"Please remain in your present location. Officers will be dispatched."

"Look we can't stay here. There may be more gunmen. We're heading into Rachel. I figure that we'll be safest in town." A movement by the RV caught his eye. Andrea was standing over the body of the man Clay had killed, peering at the ruined face. He watched as she rested her foot on the corpse's throat, bringing it down tentatively at first, then harder. Then she raised her foot and stamped down over and over again. She threw back her head and screamed.

Danny levelled the MP5K as Andrea's cry cut through the night air. He knew the sound well. Fury and despair; a desperate need for revenge.

A distinctive rumbling pulled his attention away from Andrea. A bright spot of light low to the road. "Andrea, get back in the RV." She paused only long enough to spit on the corpse, then did as she was told.

The radio on Danny's belt crackled to life. "We're one minute out."

He scowled but keyed the mike in response, trying to keep his accent neutral. "Roger that." He saw Clay making his way back from the police car and signalled at him: *Incoming.* Danny knew that there would be at least another two men. This type of operative never travelled without adequate backup. They would be equipped to the same standard as the two dead men. He hefted the MP5K against his shoulder.

His mouth twitched. Hope for the best, prepare for the worst.

"How do you want to play this?" asked Clay. He hauled himself into the RV, Danny following.

"A moving target is harder to hit."

Clay nodded. "So let's get moving." He turned the key and shifted the RV into drive. He coaxed the cumbersome vehicle into a wide arc around the dead bodies and the patrol car, then pushed the gas pedal hard against the floor. The windscreen held firm despite the countless rounds Clay and the gunman had put through it.

"Lie down here." Danny gestured between the rear seats, and Andrea did as she was told, cradling her laptop bag in her arms. He pushed down the cushions from the seats, arranging them to provide a meagre degree of shock absorption. They certainly wouldn't stop a bullet but they would help to prevent her being tossed around when the going got rough. Her eyes were glassy and they kept flicking to the weapon in his hand. She must be wondering what the hell kind of men they were.

Clay's gruff baritone echoed down the galley. "We got lights coming up fast."

Dust and grit spread in a plume behind the ATV. Mark hung on grimly as Luke powered after the target vehicle. Suddenly the bike slowed—bodies in the road. Luke steered towards the nearest and leant over, foot braced on the blacktop. Mark heard a sharp intake of breath, then a torrent of syllables. Mark's grasp of Québécois was meagre at best but his companion's tone was unmistakable. Swearing sounds pretty much the same in any language.

"Both of them?"

"Both." Another stream of curses.

"We gotta kill these motherfuckers and end this mission now!"

Luke was still swearing in his native tongue but he nodded in agreement. The powerful Kawasaki engine roared like an injured cougar as he opened up to full speed. Soon the RV was back in their line of sight.

Twenty feet behind the Winnebago, Mark aimed his weapon at the rear right tyre. It was big and wide: an easy target. The heavy rubber was no match for the 9mm projectiles and in seconds the rear of the vehicle had dipped awkwardly.

Luke slewed the bike to the left and Mark repeated the routine on the left wheel. Now the whole rear of the Winnebago dropped and bounced as it fought for traction, its tail sending up intermittent showers of sparks.

"Kill the driver!" yelled Luke.

Mark tucked the weapon tight into his shoulder as they drew level with the cabin of the RV. "He's already dead, he's just too dumb to realise it." He looked into the wide eyes of the driver—a big man with close-cropped blond hair—his finger hovering over the trigger.

Then the bulk of the bus lurched into a tight arc towards the bike. Mark grabbed onto Luke's back as the wheels of the Kawasaki passed momentarily under the scarred aluminium body. He felt rather than saw the bike break free with a shriek of grinding metal. He heard shots and Mark felt a heavy calibre bullet pass dangerously close to his head and steadied his own weapon as best he could. A tight three-burst round succeeded in reducing the right wing mirror to a twisted spur of metal. He aimed along the weapon's stubby barrel.

11

Danny was thrown off balance as the Winnebago slewed from side to side, its suspension worse than useless, every minor bump in the road making it lurch and shudder. The stream of enemy bullets was keeping Clay on the defensive and he could see his brother constantly overcorrecting his steering. The RV was fishtailing in ever-widening arcs; it seemed only a matter of time before they crashed or Clay was shredded.

Danny shouldered open the rear window in the dining area. He could now see their pursuers: two men on a high-powered quad bike. Using the window frame as support he shot with the MP5K. The gunman riding pillion turned, scowling at the new threat. He leaned back and sent a flurry of rounds at Danny, who dropped to his knees, then rose to return fire. Both men unleashed staccato bursts of lead. Neither was successful in hitting their mark. Then the front rider pulled his own sub-machine gun and fired a burst. From his vantage point Danny could not see the shots hit home, but the sudden jerk of the RV nearly knocked him flying. They had taken out the front right tyre. The crippled vehicle skidded a quarter turn and with a squeal of metal, shuddered to a halt.

There was a roar as the bike came alongside, then the crack of shots. More holes appeared in the walls and Danny threw himself to the floor. He turned his head to see Andrea's face pressed hard against the vinyl floor tiles. The cushions around her spat out wads of stuffing.

Something in the galley kitchen burst into flames, sending sparks and orange tendrils down towards the woman's head. Danny scrambled up.

"Over here!" He beckoned to her, then leapt over her. Standing momentarily on the seats, he planted a boot into the rear window.

The latch of the window popped under the sudden pressure and he rolled sideways through the improvised exit. Andrea didn't need his words of encouragement to follow, her laptop bag swinging behind her. Another two booming shots sounded from Clay's revolver then he too tumbled bodily from the window. But where Danny had landed with feline grace, Clay fell sideways as a tuft of hair was sheared from his head by a wild ricochet and he landed heavily on his back. Danny grabbed his older brother's arm and hauled him to his feet. Bullets continued to rip through the body of the RV as the three crouched and ran towards a shallow culvert at the side of the road.

The two gunmen met at the front of the Winnebago and watched the spreading flames with satisfaction. Mark scanned the road either side of the ruined RV as Luke speed-changed his magazine and emptied it into the vehicle on full auto with a roar of angry contempt. His head snapped up as a blur of movement caught his attention. He slapped Mark's shoulder and made two brief chopping motions in the direction of the blur. Both men advanced as one. Luke sighted down the stubby barrel of his weapon, eyes straining in the darkness. Mark moved low and quick, aiming too into the roadside. Nothing moved, no target presented itself. They knew better than to try a blind charge. Luke reached into a pouch at his waist and pulled his night-vision goggles clear. The night turned a curious hue of green. He scanned the roadside from left to right.

There!

Thirty feet away. The woman crawling away, moving fast despite her ass being stuck way up in the air. Where were the men from the RV? *Make sure they're dead, then pick up the girl*, Luke thought.

Move!

A brief flash from his left flank and a round entered Mark's neck just below the ear. In a moment of curious detachment Luke realised that it must have been a big one. A fist-sized chunk of blood and bone was ejected as his comrade pitched onto his knees. Then he slumped forward, forehead hitting the asphalt.

Luke pivoted towards the sound of the shot and pulled the trigger, emptying the magazine into the darkness.

Danny emerged from cover as the gunman let the empty magazine clatter to the ground. He put a three-burst into the man's right shoulder from his MP5K, knocking him to the ground. The man was still valiantly trying to swap his weapon to his left hand as Danny pressed the muzzle into his ear. "Enough!"

The gunman released his weapon and clamped both hands over his right pectorals. Blood seeped between his fingers.

"Aye, you've been shot, fucknuts!" Danny's Scottish brogue was thick with contempt as he kicked the man's submachine gun to one side. "The cops should be along soon, but between now and then we're going to have a wee chit-chat."

Clay appeared from the darkness. "Chit-chat my ass. I've got one left in the chamber for this asshole. I say we ventilate his head just like his buddy, make a matching pair." Clay levelled his huge revolver at the injured man's face.

"You've got one chance or it's the end of the road for you," warned Danny.

The man gasped for breath, a bloody froth at his lips.

"You've taken one in the lung. Pretty soon you'll be drowning in your own blood. Not a good way to go. Now, who sent you and what do you want with the woman?"

The response was a blood-choked gurgle. The gunman spat out a gobbet of blood then began to talk, his voice barely above a whisper. "She's got something that doesn't belong to her…"

Behind them, the RV was now sheathed in flames, acrid plumes of smoke tainting the night.

"And what *has* she got?"

The words were quieter again, barely audible. Danny, on one knee, leaned in a fraction to hear. Then a switchblade that had been concealed in the gunman's chest webbing ripped up at his exposed throat. The blade nicked Danny's cheek as he snapped his head away. He slammed the stock of his weapon into the man's mouth. The knife dropped.

Danny looked back at Clay and shrugged. "You try to be civilised…"

The gunman launched into a torrent of vile language, some English, some French, all unmistakable in context.

"One last try. What has the girl got? Why do you want her so bad?"

"Fuck you! Burn in hell. Burn in hell!"

"Are there any more of you out here?"

"Burn in hell!" The man repeated the fiery mantra over and over.

Danny saw his hand feeling for the switchblade and hauled the man to his feet by the throat. "You're going to the electric chair for this."

The gunman's left hand snaked to his collar and another blade flashed, but this time Danny was ready. He pivoted into a classic combat throw. Locking his opponent's extended elbow over his own shoulder, Danny snapped the top half of his body forward. The man was pitched bodily into the blacktop. His head and neck snapped back with a crunch of separating vertebrae as the rest of his body tumbled over in a loosening of limbs.

Clay sauntered over and regarded the twisted body. He looked into Danny's eyes but said nothing. Sometimes no words were required.

"Are they both dead?" asked Andrea. She had appeared at Clay's side.

"As disco-dancing dodos. Serves them right for what they did to my bus."

"What do we do now?"

Both men turned to look at her. She was covered in blood and dirt. Her pale-blue eyes reflected the flames licking out of the Winnebago.

"Two choices: stay and wait for the cops, or put as much distance between us and them as possible," Danny replied. He tapped the dead man's face with his foot. "I thought heading for Rachel was best, but if there are more of these out there, I vote for heading south as fast as we can hustle."

"What about the police? Won't they be after us as well?" Andrea asked.

"For questioning? Definitely. But I think that once they see the video from Ryback's car they'll know that we weren't the bad guys here." Clay pointed back down the road. The red and blue lights still flashed in the distance.

Danny touched the bloody nick on his cheek. "I'd rather explain from another state. Just in case we meet any overzealous troopers before this gets sorted out. Jail time in Nevada is no joke. Not something I'd like to sample while the lawyers duke it out."

"Prison? Why would we..." Andrea gripped Danny's arm, her eyes wide with dismay.

"Because they'd bang us up in the state pen while they sorted through all of this, just to be on the safe side."

"But they did this to *us*..."

"*We* know that, but the investigation could take months," warned Danny.

"Years, even. These Nevada boys aren't the quickest out of the stalls," added Clay.

Andrea's expression was one of incredulous disbelief.

Then she shook her head. "No, I'm not being locked up for any of this. No way! Once they see what those lunatics did, the police will understand."

"Yes. *Eventually*. That's my point. In the mean time we'll be wearing orange jumpsuits and hiding our valuables up our arses."

"But I'm English—" she turned to Danny "—and you're Scottish, aren't you? Are they allowed to put us in an American prison?"

Clay laughed at her naivety. "There's people locked up in this country for looking the wrong way at the judge. Besides—" he gestured at Danny "—we're both half-breeds. Dual citizens. He's just got a dumb accent." Danny's expression made Clay laugh louder.

"But…"

"But nothing; trust me, you do not want to spend any time in a Nevada clubhouse. They make Shawshank look like the Marriott."

"So what am I supposed to do?" asked Andrea, her face contorted with worry. "I'm just here to do a story for a magazine. Now I'm supposed to go on the lam with two men I've just met?"

"*Two* men who've just killed the *four* men that were trying to do God knows what to you!" spat Danny. He felt the muscles in his jaw bunching in annoyance.

"I know I'd probably be dead if you hadn't picked me up. I know that. It's just that this is fucking crazy." Andrea wiped her eyes with the back of her hand. Her shoulders slumped. "I'm just a features journalist. Film reviews and the odd city guide, for God's sake. I'm not an investigative reporter. I don't understand why anyone would want to hurt me!"

Danny relented. "He said that you had something that didn't belong to you. Have you taken anything that you can think of… stolen anything?"

"Stolen? I've never stolen anything in my life." Andrea's voice rose in pitch. "I never did anything to those men."

"Okay, look we can thrash this out later. First we better hit the road and get somewhere safe," Danny cut in, placing a hand on her shoulder. He looked deep into her eyes, and could imagine what she saw—his face streaked with blood, probably almost as terrifying as the men they'd just killed. If she was smart she would be thankful that he and Clay were on her side.

"So where can we go?" asked Andrea. "And how do we get there?"

Danny pointed to the gunmen's abandoned quad bike. "Did you ever see that old cartoon *The Hair Bear Bunch*?"

Clay shared the joke and nodded. "Three on a bike, right?"

"Not the most comfortable wheels ever, but it'll get us on our way. We can boost a car further on down the road." Danny dropped to one knee and rolled the dead man, relieving him of his backpack and searching through his chest webbing. "Clay, go see what the other joker has on him. We can't carry more than two of the subs on the bike, but any extra ammo or pistols could come in handy." As Clay walked to the other body, Danny took a Glock 37 and its holster from his dead opponent's hip, pulled its twin from his waistband, and put both in the backpack, along with the spare ammunition and satellite phone. He pulled the walkie-talkie from his belt and tossed it to the ground, then picked up the man's MP5K and slung it across his back with his own. Clay returned, carrying another Glock and two MP5K magazines. He was chewing a Butterfinger.

"We should send these guys a thank-you letter for all this free hardware," he said between bites, putting his haul into the backpack.

"Not to mention the candy." Danny grinned.

"So again, where can we go?" asked Andrea. "All I have is my MacBook, for all that's worth. I left everything else, my phone, my passport, my money..." There was a hitch in her voice. "My brother..."

"But you're still alive," said Clay. "That means you've still got a chance to put things right." He turned to Danny. "I say we head for Tansen's place. He lives so far out no one will find us. It's a long haul but he has a lot of resources. If we need to, I'm sure he could set us up to fly down to Mexico until we get this sorted." He grinned wryly. "Let's just hope he's forgiven me for that incident with the bowie knife."

Danny grinned at his brother. "Agreed. And I think you should go up front. Be our windbreak."

Clay mounted the bike and revved it experimentally. "Three-quarter tank. We're in luck." Andrea took her place behind him, and slipped her arms around Clay's wide torso. Finally, Danny, with the backpack and looted weapons slung over his shoulders, took up the rearmost position.

Slowly at first, then accelerating rapidly, Clay took the road south.

12

Tansen Tibrikot watched the approaching car with a detached interest. Almost no one drove out to his house; at least not on purpose, and not this early. From the red stone boulder upon which he sat, he had followed the vehicle's progress along the single-track road for most of the four miles that it stretched from the main highway. Tansen's only regular visitors were UPS drivers, and the deep-blue saloon didn't much look like it was in the parcel-delivery business. The morning sun provided a pleasant warmth on his back and he was loath to leave his position. The surface of the rock had been eroded by wind and rain over millennia into a natural curve that served as a perfectly comfortable seat.

Ten minutes later the battered Honda Accord rolled to a stop next to Tansen's own vehicle. The dirt-encrusted import looked like a thrift-store reject next to the gleaming bronze of the H1 Hummer.

Tansen tipped his tan Stetson back on his head and spat out a chewed matchstick. From his vantage point he looked down on the three occupants of the car as they disembarked and approached his home. The single-storey house was built in the style of an old cattle ranch but no livestock had ever been kept there. The original nondescript building had once served as a way station for Wells Fargo Bank, but Tansen had done extensive renovation work, transforming it to resemble the idealised structures he'd seen on *Bonanza* and *The Virginian*.

He squinted at the three figures. One was a woman he didn't recognise, with blonde hair and a trim figure. She was clutching a rectangular padded bag, and even from a distance, Tansen recognised the expression on her face. He knew fear when he saw it. The other two he knew all too well. Clay Gunn, tall and broad, his hair close cropped. He'd have words with that cowboy. And behind him the smaller figure of Danny. He grinned. He'd first met a young Daniel Gunn while serving with the British Army as part of the Royal Gurkha Rifles, alongside the Royal Green Jackets, Danny's regiment. The Green Jackets were skirmishers, frontline shock troops like his own Gurkha brothers. Under a blazing African sun the two men had stood together, low on ammunition, against a superior force, yet neither had backed down. Gunn had dropped target after target, choosing each shot with care. One bullet, one kill. Tansen too had made each and every shot count. Between them they had killed seventeen enemy combatants. The last two Tansen had cut down with his kukri, the fearsome curved knife carried by every Gurkha soldier. Both had held their nerve. Both had lived to fight another day.

He slipped down the weathered rock.

* * *

Clay's spirits rose as he saw Tansen approach. To a casual observer, his old friend might pass as a Native American, with his broad flat face and brown skin. But Tansen had been born and raised on the other side of the world.

"Howdy."

"Right back at ya, Tan-man." Clay stepped forward, hand extended in greeting. He stood immobile for long seconds before Tansen's hand met his. Behind him, he heard Danny let out a held breath. Although rather portly in stature and standing no taller than five-three in his cowboy boots, both brothers knew that the man before them, when pushed, was a stone-cold killer.

Tansen's features softened and a smile not unlike that of the Cheshire Cat spread across his face. "You look like a bear ate you up and shit you out!"

"Well, we're trying for the grunge look. I hear it's all the rage with the kids these days," replied Clay.

Tansen removed his hat revealing his jet-black hair, cropped short as always. "Did you bring it?"

"No I haven't got it with me."

"Shame. We could have settled it once and for all."

Clay shrugged. "It's already settled in my mind. You won. I was being an ass."

"Yes."

"Call it national pride. You know how patriotic we get… and I guess Texans are the worst of all."

"Yes."

"Tansen, old buddy, we need your help."

The smile crept into Tansen's deep-brown eyes. "Come on in. I've got fresh coffee if you want to sit awhile."

Andrea hung back as Clay and his friend went into the house, Clay's arm slung around the shorter man's shoulders. The older Gunn brother towered over the other man, yet Tansen's presence easily matched that of the muscular Texan. She whispered to Danny, "Is it going to be okay?"

"Looks like it. They just needed a minute."

"Who is he?"

"Tansen, an old Gurkha friend of ours."

"Like in the army?" Andrea had a vague mental picture of dark-skinned men in green fatigues. "Are they the ones from Nepal?"

"That's right."

They followed the others into the house. Andrea noted that Tansen was dressed like an extra from an old Western, in dark jeans, a red check shirt with a faded leather waistcoat. Intricately embroidered cowboy boots with ornate steel caps at the end of the toes completed his ensemble. Inside, the house was a shrine to the Wild West. Dozens of vintage revolvers sat in display cases both free-standing and wall-mounted. Andrea knew very little about guns but stared with interest at the nearest weapon. The small brass plaque at the base of the weapon told her it was a Colt 1851 Navy Revolver. The barrel was the longest she'd ever seen on a handgun.

"Tansen has got the biggest collection of Old West memorabilia that I've ever seen. The museum in Dallas could learn a thing or two from this man."

Tansen grinned appreciatively at Clay's comment. "Best in the West…"

Andrea smiled a hint of a smile, not knowing quite how to respond.

"We're sorry to land on you Tansen, but we're in a real hole," offered Danny.

Tansen waved his hand to dispel the apology. "Now, who is your lovely lady friend?"

She stepped forward. "Andrea Chambers." She smiled, caught unawares as their host kissed her hand as she extended it to shake.

Tansen waved for them to sit and then busied himself in the kitchen area. Minutes later he placed four steaming mugs of coffee on the table, which was made from an old wagon wheel capped with a sheet of smoked glass. The cavities between each spoke of the wheel were filled with spent bullet casings. Andrea tried not to smile, thinking of *When Harry Met Sally*. She thought it best not to ask if he'd gotten it from Roy Rogers' garage sale.

"Now then, what brings you to my neck of the woods?"

Andrea sank back into the sofa as Danny told their story, letting it wash over her. Tansen did not speak until Danny was finished, only nodding occasionally, his face stoical.

"So what can I do to help?" he asked. Andrea noticed that his Nepalese accent was hardly perceptible.

"We need to lie low while we figure out who these guys were and just what they were after," Danny said. "They were well trained and well equipped. I'm sure if they had just wanted to kill us and not take Andrea alive, we'd all be taking the longest dirt nap in the desert. One of the shooters said Andrea had something that didn't belong to her but she's got nothing."

"Could you have had this 'something' and lost it?" asked Tansen, turning his dark eyes to Andrea.

Andrea sat up. "I really don't know. They came out of nowhere and started shooting. They could have just pointed their guns at us and we would have given them anything they'd asked for." The memory of Greg's dead face made her fall silent again, her stomach churning.

"Well, let's look at what we know." Tansen counted off the points on his fingers. "One: They were well trained. That probably means military or ex-military. Two: they had the latest professional equipment. That means they are well financed. Three—" he turned to Andrea again "—they killed at least three people that you had contact with, one of them a cop. And they tried to kill Clay and Danny too. So they are prepared to do anything to achieve their goal. Four: whoever went to the trouble of employing a fire team to capture you will not just give up. Whoever is behind this probably has the resources to send out more teams."

Andrea brushed her fingers distractedly through her dirt-encrusted hair. "I still don't understand why this is happening to me."

Danny finished the dregs of his coffee. "Well, if we come across any more of these fuckers I'll be sure to find out."

"You can all lie low here for as long as you need. You can get cleaned up and Danny and I will go into town and get some new clothes for you all. It's probably best if the pair of you—" he nodded at Andrea and Clay "—stay here." Andrea saw Tansen eye Clay's considerable bulk and was suddenly keenly aware of her torn and dirty clothing. "You two are more noticeable."

Danny smiled. "Are you saying that I'm a plain Jane?"

"No, I'm saying that people are more likely to notice

beauty and the beast if they wander around in Castillo." That made Andrea feel a little better.

Tansen pointed the way to the bathroom, handing her a towel and first-aid kit. Accompanied by the steady timpani of running water, Andrea let the last of her tears fall to mingle with the blood and dirt. The water was the colour of weak tea as it swirled down the plughole. She rubbed scented shampoo deep into her hair, enjoying the smell of apples, rinsed and repeated. She examined her scrapes and cuts, which stung sharply as the hot water and shower gel made contact. The wounds on her leg and ribcage were still so painful she could barely touch them. The torn skin on her ribs was red and puckered and her leg burned in a strange numb way. After long minutes of standing immobile, head bowed, she turned off the water.

She towelled herself dry, taking extra care around the more painful areas. She delved into the industrial-sized first-aid kit Tansen had provided and wound a new length of bandage around her leg, then added a couple of large Band-Aids to her ribs. Her thoughts crept to her parents back in England. Had the news of Greg's death reached them yet? Probably not. How would they cope when they did hear? Her mother cried at Red Cross commercials, for God's sake; this would break her. Maybe she could phone home and at least let them know *she* was still alive. She decided she would ask Tansen later.

She didn't want to dress in her soiled clothing but had no alternative. Everything she'd brought with her was in the rental Jeep. All she had left was her MacBook, which was probably broken anyway, and thirty bucks plus change that had been stuffed in her trouser pockets. She didn't even have her phone, for God's sake.

Shit. What a nightmare. Again she found herself looking down at her countless scrapes. She would have been dead for sure if she hadn't found the Gunn brothers. The two men had proved very resourceful.

Yet what did she know about them? Next to nothing. They called each other brother yet Danny was clearly Scottish and Clay was Texan through and through. Even when they'd had time to talk they had not revealed much about themselves. All that she'd gleaned was that Danny had recently been in the Middle East. He hadn't elaborated as to which country. Her journalistic instinct stirred. Maybe she'd get more information now they were safe at this strange ranch.

Which was another question in itself: what the hell was a Nepalese Gurkha doing out in the American desert, miles from the nearest town? More questions than her mind had patience for.

The long shower had revived her somewhat and she realised how hungry she was. She hadn't eaten anything for over twenty-four hours. The breakfast buffet in the Vegas hotel seemed so long ago. As if on cue, her stomach rumbled.

A light knocking at the door brought her back to the moment. Tansen's voice enquired, "Are you okay in there?"

Andrea pulled on her clothes. "I'll be out in a minute."

In the living room the men downed their third coffee. Danny was explaining to Tansen how they'd raced away from the burning RV, all three perched on the quad bike. They'd driven flat out any time they'd been on blacktop, with frequent detours to avoid oncoming traffic, veering onto a path that ran parallel to the road. After catching four hours of sleep on the hard ground, Clay had hot-wired a car in a motel parking lot. One guest would be wondering who had enough bad taste to pilfer their beat-up jalopy. With any luck it wouldn't have been reported stolen until this morning. Danny and Andrea had travelled in the aged Honda while Clay had followed them on the quad bike. He'd then abandoned it in a low depression out of view from the road. That way the two vehicles were less likely to be linked by the cops, or more importantly, any operatives on their trail.

As Andrea emerged from the bathroom the three men stopped their conversation mid-flow. Although still dressed in her tattered clothes, her face was almost unrecognisable, free from blood and dirt. She was attractive in a natural and unpretentious way. Clearly a little self-conscious at the stares, she took a seat next to Danny on the sofa.

Danny was the first to catch himself. "Feel any better for that?"

"Almost human again." She smiled, with her mouth if not her eyes.

Danny motioned to Clay. "You go next if you want, I'm going to check out the news. See if we're on it yet."

Clay shrugged himself out of his seat and moved towards the bathroom without further comment.

Tansen handed Danny the remote control for the wide-screen television. After clicking through a dozen channels, bypassing obligatory reruns of *Judge Judy* and *Everybody Loves Raymond*, he found the local morning news. After a short feature on a supposed military victory in Libya, the next story made him sit up. A blonde news anchor was doing her utmost to project gravitas. There was footage of Highway 375 and Officer Ryback's patrol car. Her report was full of key media buzzwords—*murder, missing suspects, death toll, terror, destruction*—without giving any real facts. Two men found dead at the scene were as yet unidentified, she said. The camera panned in for lingering close-ups. Their bodies had been covered with sheets; only their boots could be seen.

The third victim *had* been identified. A formal picture of Officer Ryback in uniform flashed on the screen. Then a picture showing the dead trooper standing with his wife and a young boy, all three smiling broadly. Andrea shifted in her seat. Danny could see she was upset—after all, the cop had died because *she* was a target. It wasn't her fault but Danny knew that wouldn't stop the guilt. Then again, what did he really know about her?

The story flashed back to the anchor, her eyes opening dramatically as she picked up her dialogue. She promised the viewers that they would be going live to that location after the commercial break.

Danny switched channels as the Nesquik Bunny broke into a song about chocolate milk. The next news channel had more information. Police were searching the area for the occupants of the Winnebago, now feared dead. No names were given, only that there were thought to be at least two men involved. There was no mention of Greg and Bruce. Clearly the police hadn't connected the two crime scenes. Danny frowned. Unless the first crime scene hadn't yet been found. He turned off the TV and turned to Andrea.

"Well, they haven't named anybody yet."

Andrea shook her head. "What about Greg and Bruce? Do you think that means they haven't found them?" She looked pale, and Danny thought he knew what she was thinking: bodies in the heat of the desert would go downhill fast.

He was saved from answering when Clay emerged from the bathroom, still towelling his hair. "Your turn."

With the bathroom door shut, Danny stripped off his dirty clothes. He moved his fingers over the large area of pink skin that stretched down his left side, mid-ribs to hip. The injury was the reason behind his visit to the States. See Clay. Heal. R & R…

"An' how's that workin' out for you?" he asked his reflection.

"Holy shit, what the hell happened to you?" Andrea couldn't stop herself. Danny had stepped from the bathroom dressed only in his jeans, his shirt and boots dangling from one hand. The sight of his scarred torso elicited a visceral reaction. She felt her cheeks flushing a deep red. "I'm sorry, I didn't mean…"

Danny waved his hand. "Don't worry about it. I picked these up before we met. These babies are nothing to do with last night."

When Danny didn't offer any more information, she looked at Clay for further clarification. Neither man elaborated, so she let the subject drop.

Tansen filled the awkward silence. "Help yourselves to any food you want. Danny and I will head into town and get some new clothes. What sizes do you all take?"

Andrea and Clay wrote down their measurements on a sheet of notepaper. Tansen read the figures and smiled. "You'll just have to trust me on colours and fashions."

Danny had finished dressing and was lacing his boots. He slipped the denim shirt offered by Tansen over his stained T-shirt. "I'm good to go."

The two men left without any further ceremony. Moments later Andrea heard the Hummer rumble into life.

"Hungry?" asked Clay.

"I could eat my fingers."

Clay opened the large refrigerator door and pulled out two thick pre-packed rump steaks. He smiled. "I think I can help you out with that."

Andrea took a seat at the breakfast bar. She felt herself warm to Clay; he seemed more open than his younger brother. "You're taking this in your stride. Most people would have run a mile. I know I was scared to death."

Clay shrugged as he busied himself in the kitchen. "This ain't my first rodeo."

"Sort of guessed that. Were you in the army or something?"

Clay smiled and flicked a casual salute. "Six years as a Ranger."

"I've seen those on TV. Rangers lead the way, right?"

"Booyah!"

"So what's the story?"

"Story?"

"You said that you and Danny are brothers…"

Clay smiled knowingly. "Yet he's Scottish and I'm American, right?"

"It's kind of got me puzzled."

"I'll give you the short version." Clay busied himself with the steaks. "Our father was a medic in the US Navy. He met Mom in a little place called Dunoon in Scotland. The Navy has a base there. They married. Had the two of us. Later they split... Mom never got used to the constant upheaval of a new home every year. Well, there was more to it than that of course. They divorced in the end. I was old enough to choose where I went. I chose the States. Danny wasn't old enough and went back to Scotland with Mom. We tried to stay in touch but I had joined up by then and was living my own life."

"You don't look much alike," said Andrea, eyeing the scars that decorated the big man's features.

"Suppose not. Dad was a typical Texan. I guess I got more from his gene pool. Danny takes after our Scottish side. Small and mean!" Clay smiled.

Andrea grinned back. "He only looks small when he's next to you."

Hooking his thumbs into his belt, cowboy style, Clay gave a little swagger. "Yeah, we're built big all over in Texas."

Andrea leaned over and swatted at his shoulder. She was suddenly completely at ease for the first time in what felt like a lifetime. "Really."

"I never lie to a pretty gal."

"Now there's a lie if I ever heard one!"

Clay's smile spread across his whole face. "Damn you, woman. Rumbled again."

"Just get cooking!" She looked as stern as possible for a couple of seconds, then both of them laughed out loud.

13

The man known to his subordinates as "Topcat" tapped the antique bayonet blade against the palm of his left hand. The familiar cold of the steel helped him to think. The contract should have been completed, yet still contact had not been re-established. The four men Magson had assigned were more than capable of such a routine mission. All had terminated targets previously. All would kill without hesitation if the contract called for it.

Andrea Chambers was a major security risk, that was clear from the dossier on his desk. She was in possession of highly sensitive stolen data linked to the security of both the United Kingdom and the United States. The report did not specify what the data was or what it could be used for. That didn't trouble him. Many contracts were accepted without such information. They gave a clear objective and a time-scale. No embellishments. All the dossier told him was that she'd received a USB flash drive from another terrorist collaborator and was transporting it to an unknown contact in America.

Topcat had been playing catch-up from the start.

Chambers had already flown from Heathrow to Las Vegas by the time the contract had been issued. Time was of the essence: find the woman, recover the flash drive. Once the latter had been achieved, terminate the target.

The team had been assembled quickly. He'd picked four men from a possible twenty. Two he'd used several times before, the other two he had chosen on the recommendation of one of his squad leaders. All four were seasoned operatives. All had served in the armed forces of their respective homelands. The orders were clear and basic: a simple snatch and grab. Elimination of any other persons who may have seen or come into contact with the target or the data on the drive was authorised. Elimination of the target once the package was secured.

The clunky handset of his Iridium 9600 satellite phone remained defiantly silent, propped against well-worn hardback copies of Stephen King's *The Stand* and Jane's *Guns Recognition Guide*. Quality reading material when things were slow.

The bayonet tapped out an impatient rhythm on his palm once again. He glanced first at the wall clock, then his wristwatch. Both told the same time. His cheek twitched as he considered his options. Still the handset remained silent.

With a grunt, Topcat sheathed the bayonet in its leather case. He turned to his desktop computer and tapped in a sequence of numbers, letters and symbols. The screen accepted his password and another couple of agitated taps loaded a global tracking program.

The four men whom he'd dubbed "the Apostles" had not yet been chipped with RFID implants but the satellite phone that Matthew carried was tracker enabled, even when powered off. That, at least, would show the general location of the team. The screen displayed a satellite view of North America. He tapped the zoom icon. The screen blurred for a few seconds then cleared to show the state of Nevada. Another zoom. The screen now showed an area to the north-west of Las Vegas. He huffed and leaned in. If contact had not been made by the unit within another quarter-hour then Topcat resolved to break protocol and phone *them* to demand a status report. He'd not had complete faith in Matthew's leadership capabilities but knew that some men flourished in the field. He himself had been held in contempt by some of his commanding officers during his time with the Parachute Regiment. He also knew from personal experience that those who excelled in the classroom were not always the same men who did so under fire. So he'd given Matthew a shot at running his own squad.

He looked again at the contract dossier. It had come to him via Charles Banks of the CHSS, who had passed more than a few unofficial jobs his way over the years. Lucrative for TSI, but Banks made his skin crawl. Not a soldier, that was certain. The men of the Coalition and Homeland Security Service worked in the shadows. Trident Solutions International at least kept *part* of its work in the public eye.

Sharon poked her head through the door with a quizzical expression. "Did you call, Mr Carter?"

He looked up, not realising he'd spoken out loud. "No, just clearing my throat." Then as an afterthought, "I could use a cup of coffee about now."

His secretary smiled, nodded in acquiescence and left the

room. Less than a minute later a silver coffee pot and a plate of digestive biscuits were placed on his desk. He smiled at her in appreciation and waved her away when she offered to pour. The door closed silently behind her. He broke a biscuit in half and let it sit on his tongue. Delicious. Soldiers, biscuits and beer: three of the few things Britain was still good at producing.

When the coffee was finished he checked the clock again and picked up the satellite handset. The four-digit code lit up the display and a soft continuous purring ensued. No answer. The receiving phone half a world away was still switched off. A chill crawled its way up his spine. In his considerable experience, he knew silence was seldom golden.

"Shit!"

Sharon's head appeared at the door again. "Sir?"

"Get Magson on the phone. We may need another team."

14

Danny rested his arm on the Hummer's window frame as he and Tansen rolled into town. The main street of Castillo was a low-key affair. Single-storey buildings lined both sides of the two-lane road. It was one of the few towns left in the civilised world without a Starbucks or a McDonald's. Danny smiled as they passed a White Castle burger joint and a coffee house called Tarbucks. The big boys would arrive eventually, sure as dry rot.

The town was a world away from its flamboyant neighbour, Las Vegas. A single lone casino sat quiet on the east side of town and it had none of the glitz of the Vegas equivalents. It was a dull breezeblock building with a red pagoda-style roof, now weathered to an anaemic pink. A manic-looking plastic rabbit peeked out from the flickering neon sign.

A bored doorman leaned against the wall at the main entrance and smoked a stubby cigar. He glanced momentarily at Tansen's Hummer, perhaps wondering if they were going to stop, then went back to his smoke. Danny avoided eye contact. Doormen and meter maids tended to remember new faces and it suited Gunn not to be noticed.

"You've really taken to the life out here."

Tansen smiled. "I love it. Nobody bothers me. I can ride a horse whenever I want, and shoot my pistols without getting a visit from the law."

"I was sorry to hear about Raj. She was a lovely lady."

"She only had three years in America but she loved every minute." He shook his head, dark shadows for eyes. "Lung cancer, and she never smoked a cigarette in her life."

"Life's one strange highway, all right." Danny studied the passing buildings, his soldier's instinct never dormant. "Hey, you're still a young man, I'm sure there's plenty of cowgirls more than willing to take you for a test drive."

Tansen cocked his head to one side. "Nah, I married my Raj for life. I know she's dead but I still consider myself married. Does that make sense to you?"

"It does." Danny dropped the subject, leaving his Nepalese friend to his own thoughts.

The Hummer rolled to a gentle stop in front of a double-fronted clothing store. The store sign read BRANNIGAN'S in bold Western script. An old-fashioned spring-mounted bell over the door tinkled as they entered. They were met by a pleasant aroma of sandalwood and leather.

Danny chose two mid-sized backpacks for Clay and Andrea, then moved to the ladieswear section. He glanced at the sizes that Andrea had written on the slip of paper. He made a few calculations, doing his best to convert the UK sizes that she'd supplied to their US equivalents. He picked out one pair of black canvas trousers and a dark-blue pair of Wranglers. A green tartan blouse and a black sweatshirt went into the basket as well. Two plain white T-shirts followed. As an afterthought he picked out a multipack of plain black briefs and two six-packs of socks. He then moved to the men's section. While Tansen was picking out Clay's clothing, Danny took his time selecting his own choices. It was probably unnecessary but Danny thought it best if they appeared as two separate customers. With that in mind he circled the store, waiting for Tansen to make his purchases before approaching the cashier himself. He declined the chance of a Brannigan's loyalty card despite the chance of saving ten per cent on his next purchase.

The two men met up at the Hummer, where Danny loaded the bag of clothes and the backpacks into the tailgate. "Is there a RadioShack in town?"

Tansen pointed to the opposite side of the street. "There's a store that sells electronics at the end of the block."

"Good, I just need a couple of throwaway cell phones."

"I'll wait for you in here." The Gurkha wiped the beads of sweat from his forehead.

Danny heard the air con spring into life as Tansen clambered back into the vehicle. Danny smiled to himself. *How quickly we grow accustomed to the comforts of life*, he mused. A few years ago Tansen could have traversed Death Valley in his jockey shorts with nothing more than his knife and a litre of water for company. Maybe they were all getting soft in their old age.

The electronics shop was well stocked and carried a wide range of audio and video equipment. Bypassing the latest iPhones and tablets, Danny strolled over to a revolving display stand that was filled with pre-paid cell phones. He selected three cheap Motorola handsets. They were probably a few years out of style but Danny was not interested in appearances. He returned the smile that the girl behind the counter gave him. She was very pretty and reminded Danny of a young Julia Roberts. She had that same extra-wide smile going on. "Have you got car chargers for these?"

The girl turned to the shelf behind her, sending her long ponytail swinging through the air. "This is a universal charger. You just select the appropriate jack adapter to fit your model of phone. That should work."

"Great, I'll take three."

He was rewarded with another winning smile. The overhead lights reflected as bright spots in the slim-lensed glasses that she sported.

"That'll be eighty-seven dollars."

Danny counted out nine ten-dollar bills and handed them over. As an afterthought he added, "Do you carry Tasers or anything like that?"

"Sure." The ponytail swished again as she moved from behind the counter towards an enclosed display unit further into the store. "We have these."

Danny looked into the case. The dozen or so stun guns lay next to a range of lock knives and pepper sprays. "My niece is going to college soon… I want her to be safe, you know."

Ponytail bobbed her head in understanding. "Yeah, you can't be too careful."

"I don't know much about them. Which is the strongest?"

"This is a good one." She reached into the case and retrieved a unit that resembled an ammo clip. Two silver prongs extended a half-inch from the top of the handle. "This Sabre model can deliver multiple shocks on one charge. The battery life is excellent as well."

"How much?"

Ponytail smiled, a flirtatious glint in her eye. "Well, seeing as you've spent lots already I could let you have this for a straight fifty bucks."

"How much is it normally?"

"Forty-nine ninety-nine!"

"Wow, a real bargain."

"Better believe it."

After paying, Danny left the store with his purchases and Ponytail gave him a little finger wave as he glanced back at her. Seconds later she was busy opening stock boxes.

"She loves me, she loves me not," he said, smiling to himself.

Tansen was eating a chocolate bar with gusto when Danny returned to the Hummer. Danny declined a bite of the rapidly disappearing Hershey bar, and Tansen swallowed the last inch and a half in one mouthful. After wiping his hands on the legs of his jeans, Tansen slipped the Hummer into drive and they headed out of town. The casino doorman had disappeared, smoke break over. The weather-worn plastic rabbit had not lost his manic expression.

As they followed the road back to the house, Danny pondered the events of the previous night again and the many possible futures. "We'll be moving on as soon as possible," he said.

Glancing over, his dark Nepalese eyes inscrutable as always, Tansen gave a half shrug. "You're welcome at my place as long as you need. You know that."

"And appreciate it. But there's a very good chance that a shitstorm is following on our heels. I don't want to get you caught up in it as well. If we'd had options we'd never have bothered you."

"I'm glad to have you. We've both been through storms before; one more wouldn't kill us." Tansen's laugh lightened the mood.

"Nah, jokes aside, we don't know what the hell we're up against. I think the best strategy is to keep on the move until we've got more intel on these guys. I need to figure out who they are, what resources they have and how to get them off our backs."

"Devil's advocate?"

"Sure, go ahead."

"Drop Andrea off at the main precinct in Vegas. Let the cops earn their money. You and Clay go on an extended vacation. I hear Italy is nice this time of year."

"I couldn't just walk away. She has no one over here. She's desperate."

Tansen slowed the Hummer. "What do you really know about this girl?"

"How do you mean?"

"How do you know she isn't a criminal on the run? Let's face it, military teams do not go out on thrill-kill vacations. They were assigned for a reason, and there's no *good* reason I can think of."

Danny rubbed his face. He suddenly felt very tired. "I don't know, she seems genuine to me. She was half dead last night."

"I'm not doubting the effect, I just want you to consider the cause."

"My gut tells me she's telling the truth."

"Okay," Tansen replied. "I had to say it. Just covering all the bases."

"I know."

"One last question."

"Shoot."

"If it had been a *man* that had come to you for help, would you be going to the same lengths to protect him?"

Danny huffed. "I'm not doing it for a shot at some action."

"Then why?"

"Why did you stand up on that train in India?"

Tansen's head dipped as he remembered the situation that had brought him to America. "Because no one else was going to."

Danny spread his hands and gave a slight nod. "Exactly."

"Okay."

"Oh, and stop playing devil's advocate now. You're way too good at it."

15

Andrea wolfed down the food that Clay had prepared. The steak and salad really hit the spot. She found herself talking through mouthfuls of beef and lettuce. "So I get you and Danny now, but I'm still at a loss with Tansen."

"Ah, that man takes a bit of explaining."

"You seemed very cautious when we first arrived. What was that about?"

Clay cut a square from his steak, the fork hovering near his lips. "Last year we were having a beer together and I made the mistake of saying that the Bowie knife was the best knife in the world."

"And...?"

"You know what a Gurkha knife is, right?"

"Yeah, it's like a banana-shaped machete."

"Well, you should never mix beer and knives. Five minutes later we were in the bar's parking lot. Tansen was stabbing his kukri through an old oil drum, cutting it to scrap. I tried to do the same with my Bowie. The first slash bounced off the drum and cut his arm open."

"Oh."

"Tansen would have killed anyone else where they stood. He just glared at me, then jumped into his car and left."

"Have you spoken since?"

"Not until today."

Andrea chewed, considering. "Lessons learned then, huh?"

"Damn right."

"So how did he end up out here? Gurkhas hardly get let into *Britain* and they serve in our army."

Clay smiled again. "Tansen's a rare thing. A genuine hero."

"How so?"

"A few years ago there was a train going across India. At a stop in a remote village, a gang of about fifty bandits boarded. They moved through the train, robbing everyone and beating those who tried to resist. And you have to understand that these were real cut-throats. A lot of people were hurt."

Andrea put down her fork. "Jeez."

"There were two American students. Girls backpacking their way across Asia. One of the girls was blonde and stood out like a sore thumb. Some of the bandits decided that they were going to do more than rob them."

"Oh, God…" Andrea knew what was coming next.

"As they started ripping off the girls' clothes, one man stood up."

"Tansen."

Clay's voice was low with respect. Andrea held her breath. "He killed three men before they knew what was happening. Damn near chopped the first guy's head off."

Andrea's meal was temporarily forgotten. She was surprised to feel warm tears in her eyes.

"The rest of the bandits went for him. A few of them had guns but couldn't get a clear shot." Clay gestured with his hands "Confined space, y'know? They kept attacking him with their sticks and knives and he kept chopping them up. By the time the police arrived they'd had enough and made a run for it." Clay grinned wryly. "Well, apart from the ones he'd sliced and diced. He killed three and seriously injured another eight."

Andrea grimaced. An image of her own blood-soaked attackers flashed through her mind.

"When the police and the newspapers interviewed him later, he said he was prepared to be robbed but not to watch girls be brutalised." Clay pointed to his own elbow. "The tendons in his left arm were severed in the attack. His surgery was paid for in a private hospital and he was given a medal by the Indian government for his bravery... oh, and free travel on India's rail network for life."

"I should think so, too. So how did he end up out here?"

"One of the students he saved was the daughter—the only child—of a Nevada congressman. A guy called Lew Phillips. He pulled some strings and Tansen was granted American citizenship."

"I had no idea. That was never reported on our news."

"It only made ours because Phillips *made* it news. So Tansen and his wife, Raj, moved out here. As you can see he really likes his cowboy folklore."

"So he's a man to be reckoned with." She resumed eating.

"And then some."

"That's a hell of a story."

"Hell of a man."

Andrea finished her food in quiet thought. She washed up the dishes and utensils then switched the TV back to the news channels. Another ten minutes of channel hopping provided no more new details than the earlier reports. Many of the segments were the same ones as they'd already watched. News on a loop. Same words, same faces, no new information. She hit the mute button.

Clay turned from the window where he'd been standing. "The guys are back."

She stood next to the big Texan and peered through the window. The bulky Hummer was parked outside. A cloud of dust mushroomed around the vehicle for a couple of seconds then drifted lazily to the ground. She watched with new eyes as Danny and Tansen collected brown paper bags from the rear hatch. She felt a lump form in her throat. She knew she'd be dead already if she hadn't happened upon the mismatched brothers, and here was another deadly man seemingly willing to help. She'd never believed in fate, unwilling to accept that one's life path was predestined. Yet after watching her brother murdered, she had stumbled upon three warriors with not only the skills, but the fortitude to keep her alive. Andrea allowed her eyes to close in prayer. Maybe there was a chance, however slim, she would survive.

Tansen stormed through the door, his waddling walk accentuated by the armful of bags he carried. Danny gave her a smile and handed her a cardboard box. She turned it over in her hands.

"Sabre? What is this, a stun gun?"

"Just in case."

The clothes were deposited on the wagon-wheel table. Andrea picked out a pair of jeans, a tartan blouse and a T-shirt. She took fresh underwear and socks from the packs and returned to the bathroom. Five minutes later she emerged looking and feeling like a changed person.

"They fit okay?" asked Danny.

"The waist's a bit big, but they're fine." She turned to Tansen. "Where can I dump these?" She held her soiled garments in a loose bundle.

"Just put them next to the back door. I'll toss them on the fire later."

"What should I do with the rest of the clothes?"

Danny passed her a backpack, the store tags still in place. "Put anything you're not wearing in here. Clay, there's one for you too."

As the Gunn brothers took turns in the bathroom to change into their new gear, Andrea tried booting up her battered MacBook. A crack ran diagonally from corner to corner across the screen. Given how much it had been through, she was amazed the laptop was even in one piece. After a short burst of whirring and several beeps, the screen flashed, then went black.

"Damn it!"

Tansen raised his eyebrows. "No good?"

"It's toast. A technician could probably duplicate the hard drive, so it doesn't mean everything's gone, I just can't get to it. When I get home..." She stopped herself. "It doesn't matter. Everything important is in the Cloud." She straightened her shoulders. "It's just junk now. No point carrying it around. Do you have a computer I could use?"

"Sorry, I never had much use for one."

Andrea nodded. "Could I use your phone? I need to let my parents know what's happened."

Tansen silently pointed to a wall-mounted phone. She rose and walked over, lifting the cordless handset clear. She looked back at her host. "Is there somewhere I can speak in private?"

"Sure." Tansen led her to a bedroom. He closed the door as she began to dial the number.

Andrea waited nervously. *What can I tell my parents?* She was scared of choking on the awful words. The soft ringing began in her ear. Her stomach flipped. She allowed the phone to ring ten times before hanging up. A strange mixture of guilt and relief swept over her. She knew she'd have to speak to them, but was glad that the moment had been delayed. She sat on the bed and allowed her chin to drop, her hair hanging down over her face. Sobs racked her chest. Fatigue leached through her body, suddenly, unrelentingly. Andrea realised her eyes were closed, yet didn't seem to have the strength to open them again. She curled up at the bottom of the bed like a child and let sleep take her.

16

"Mr Carter, I have Magson on line two for you."

Topcat pressed the reply button on his intercom unit. "Put him through."

Magson's voice was raspy from thirty years of a twenty-a-day habit. "Top?"

"I believe the Nevada assignment has been compromised."

"Compromised?"

"I've been unable to contact the team as expected."

"Unable?"

"Jesus, Magson, are you just going to repeat random words back to me or are you going to get on this?"

"You want a second team on it?" His second-in-command coughed noisily down the phone, causing Carter to swear silently at the handset.

"Yes, I want a second team assigned and on the trail within the hour. Who else have we got in that neck of the woods?"

"We've got six in Los Angeles, just back from Pakistan.

They're all old hands. They'll be good to go."

"Who?" Carter asked curtly.

"You know them, Top, the Presidents."

Carter smiled. He did indeed know the team well. He tapped the team name and individual tags into his computer and a set of six profiles appeared on screen. He studied the faces before him. Six men, all sharing a common feature. Their eyes spoke of an immeasurable yet controllable capacity for violence. Killers' eyes. "Get Lincoln on the line. I want his team ready to roll ASAP."

"I'll get right on it."

"Send the mission briefing to him. Give him a status report. Call me back when they're moving."

"Will do, Top."

Carter studied the screen again. The short list of operator names blinked green. The green highlights told him that they were all live and active. A single click on each of the highlighted names would open their personnel files giving full names, military histories and contact details. But Carter knew most of the details already. He scanned the call signs and allowed himself a tight-lipped smile. He was confident that the Presidents would get the job done.

He considered the Apostles for a moment. The four-man team, if still operational, could assist the replacement team. That would give a mobile force of ten. Carter had witnessed fire teams of less raze entire villages during his time in Africa.

The six names continued to blink green. *Lincoln. Washington. Bush. Clinton. Kennedy. Roosevelt.* All were highly qualified. He moved the cursor and clicked on an icon showing the other team. The call signs of the Apostles appeared. The four names blinked green. Carter scowled slightly, considering. Would he have to close the file on Matthew, Mark, Luke and John? Only time would tell. If they *were* still alive and had dropped the ball, he would deliver some old-style biblical wrath himself.

Twenty minutes and another pot of coffee later, Magson confirmed that the Presidents had received and accepted the assignment. Thomas Carter, known to his teams as Topcat, allowed himself to smile fully for the first time that day.

17

Andrea's scream tore through the house. Danny was the first through the bedroom door, his hair mussed from sleep but his muscles coiled and ready to spring. Just as quickly he relaxed and waved at Clay and Tansen—who was wearing pyjama bottoms decorated with rodeo clowns—gesturing them to hold back. "She's all right."

Andrea was on the floor, her arms wrapped around her knees. She rocked back and forth, tears fresh on her face.

"Oh, Jesus. It was all real."

Danny sat on the floor next to her. "Are you okay?" He knew how inane the question sounded, yet had to ask.

"I was dreaming. But it was real."

Danny looked into her eyes, trying to think of some comforting words. None came easy to him. "I—we—*will* make them pay."

Andrea swallowed. It sounded like there was a lump in her throat big enough to choke her.

His voice was as sharp as flint as he repeated his words.

"Why would you? You don't owe me anything. You

don't know anything about me. Why would you risk your life for a stranger?"

"I guess we all have to stand up on a train once in our lives."

Andrea smiled weakly. "Yeah. Clay told me about that."

She scrutinised him. Danny could guess what attracted her gaze—the scars around his eyebrows, old scars, like those of a boxer. She dropped her eyes. "Help me up?"

Danny stood and offered his hand. As she gained her feet, she reached out tentatively, her fingers stopping a fraction of an inch short of his face. "Danny…"

He pulled away gently. "Come on. You've been asleep for nearly fifteen hours. You need to catch up with the team. We shouldn't have stayed this long but we thought you needed the rest. Hell, so did we." He looked at his watch. "It's nearly six a.m. Time to get moving."

Andrea looked shocked. "Really? I feel like I've hardly closed my eyes."

"That's the effect of shock. Your mind just wants to shut down and block out all the bad shit."

"I feel numb. Not just emotionally but bodily as well." Andrea clenched and unclenched her hands several times as if trying to restore some feeling to her limbs.

"The worst thing about shock is it can sneak up on you when you're least expecting it. You think you're back to normal then realise you're about to walk in front of a truck. It tends to shut down your perceptions." He realised he sounded like he was speaking from experience. He was.

Andrea smiled weakly again. "At least there aren't many trucks out here."

"I know it doesn't ease the hurt. I was just trying to explain the effects."

Andrea reached out again; this time her fingers did stroke his face. "I know. You've already done so much. It's unbelievable. I don't know how I'm ever going to thank you all for saving my life."

Danny moved back, breaking the contact. "Come on, I want you to hear about our next move. The guys are waiting for us." Danny led her back into the living room. Clay and Tansen were now dressed and both had mugs of coffee in their hands. Tansen wordlessly fetched another and handed one to Andrea.

Clay was the first to speak. "We've been talking about our next move. I need to pick up some cash from a safety-deposit box I have tucked away in Vegas. That'll keep us going for quite a while. That way we can stay off the grid. We don't know how far of a reach these guys have. It's better if we don't use credit cards. It could be an unnecessary precaution, but better safe than sorry."

"Vegas!" Andrea blurted out the word louder than she'd intended. "My passport is still in the hotel room's safe!"

The men glanced at one another.

Andrea continued, "I'd forgotten—the rooms are booked until the end of the week. The trips up to Area 51 were supposed to be spread over four days, but we were going to go back to the hotel each night."

"It's risky to go back to your hotel. If there're more men after you they're probably watching it," said Danny.

"But I'll need my passport to get home." Andrea looked panicked. "I can't stay over here on the run for ever."

"Going back to the hotel might do away with that option if they're waiting for you." Danny was aware that his voice had none of the tenderness it had had in the bedroom. A single tear ran down Andrea's face. He cursed himself. She was still too fragile; he had to go easy on her.

Clay shifted in his seat. "I guess we could check it out. Take a look-see. If the coast is clear, we go in. If not, we head for the hills."

Danny shrugged. Having said his piece, he was now resigned to the plan. "We should ditch the car. Leave as few tracks as possible. If I think it's safe, Andrea and I will go to the hotel. Clay you pick up the money. If it's not safe we all leave town pronto, no arguments." He turned to Andrea. "Your passport is no good to you if you're dead."

Tansen spoke up. "I have an old pickup truck out back. You can have that. I just use it for lugging around horse feed and fence posts. It's not pretty but it'll get you where you need to go." Tansen retrieved a set of keys from a drawer. "It's four-wheel drive as well. It might come in handy. Just give me a hand to clear my stuff out of the back."

Clay volunteered to help. The two men left the house by the rear door, leaving Andrea and Danny alone again.

"I tried to call my parents yesterday but they didn't answer. If the news has reached them they must be sick with worry."

Danny tried to control his face. She clearly didn't know what a stupid thing she'd done. "It's a good thing they didn't. You can't do that again. I know it seems hard, but I'm just trying to keep us all alive long enough to figure this out."

"I just need to let Mum and Dad know that I'm still alive."

Danny shook his head. "We don't know how far the web stretches. These guys may have the resources to listen in on your parents' phone. Believe me, it's pretty easy to do these days. Until we find out exactly what they want with you, it's best to stay off the grid as much as possible. So no phone calls, no emails, no social media, nothing."

Danny was almost impressed at the way Andrea stuck out her chin defiantly. "But Clay is going into a bank to get cash. What if they're tracking *him* now as well?"

"He's going to get cash from a private safety-deposit box. He keeps it under a false name." Danny smiled at the puzzled look she gave him. "Clay is very wealthy. It amuses him to keep stashes in different countries."

"How rich is he?" Andrea flushed. "I don't mean to be rude."

"Even I don't know what he's worth. But I like to remind him that he's got way more money than sense."

"Did he strike oil in Texas or something?" Andrea asked.

"No, not exactly. It's a sad story really. Just after he left the Rangers, he met and married Diana. She was a real techno-geek and was one of the first dot-com millionaires. She had a company that patented a search algorithm that's still used in most search engines. I don't know much more technical detail, just that she sold the company for more money than you could spend in a lifetime."

"Wow. Where's Diana now?"

"That's the sad part. Clay and Diana were only married for two years then she was killed in a hit and run just outside of Dallas."

"Did they get the driver who killed her?"

"No. The cops found the car burned out a few days later, but they never found the driver."

"That's so shitty."

"Diana was an only child so Clay got everything, which turned out to be way more than even he knew about."

Andrea puffed out her cheeks. She clearly did not know what else to say.

Danny walked to the front door and peered through. "They've brought the pickup around. You can help me load up if you want to."

"Sure."

Danny hefted the two backpacks of clothes and nodded at the paper bag of disposable cell phones. "You take that."

Once outside, Danny popped the trunk of the stolen car and pulled out the two MP5Ks and the dead man's backpack of assorted handguns and ammunition. He laid them on the flat-bed of Tansen's truck. The Dodge Dakota pickup was dented in several places, and its faded yellow paintwork sported more than a few scrapes. It looked like what it was, a well-used utility vehicle. A thousand like it traversed Nevada daily. It would not draw any unwanted attention.

The sub-machine guns made muted clunks as he laid them out. Andrea looked at the angular weapons with curiosity. She touched one of the MP5Ks with a tentative finger. "Could you show me how to use one of these?"

Danny raised an eyebrow. "I could, but it's probably not a good idea. I'll ask Tansen for something more your size when we get finished."

"I'm not a wimp, you know!"

Danny turned to face her. "I didn't say that. But different

weapons suit different people. I'm not trying to fob you off. I'm not against you having a weapon, just not one of these."

Andrea huffed and let her hand linger on the sub-machine gun a little longer.

Tansen appeared at her side. "Ask Tansen for what?" He tossed a duffle bag at Danny. "Here. You probably shouldn't have a platoon's-worth of firepower rattling around for all the world to see."

"Do you have anything that will fit Andrea's hand?" asked Danny.

A grin like the proverbial cat that ate the cream lit up Tansen's face. "Oh I'm sure I have. But we'll have to test-fire a few to get the right match." He took Andrea by the arm and led her back into the ranch house.

Danny motioned to Clay, who had ambled over. "Well that's Tansen happy for half an hour." He started packing the MP5Ks and the backpack into the duffle bag, along with the new cell phones, then pulled the satellite phone from his pocket. He checked that it was still powered off, then tossed it in too.

Within minutes single shots began to ring out from behind the house. The brothers smiled at each other. The tones of the retorts changed after every six or eight shots. Danny knew that Tansen would be working his way through a suitcase full of assorted pistols and revolvers. With the steady echo of gunshots in the background, he and Clay finished loading the pickup.

Clay wiped dust from his face. "Let's dump the car while they're out back shooting."

Danny drove the Honda back into Castillo, Clay

following in the pickup. He parked the stolen car in a side street near the Tarbucks coffee house and left the keys in the ignition. With a bit of luck the car would be stolen again and end up many miles away.

When they arrived back at the ranch, Tansen and Andrea emerged from the front door. Danny leaned out of the window and gave her his best cheesy grin. "Hi honey, I'm home. Did you find something neat at Guns 'R' Us?"

Andrea angled herself, holding a small gun pointed down at forty-five degrees. The compact revolver looked like it belonged in her hands. "Tansen gave me a Taurus." She turned to Tansen. "What did you say it's called?"

"A Model 856. .85 Special ammo, chambers six rounds."

She grinned, and pulled a small cardboard box out of her pocket. "And he gave me extra bullets."

"Looks good on you, and you learned your lessons well, I see." Danny nodded in appreciation of the safety stance.

"She was a good student," Tansen added in affirmation. "Shame you can't stay a few days. I'd have her shooting the wings off flies. Here." He handed Andrea a small holster. "It's Velcro, easy on, easy off."

Andrea secured the holster around her belt at the hip, then slid the small weapon into its pouch. "I feel like a cowboy!"

"And you look like one—but you're a cowboy who doesn't have a licence to carry." Clay grinned. "Better put it in the bag with the rest of the hardware for now." As Andrea reluctantly removed the holster, Clay stepped forward and extended his hand to Tansen. "I'll be back to pay for all of this as soon as I can."

Tansen waved him away. "No need. Just stay alive. Come and see me again once this has all died down. I'll have a crate of beer in the fridge with your names on it."

"We can't thank you enough, Tan. We'll be back this way as soon as it's safe," said Clay. The men embraced. Danny offered his own thanks. Then Andrea stepped close and took the Gurkha's face in her hands. She kissed him on the cheek and gave him a long affectionate hug.

Tansen felt himself blushing as the woman climbed into the pickup truck.

"Bye y'all." His voice was drowned out as the Dodge pulled away. A waving hand came from each of the front windows.

He made his way back inside the house. He sat in his favourite chair and looked at the picture of his wife.

"Well Raj, I guess it's just you and me for supper." Raj stared back silently, the half smile for ever frozen on her lips.

18

The Western Lakeview Resort and Spa sat a few blocks west of the main Las Vegas strip. The lake itself was a man-made affair much like the rest of the city, although to call the two thousand square feet of water a lake would have been creative licence anywhere else, at least as far as Danny was concerned.

The hotel sat in the shadow of the giants: the Bellagio and the Wynn Las Vegas, and many other multi-million-dollar casino resorts were just a throw of a poker chip away. The six storeys of the Lakeview paled in comparison. Clay drove them up East Flamingo Road and Danny and Andrea got out of the pickup in the parking lot of the Earl E. Wilson stadium. It was half full of vehicles displaying licence plates from every state in the continental US.

Danny opened the duffle bag and pulled out the three Motorola disposable cell phones, all freshly charged. He slipped one in his pocket, then handed the others to Clay and Andrea.

"You give me a holler at the first sign of any trouble and I'll be back." Clay gripped Danny's shoulder as he spoke.

The side of Danny's mouth twitched into a smile. "You're one of only two numbers in my speed dial."

"Damn right. Be careful. I'll be back in half an hour." Clay drove off without further comment.

Andrea and Danny crossed the parking lot and then the main road at a trot. "You stay here. I'll take a look," said Danny. He punched a couple of buttons on his Motorola. Andrea's identical handset began ringing.

"Like walkie-talkies?"

"Exactly," said Danny. Andrea nodded and went to stand in the shade of the building. She pulled the straw cowboy hat she'd found in Tansen's truck lower over her hair to shield as much of her face from passers-by as possible.

Danny rolled his neck and shoulders then arched his back. Both the muscles and skin around his midsection were tender but wouldn't stop him moving fast if required. After taking a deep breath through his nose, Danny stepped from the burning heat into the coolness of the hotel. He allowed his eyes to adapt to the change of light as he looked around the lobby.

The interior of the hotel was a combination of postmodern bland with occasional nautical themes. Framed pictures of ropes knotted into intricate patterns marked the junctions in the corridors and several decorated the area behind the check-in desk, which occupied a third of the lobby. Three members of staff were busy behind the desk, two attractive women checking guests in, and a heavy-set black man who was probably security, flicked through a filing cabinet, his back to Danny. The man's shoulders were much wider than the cabinet.

Danny scanned the room. Nothing alerted him to any danger. No tough-looking men with bulges under their jackets stared back. Just a normal smattering of couples and families on vacation. One man sat alone at a low table, a small cup of coffee untouched in front of him. The man held his head in his hands. Danny had two guesses: heavy losses at the casino or a heavy night last night.

Danny lifted his cell phone to his mouth. "Clear."

Thirty seconds later Andrea entered the lobby, passed Danny without making eye contact and approached the desk. A woman whose name badge identified her as Tania, smiled at her. "Hi, welcome to the Lakeview. How may I help?"

Danny saw the tension in Andrea's shoulders. *Breathe.* "I'm in room 4495. I left my room key here while I was visiting the Hoover Dam."

"It's incredible, isn't it?"

"Yeah, it's something to see."

Danny saw Tania hand over an old-style key complete with a red plastic fob. Not many hotels still used the traditional key; most had long since moved over to the key card.

"Is there anything else I can help you with today?"

"No that's everything thank you." Andrea began to turn away.

"Oh, Miss Chambers, you have a letter. This came in two days ago for you. I'm sorry, my colleagues should have given it to you when you checked in." Tania produced a large padded envelope emblazoned with the FedEx logo and handed it over with a smile. Andrea thanked her and walked towards the elevator doors.

Danny slipped his hand into the crook of her elbow as

she pressed the call button. "We should take the stairs."

Andrea glanced around the lobby. "Is there anybody here?"

"I don't think so. I just don't like being boxed in if there's even a slight chance of danger. I'll go first. Stay about six feet behind me."

They climbed the stairs without incident. As they reached the fourth floor Danny paused at the stairwell door, listening. Nothing. He waved Andrea forward as he slipped into the corridor.

"It's down here."

When they reached the room Danny held his hand out for the key. Andrea handed it over without comment and took a few steps back. Danny drew the Glock 37 he'd taken from one of the dead gunmen. He'd checked the clip earlier and knew it to be full. The Glock contained ten .45 calibre rounds, each one more than enough to kill. He put the key in the lock without a sound and turned it, then pushed the door ajar with his foot, allowing it to swing fully open before crouching and scooting inside. A rapid sweep of the room followed. His whole body worked as a single unit. Wherever his eyes went the Glock travelled simultaneously.

"Clear."

Andrea followed him into the room and he locked the door behind her. Maid service had been; the bed was made, the room neat and orderly. She opened the closet to reveal a safe, punched in the four-digit code and it opened with an audible clunk. After removing her passport and a document wallet she sat on the bed. She opened the wallet and wordlessly showed Danny the contents: money, medical insurance card, plane tickets. He nodded, and she began pocketing the paperwork.

"Is that everything?" asked Danny. He received a nod in response. "Good, let's go."

Suddenly Danny pivoted, gun at the ready, as a repeated scraping sound came from the door. Danny recognised the sound. Someone was using a lock-pick gun. Certainly no staff member would use such a tool.

The door began to open.

19

The ringtone on his phone played the first three lines of "Jailhouse Rock" before he answered. He gave his surname by way of response. "Lincoln."

"Go secure."

Lincoln entered a five-digit code and a red light on the display lit up brightly. "Secure."

"I've got an assignment for you. Are your team good to go?"

"Always."

"This is a highest priority. A previous team may have dropped the ball, we need a swift resolution."

"Brief?"

"I'm sending through the dossier now. Read it and respond within the next thirty minutes."

Lincoln returned Magson's call twenty-two minutes later. "Mission understood and accepted. The team's good to go."

"Do you require any ordnance?"

"Negative, we're fully equipped. Just have the pay cheques ready."

"Of course."

"Oh, we'll need transport once we hit Vegas: one truck and one bike that can go cross country as well."

"No problem. One of our people will meet you at the airstrip. Your transport will be waiting."

The man known to his employers as "Lincoln" downed the last inch of Wild Turkey in one gulp. He turned to his long-time friend and fellow President, "Washington". "Round up the guys. We saddle up in an hour."

Washington nodded as he uncurled his huge frame from the easy chair. He gave one last lingering look at the *Girls Gone Wild: Spring Break Special* DVD he'd been watching, then headed for the parking bay of Lincoln's LA duplex.

The rest of the team assembled. Only "Clinton" proved difficult to locate. This was due to his being otherwise occupied with two Russian prostitutes on Wilshire Boulevard. He finally answered his phone with an annoyed gasp and grudgingly arranged a rendezvous with the rest of the team at a diner next to the Pavilion for Japanese Art. The five men—Clinton, Washington, Roosevelt, Kennedy and Bush—listened with detached acceptance as Lincoln gave the mission brief. Then Clinton began to describe, in intimate detail, the depraved act that the summons had interrupted.

It was a short hop on a private plane from the City of Angels to North Las Vegas Airport. Situated in what the locals referred to as Northtown, the airport catered for private and business flights far more readily than the larger McCarran International Airport. As promised, there was an SUV waiting for them in a hangar. Parked next to the Toyota Land Cruiser was a Harley-Davidson; the operative known as Bush preferred the extra mobility.

The men gathered around the SUV, unpacking their go-bags, strapping on body armour, checking weaponry. Washington booted up a laptop and launched tracking software. Bush examined the Harley and pronounced it serviceable, then he and Clinton prepared to leave. They were to do a sweep of the target's last known residence—the Lakeview Hotel. Within minutes of the plane landing, the bike was tearing out of the airport via a service road. Bush leaned into the wind, enjoying the speed. Clinton clung on behind him.

The Lakeview didn't impress either man as they sailed past the baseball stadium, hung a tight U-turn and pulled into the parking lot. The target, Andrea Chambers, had already left the hotel by time the first team had arrived on the scene. The chances of her returning were slim but both men had learnt not to underestimate the stupidity of a fleeing target.

They entered the lobby and strolled past the check-in desk as if they were guests. A pretty Latina on the desk flashed them a smile as they passed. Clinton pressed for the elevator. He glanced back at the woman. He hadn't ridden a Latina for a while.

The ride between floors was short and they stepped out onto the carpeted hallway. A large man wearing a Hawaiian shirt and a Penn & Teller cap brushed past them and took up most of the elevator himself.

Bush smiled as the elevator doors closed behind him. "Buffet must be open."

Clinton coughed into his hand. "Fat fuck."

"Did you see that shirt? Guess he thinks *Magnum, PI* is still cool."

Clinton shook his head. "He looks like he ate Magnum."

The men chuckled as they approached room 4495. Bush lowered his voice to a whisper. "You do the honours. I'll keep an eye out."

Clinton produced a small pistol-shaped tool. After slipping the narrow blade into the lock, he depressed the trigger repeatedly as fast as he could move his fingers. The lock-pick worked a treat. The tumblers in the lock relinquished their grip and the door opened an inch. He gave Bush a satisfied nod after stashing the lock-pick and drawing his Kel-Tec PF9. He favoured the pistol due to the fact it was easily concealed and had real stopping power at the ranges he worked at. He liked to be within spitting distance of his target and prided himself on his one-shot, one-kill prowess. Bush too carried a Kel-Tec, but his chosen model was the futuristic looking PMR-30, due to the thirty .22 Magnum rounds it held. His rule of thumb was, if you can put one bullet in your man, you can put in ten for good measure.

Clinton dropped into a practised crouch and listened. The room beyond was silent. He pushed the door open with his foot and took two steps inside. The warning shout caught in his throat as something slammed hard into his face. As he brought up his pistol and squeezed the trigger, the door slammed behind him.

20

As he threw the coffee machine at the intruder's head, Danny Gunn burst out of the hotel bathroom. From the corridor he could hear another man's voice yelling a name—Clinton? *No time.* He moved low and fast, one hand sweeping down onto the gunman's wrist, as the other slammed into his throat. Danny aimed the blow so the web of his hand between the thumb and forefinger would crush the trachea.

But it was clear that this "Clinton" was no novice. He angled away from the blow, tucking in his chin. Danny pivoted as he fought to remain out of the line of fire. Clinton also pivoted, squeezing the trigger of his weapon. One bullet punched a hole into the headboard of the bed, while another went wide and hit the telephone, making it leap into the air. The two men whirled in a tight circle.

Danny felt a lance of pain shoot up his leg as Clinton landed a boot just below the knee. Momentarily distracted, he didn't rock back far enough to avoid two glancing blows to his jaw and cheek. He sensed the weight shift as Clinton began to launch another kick. Knowing that if he went down, a bullet in the head was sure to follow, Danny stamped down on Clinton's foot, stopping the kick before it started. As Clinton struggled to maintain his balance, Danny slammed his forehead into the man's nose. Not a graceful move by any stretch, but it had the desired effect. At close quarters, the head-butt along with the elbow and the knee were the weapons of choice.

Clinton slumped with his back against the door. Danny clamped down on the man's gun hand with his teeth, half the thumb in his mouth. After a couple of shark-like shakes of his head, a Kel-Tec PF9 pistol dropped to the floor. Stepping back, Danny watched Clinton curl into a semi-foetal position. One hand was clamped over his ruined nose, the other cradled against his chest. Danny drew his own pistol. He jabbed it once hard into his opponent's face. "One chance! Who sent you and why do you want the woman?"

Clinton opened his mouth, seemingly ready to talk, when a series of bullets ripped through the door. One of the rounds caught him low in the back. He slumped down further.

Danny didn't wait for the second man to enter. He sent four rapid shots through the door panels: two at chest height, and two more up high. He waited two seconds then put another three rounds through the thin walls either side of the door. He knew the instinct to duck against the wall when being shot at through a door. With a solid brick wall you were relatively safe. Against a wall comprised of breeze blocks and one-inch plasterboard you were as protected as a horny teenager with a pin-pricked condom.

The shots to the right of the door were rewarded with a muffled yelp.

Andrea appeared from the bathroom, her face a mask of terror. "We better get out of here," said Danny. He desperately wanted to interrogate one of the men. Hoped that there was only one on the other side of the door.

On the floor, Clinton rolled slowly onto his back. He was trying to breathe. All he achieved was a series of short, ragged gasps. Danny knew why. Although the shooter was wearing a lightweight Kevlar vest, the effect of being shot at close range was much like being punched in the stomach by a professional boxer: heavy bruising, broken ribs and internal bleeding. He was not a threat, at least for the moment.

"Stay behind me," Danny said to Andrea. His voice held no room for negotiation and she nodded. He reached for the ruined door handle. He knew that the gunman in the corridor was probably not dead. There was a strong chance of being shot at as they exited the room. He could try sticking his pistol around the door and firing a few blind shots, but a trained operative would most likely respond by blowing his hand off.

"Wait!" Andrea grabbed his arm. "Greg and Bruce had the adjoining room."

On the floor, Clinton was struggling to sit up. Danny had no time to spare; he kicked the man full in the face. He went back down with a pained grunt. He wasn't completely unconscious but wasn't about to do a tap dance either. Danny put his heel hard into his face again, then turned to see Andrea opening the connecting door.

They stepped through into a mirror image of her room. Men's clothes dangled loose over the back of one of the chairs. A faint smell of Hugo Boss aftershave hung in the air.

A bottle of tequila stood on a bedside table with less than a quarter of its contents remaining. Andrea looked around wordlessly. Danny could imagine what she was thinking—relics from before the unthinkable happened.

Danny moved over to the room's main door. He knew there was still a chance that he'd be in the unseen gunman's sights if he stepped out into the corridor. But he was out of options. The windows were sealed and they were on the fourth floor anyhow. He eased the door open an inch. A man in Kevlar was lying against the wall opposite, his legs splayed out into a wide V. His gun was trained on the door of Andrea's room. His eyes spoke of murderous intent.

Danny stepped out at an almost casual pace and had his pistol levelled at the gunman's head as it turned towards him in recognition of the situation.

"Slippery bastard."

Danny tilted his head, accepting the curse as a compliment.

"You've got balls, I'll give you that," said the recumbent shooter. Danny could see a dark crimson patch spreading across the top of his left hip. "Just step out all casual like so you don't trigger my point-and-shoot."

Danny motioned to the man's semi-automatic. "Throw that over here. Easy."

The man clearly considered going for it for a second or two, then tossed the pistol. It made a dull thud as it landed on the carpeted floor. Danny used his heel to carefully slide the weapon backwards through the open door.

"Your man—Clinton was it?—is finished. He didn't give me the answers I was looking for. Your turn. What's your name? Why are you after the woman?"

The man looked down at his bloody hip, grinned humourlessly. "I'm Bush. She's carrying stolen intel. She's a fucking traitor to the flag. Guess that makes you a traitor too. And a shit-poor shot. Just a graze."

Andrea stepped out into the corridor, holding Bush's gun. "Liar! I don't know anything about stolen intel!"

"Bush" shook his head, a disgusted expression on his face. "Hey we're not talking WikiLeaks here. You were reported as trafficking stolen data vital to the defence of the UK and US alliance. If the Taliban or IS got hold of it thousands of people would be at risk. But you know that already, that's why you're selling it to a known sympathiser. Piece-of-shit bitch."

Andrea stared at the gunman, her mouth hanging open in shock. She pointed the Kel-Tec at him for a moment then lowered it again. "What the fuck?"

Danny shook his head. "You've got the wrong woman. She's a civilian. She wouldn't know the Taliban from turpentine. Look, I'm not going to kill you. But I need you to report back to your superiors. Back off. Re-examine your intel. You've got the wrong target."

Bush screwed up his face. "Are you in the game? What are you, freelance for hire? Ex-army? Special Forces?"

Danny didn't answer. He didn't have to.

"I thought so. Then you know the drill: we don't get to pick through the assignment files. The boss says go and do, so we go and do."

Danny pushed the pistol towards his face again. "Tell them what I said."

"Do you really think they'll listen to a grunt like me?

She's been targeted from the top. Government-issue. She's never walking away from this, even if she succeeds in handing over the data. We'll hunt her to the ends of the earth. Can you spell Guantanamo?" He looked directly at Andrea. "You're gonna fry for this."

Without warning, Danny stepped forward and ploughed his boot under Bush's chin. His open mouth snapped shut and he slid sideways down the wall.

"Talk time is over. Come on." Danny pulled his cell phone from his pocket and hit the speed dial. "Clay, we need to leave right now."

"I'm a couple of minutes out."

"We'll meet you around the back of the hotel."

"Two minutes!"

"Down the stairs." He held his pistol pressed against his thigh as he moved. Andrea stayed close behind him, their hurried steps echoing slightly in the confines of the stairwell. As they reached the ground floor, they skirted the lobby, avoiding eye contact with the staff and visitors. A quick jog took them past the swimming pool and out into the rear car park. Background music and laughter tinkled from the pool deck. A child screamed with glee and then a loud splash from the pool followed. As they stood, partially concealed between an SUV and a small camper van, Andrea gasped and panted.

"I didn't realise I was so unfit!"

Danny's mouth twitched into a smile. "Consider this aerobics with added motivation."

She bent forward at the waist, her hands resting on her knees, as she tried to slow her breathing. "You know, I don't mean to be critical but Clay told me earlier that you're a martial-arts expert, kung fu and all that. Why didn't you just chop that first guy in the room?"

Danny snorted. "Andrea, real fights are short and nasty, ugly things. If I'd tried anything fancy we'd both be dead up there."

"I wasn't being funny. I just thought—"

"It's not like it is in the movies." He glanced at the hotel. "People see Steven Seagal and Van Damme spin-kicking guys and throwing them around like it's the easiest thing in the world. The only reason we're still alive is that those guys didn't really expect us to be up there. I don't think they'll make that mistake again."

Andrea nodded. "Hey, don't get me wrong, you were great. Even if it didn't look much like kung fu." She chopped the air a couple of times with a straightened hand.

"If it makes you happy I'll try and jump-kick the next bad guy for you." Danny crossed his eyes in mock annoyance. The warm tingle that lingered in his stomach was an old familiar friend.

The pickup truck clipped the kerb as it made a sharp turn into the lot. Danny stepped out from his vantage point.

The passenger door sprang open with a screech from the unoiled hinge. Clay leaned out. "Last call for passengers: Blondie and Dagwood."

Danny pushed Andrea into the cab. He didn't have time to apologise for his hands on her ass. As he joined her he heard Clay's breath hiss between his teeth.

"Shit."

Four car spaces ahead, his face contorted in pain, Clinton was lurching towards the pickup, his pistol extended. The boot imprint on his face was raw and beginning to darken.

Danny hung on as Clay stamped down on the gas pedal. A bullet tore the wing mirror from the driver's side door, sending up a small shower of glass. Clay wrenched the steering wheel. The front grille of the pickup slammed into Clinton, catapulting him back into a parked car. His gun spun away across the parking lot as his head met the unforgiving metal of the vehicle.

"That guy's like Wile E. Coyote. Just keeps getting up for more." Danny raised his eyebrows in grudging admiration.

Clay cackled as he steered onto East Flamingo. "Guess he didn't realise I'm a real live Road Runner. Beep-beep that, you broke-assed fucker."

21

Lincoln answered his cell phone on the second ring. "Any sign of the target at the hotel?"

Bush's voice was slurred as if he was talking through tightly clenched teeth. "She was here but the guy with her got the drop on us. They're gone."

"Clinton?"

"He's still alive but down for the moment. The scumbags hit him with a car. One of them winged me, but it's only a flesh wound. She's with two men, unknown quantities. One definitely has combat experience."

Lincoln gazed at the luminescent cityscape of Las Vegas that lay beyond the airport hangar where his team had set up shop. Gleaming high-rise hotels and millions of twinkling lights. He took a long breath before speaking again. "Noted. Is Clinton shot too?"

"No. I think his ribs are broken though. He's saying he's all right but he's walking like he's in *Dawn of the Dead*. And he's got a nasty concussion."

"Can you get over to Spring Valley? We've got a man there

who'll take care of him. You remember Ricardo Chavez?"

"Yeah I remember him. Where is he?"

"He's on Fenway. Number 157. I'll call ahead and let him know you're coming."

"We'll head there now. I'll call you back as soon as I'm free."

"Will you manage with him on the bike?"

"Clinton's a tough son of a bitch. He'll make it," replied Bush.

"When you've done that, follow us," said Lincoln. He ended the call.

He turned to the rest of the team. He shook his head. "We're already one man down. Clinton."

"He gonna be okay?" asked Washington, looking up from his laptop.

"Bush says he'll live but he's out of the game for now. Bush will join up with us when he's able. Washington, I need you to work your magic on the tech. How are you doing getting a fix on the last team's sat-phone?"

Washington nodded at his laptop. "I'm narrowing it down. The main power is switched off but the secondary chip pings once every three minutes. I need to load all of yesterday's data and pinpoint where the last signal came from."

"Okay, stick with it. Then at least we'll know where the last team are and how far they tracked the target. I suppose it's too much to ask that the bitch is updating Facebook or Tweeting her coordinates?"

Washington curled his lip. "No activity since before the previous team made first contact."

"Well keep an eye on her feeds. People are stupid."

Lincoln walked out of the hangar office as he loaded the email app on his phone. It was possible that the target would try to take a flight or a bus, but there was no way his team could cover that much ground. As well as North Las Vegas Airport and McCarran International, there were dozens of smaller airfields within a hundred miles, and several major bus terminals. But Lincoln made a point of knowing the right kind of people in as many cities as possible, they could save a lot of legwork if you were running someone to ground. Hotel porters, waitresses, police officers… and transport personnel. Nobody paid them any attention but they tended to see and notice a lot. If you weren't shy with the green they could come in very handy. He sent out an email to all the relevant contacts at local airfields, bus terminals and train stations, with a photograph of the target. If she tried to use public transport, there was a good chance that one of his sources would spot her.

He turned to where Kennedy and Roosevelt were loading up their weapons. Kennedy worked the firing bolt on one of the long guns. He'd served as a Marine Corps sniper and still enjoyed the thrill of the long-range shot. It took real skill to operate as a trained sniper. Kennedy was a valuable asset. Long hours of solitude, pinpoint concentration and above all else, discipline. The gang-bangers of the world could put a bullet in an enemy but it tended to be a spray-and-pray affair. Civilians got hurt. A lot of soldiers seemed to be that way as well. But Kennedy's mantra was: *There's no such thing as friendly fire, only careless fire.* Of his seventeen confirmed kills under Lincoln's leadership, not one involved any collateral damage.

"Roosevelt" preferred it up close and personal. A Saiga-12

assault shotgun twinned with a modified Dan Wesson Valor .45 were his firearms of choice. Lincoln considered him a blunt weapon. Valuable but more expendable than Kennedy and the tech-savvy Washington.

A tapping on the glass window of the hangar office alerted Lincoln that Washington was trying to get his attention. The tech specialist had set up shop in the cramped space, and as Lincoln entered, the aroma of burned oil and stale sweat greeted him. Washington pointed to a map display on his laptop. "We've got a fix on the other team's sat-phone."

"Where?"

"Like I said, the main power is still off but the secondary chip pinged from a single location for nearly twenty-two hours. See, here's where the first team reaches the hotel, on the target's trail. Then they're on the move, out in the wild, going fast. Then the phone is static, as I said." He pointed to an area of desert. "There's nothing on the map, but it's worth a shot."

Lincoln stared at the screen for a few seconds. "They could have been parked up at a rest stop."

Washington shrugged. "Maybe."

"Or they could have been lying low at a safe house," Lincoln continued.

A smile from Washington. "Maybe."

"Worth checking out. We're a man down, and could do with their backup, and whatever intel they have on the target. She could be anywhere now, but they might have knowledge of her intended destination. Better than sitting here with our thumbs up our kazoos."

"Sir, I like a thumb up my kazoo. I've even paid for it on occasion."

Lincoln laughed. "Okay mount up. We're moving out." He left the office and repeated the order to the other two operators. Within less than a minute all four were in the SUV, with Washington at the wheel.

The Toyota gathered speed as they left the airport grounds. Washington was being guided by his GPS. The route to the satellite phone's last location skirted close to a couple of small towns. These were of no interest. The nearest relevant population centre was a small dot labelled Castillo. The phone's coordinates corresponded to a location some twenty miles past Castillo's dot. They skirted the busier roads out of Las Vegas, then joined the 157 heading east.

Roosevelt leaned forward from the back seat, growling, "I don't care who these guys are. I'm gonna deep-six every last one of them."

No one in the vehicle disagreed.

22

Danny Gunn worked his jaw, feeling the muscles begin to tighten. Clinton had caught him with a couple of solid blows. He silently berated himself. A few years ago he would have dropped the man with that first throat strike. He glanced down at his callused hands, making a promise to himself that he would sharpen up his hand-to-hand skills as soon as he was done with this shit-stick.

Clay glanced over. You okay bro?"

"Aye, I'm fine." Then he added, "Nothing a shot or two of Glenfiddich wouldn't fix."

"I'll see your Glenfiddich and raise you two Jack Daniels," quipped Clay.

Andrea glanced between brothers and added thoughtfully, "I'll see your Jack Daniels and raise you a pint of snakebite."

Danny laughed. "Classy. They don't even serve that any more at *home*. Your chances of a snakebite over here are just about zero."

Clay raised an eyebrow. "I've heard of it, never had one."

"It's lager mixed with cider, half a pint of each," said Andrea. "It's good."

"It's what's known in the trade as 'loopy juice'," Danny added.

Clay affected his best Queen's English voice. "Ah, one can't go wrong with a little loopy juice."

"Indeed," replied Danny. "Who said that, Queen Victoria?"

"Victoria Beckham."

"Damn, I was so close."

"Yeah, one is a strange old bird with only one expression—"

"—And the other was the Queen of England."

Andrea nudged Danny's shoulder. "Hey, I've met Posh and Becks, they're really nice people."

"I liked all of the Spice Girls, just couldn't eat a whole one." Danny crossed his eyes and feigned a sick expression.

"What, not even Victoria? I've seen McDonald's fries that were wider than she is."

Andrea was now laughing as well. Her voice had a strange nervous energy, almost exhilaration. "Stop it, right now." She shook her head. "I can't figure you guys out. One minute it's death and destruction, the next you're taking the piss!" After a few seconds of quiet she asked, "So where are we going now?"

Clay had manoeuvred the pickup in an arc, tracing a wide sweep first heading away from the Lakeview, then parking on the opposite side of the road. He had turned the vehicle to allow a view of both the rear and side entrances of the hotel.

"Nowhere," said Danny. "We're watching."

"Watching what? Shouldn't we be heading for the hills? You said we needed to get out of Nevada as soon as possible."

"It's better to be the hunter than the hunted. Now it's our turn," said Danny.

He pointed to where a large motorcycle was waiting to join the traffic flow from the rear car park. The bike carried two occupants. The main rider removed his helmet long enough to spit a mouth full of red saliva onto the roadside. Andrea recognised him from the hotel corridor—Bush. The passenger was slumped low, with one hand around the driver's middle and the other clutched across his own torso. Clinton.

As the bike headed west, Clay began to tail the Harley, four cars back. Danny didn't need to ask why. They both knew that the bike would remain within the speed limit. Injured hitmen and traffic police were never a good mix.

"Where do you think they're going?" asked Andrea. She glanced between the brothers.

"Taking care of their injured. So we'll see where they do that and maybe pop in and ask a couple of questions." Danny gave her his best great-white-shark smile.

Clay chuckled, his wide shoulders bouncing up and down. "Pop in, yeah, I like that. Maybe a little Gunn action is just what the doctor ordered."

Andrea shook her head again, bemused. "You guys just make stuff up as you go along."

Clay's chuckles intensified. He turned to Danny. "Hey, tell her about the thing with the car battery."

Danny shrugged, giving Andrea a sideways glance.

"Car battery?"

Clay started again. "Ah, he won't tell you but I will. Danny boy here was working in the Central African Republic a few years back—freelance, you understand, not army. His team was sent to crack down on gangs coming over the border from Sudan. On patrol one night, they happen upon a raiding party's camp." Clay looked over at his brother. "How am I doing so far?"

Danny rolled his hand in the air in an impatient gesture.

"So Danny and another couple of his guys come across one of the gangs camped at an old garage on the outskirts of town. These boys had AKs coming out their ears and were getting ready to use them."

"Stop hamming this up," interjected Danny. "There were about ten of them and three of us. They had a man on sentry posted at the front gate of the garage yard. There was no easy way to get to him. We didn't have any suppressors for our weapons and if I'd just shot him the rest of the gang would have been up and at us."

Andrea asked, "So where does a car battery come into all of this?"

Clay made a left turn, still keeping four car spaces between them and the Harley.

"The sentry was leaning against an outbuilding, smoking. We had approached from high ground and were looking down on the compound. We needed to get up to the main building as quietly as possible, so I used what was to hand."

"The battery?" she asked.

"Aye, there was an old truck battery lying next to a pile of tyres. I picked it up and dropped it on the Sudani's head from about five feet."

"Jesus, what happened next?"

"The guy went down like a bullock in a slaughterhouse. We dropped down, double-timed it over to the main building and introduced ourselves to the rest of the glee club."

"And?"

"And they never raped or killed anyone else ever again."

"When we get finished here, you can tell her about the Somali pirates. Oh and that thing with the meat grinder," said Clay. He slowed the vehicle as the motorbike rolled to a stop outside a house with a bright-yellow front door.

"Give it a rest Clay," Danny grumbled again.

Clay responded with a wink. Andrea shifted in her seat. Danny could tell that she wasn't quite sure what to say.

"Heads up. We're back on the clock."

Bush almost carried Clinton to Ricardo Chavez's front door. The ex-army medic barely raised an eyebrow as the two of them came in, and he wordlessly hooked an arm around Clinton's waist, making the man groan. He and Bush walked down the hallway that divided the squat house into two equal halves, and laid Clinton out on an examination table in a bedroom at the far end.

Chavez cut away Clinton's shirt and prodded gently at the ribcage, which was covered in angry patches of purple. Clinton drew up his knees in an attempt to ease the pain. Chavez sniffed.

"Broken ribs. Bruised kidneys. Nasty head hit. If this was kosher I'd get a scan."

Bush nodded. "How long will he be down?"

Chavez filled a hypodermic. "Hard to say." He addressed Clinton as he injected the drug. "Morphine. You're welcome." He turned back to Bush. "And you?" He gestured towards the bloodstain on Bush's hip. Bush pulled down the waistband of his trousers to reveal the long graze of a bullet wound. An inch further in and he was pretty sure his day would have been ruined. He stood impassively as Chavez cleaned the wound and slapped on a dressing.

"Thanks." He shook Chavez's hand, then grasped Clinton's shoulder. "See you soon, you lucky bastard." Clinton smiled broadly. The drugs had clearly kicked in.

Bush walked back to his bike, fists clenched. He wanted to be there when the team caught up with these fuckers. He and Clinton were tight, real buddies both on and off the clock. But he couldn't get sloppy, no alerting the cops, no speeding. Of course he was a legal firearms permit-holder. But the modified Kel-Tec and the bloodstained trousers he wore would raise a few more questions than he had patience to answer.

He pulled the bike over to the kerb as he joined the eastbound 157. He tugged his rubber-coated cell phone from a pocket and activated the the sat-nav application. Two spots were marked on the display. One, a blinking green dot, showed the position of Lincoln's vehicle. Another dot, this one red and solid, indicated his destination. After clipping the phone securely to the inside of the Harley's fairing, he accelerated so quickly that Ghost Rider would have struggled to keep up.

23

Clay ducked behind the wheel of the truck as Bush re-emerged from the house. He was obviously in a hurry to leave. A Hispanic man of about thirty stood in the doorway for a moment, then disappeared into the house. The motorbike sent up grey smoke from its wheels as it shot down the street.

"How'd you want to do this?" asked Danny.

Clay frowned for a moment then answered. "I'm gonna carry you in."

Danny looked doubtful. "What about Andrea?"

"Stays in the truck. Out of sight." Danny nodded. No doubt this time.

Andrea began to raise an objection but Danny stopped her. "We don't know how many are inside, but I really want to speak to that fucker again. If it's too hot, we'll tear out of here."

Andrea looked nervous at the prospect of being left alone but finally nodded in agreement. A smile from Clay seemed to help a little. She lay flat across the seats and pulled an old Indian blanket over herself. After a moment she scrabbled in the duffle bag and brought out Tansen's revolver and held it across her chest.

The brothers walked to the house together, Danny leaning heavily on Clay—an injured man barely able to support himself. Clay rang the bell. The Hispanic man answered almost immediately.

"You forget something?" He looked suddenly confused as he registered the new faces. Clay released his hold on Danny, who sagged into the man's arms, effectively immobilising him.

"We've got another man down," said Clay urgently. "Who are you? Get the other doctor, quick."

Their host began to haul Danny to the rear of the house. "I'm Chavez, didn't they tell you? I'm on my own. What's wrong with this one?"

Danny straightened like Lazarus on his most famous day. "Well I've got an awful stiffness in my dick. I've called Beyoncé but she just can't fit me in this week."

Chavez sprang back, his face darkening. "Get the fuck out."

Clay grinned. "We need to have a word with Mr Bump in there."

Chavez's hand crept towards his trouser pocket.

Clay whipped the Colt Python from his belt. "Unless you're thinking about showing me your private tattoos, you'd better keep your hands where I can see them. Empty your pockets with your left hand, two fingers only."

Chavez tossed his wallet and a folding knife onto the floor.

Clay shook his head in disappointment. "Do no harm. Isn't that the hippopotamus oath?"

"It's the Hippocratic Oath, asshole."

"That's what I said." Clay smiled. "Now, you're a sensible-looking *cabrón*, so just sit there and we'll be out of your hair soon enough."

The brothers exchanged a look. Danny moved down the hall, clearing each room as he passed. As he reached the recumbent patient, he turned and gave Clay the thumbs-up.

Clay addressed the medic, pointing into a bedroom with the barrel of the revolver. "Let's go in here and give those crazy kids some privacy. You know what it's like on a first date."

Danny examined the bruised body and after a short spell of consideration, tipped Clinton bodily off the padded examination table. He landed in an untidy sprawl. Danny slung the bed to the side of the room. Clinton managed to make it onto all fours before Danny's shin slammed into his damaged ribs.

"You don't write, you don't phone..."

Clinton rolled onto his back, a look of furious recognition on his face. "You!"

"Who else were you expecting? I think Dr Giggles is taking a coffee break at the moment."

Clinton sneered. "Chavez was a combat medic with the Rangers. He'll eat your man alive."

As if prearranged, a head-shaped hole appeared in the panel of the door. A second later Clay stuck his own head through. "Turns out he didn't care much for small talk. Kind of touchy, if you want my opinion. Hey, you two go ahead, I'll wait for Sleeping Beauty here to wake up."

Danny turned back to Clinton, his voice dropping an octave. "I'm going to ask you some questions and I will be getting answers before I leave. You know the drill: there's the easy way or the other way. And no one's here to bail you out. It's just me and you, Mr Magoo."

24

"There's no easy approach. We could ditch the van and close in on foot, but that could go south if we need to leave in a hurry." Washington spoke as he surveyed the landscape between the team's parked vehicle and the ranch house that corresponded to the dot on the sat-nav display. "Surely if the previous team is here they'd have decent vehicles or bikes, but there's nothing. And this doesn't look like a typical safe house. Besides, if they were here they would have checked in with Magson or Topcat."

Lincoln nodded. "I think you're right. We're not tracking the last team—we're tracking the target, or at least where she was before Clinton and Bush found her at the hotel. She or the two men she's with must have taken the sat-phone, not knowing it can be tracked. And if there's someone in the house they're sure to be watching us by now."

Washington proffered the binoculars. "It's built on an elevation. Good visibility for ten miles in every direction."

Lincoln accepted the binoculars and scanned the ranch house. "Well we're here now. Worth taking a look. It looks lived in, likely the owner helped the target—Topcat said the last team reported that she took a tumble, probably needed medical assistance. We'll go in and find out what the owner knows." He motioned at Kennedy. "I want you up on that ridge to the west. If we encounter trouble you'll be our silent support."

Kennedy made no comment, but the smile he gave told of his readiness to shoot.

A guttural rumbling announced Bush's arrival on the Harley. He dismounted and after a quick stretch updated Lincoln on Clinton's condition.

"You follow us in on the bike. Park up three hundred yards out by those trees and circle around so you're coming in from our three o'clock. Kennedy is taking the high ground. Me and Washington and Roosevelt are going in from the front. We don't know who or what we might find in there, so everyone stay sharp." Lincoln pointed to the blood that had dried into an inkblot pattern on Bush's hip. "You okay?"

"Yeah, it looks a lot worse than it is. The bullet creased my hip. Bled quite a lot but Chavez fixed me up," replied Bush.

Lincoln nodded. "Let's move in."

The SUV rolled forward at a steady twenty miles per hour. Five hundred yards from the house, Kennedy jumped from the vehicle. He hit the ground running full speed, cradling his M4, traversing the steep incline in a matter of seconds. Lincoln could see him in his mind's eye, lying prone at the highest vantage point with the main entrance in his sights through the wide-lens Schmidt & Bender scope. Kennedy was the perfect sniper.

The SUV pulled up and Lincoln, Washington and Roosevelt approached the door. They moved forward in a loose triangle formation with a few yards of open ground between each man. There were no other vehicles parked out front but that didn't mean the house was empty. There were outbuildings to the rear of the main ranch house. Any one of these could conceal a car.

Lincoln rapped on the front door after checking it was indeed locked. The phone in his pocket vibrated twice indicating that Bush was ready at the side of the house. Lincoln pressed his palm hard against the door, first at the top, next in the middle and finally at the base, gauging the give, checking for reinforcing or a triple locking bar. It felt like a standard model.

Taking one step back, he slammed his foot into the wood just under the lock. The door flew open and he moved in. The bulbous Calico pistol he carried swept an empty living room in one motion, Washington and Roosevelt following behind.

"Clear the rooms." His men nodded and moved deeper into the house. Bush appeared from a side room, sliding a large combat knife into its sheath.

"Got in through a window. Lock was child's play."

"Anything?"

Bush shook his head. "Nothing."

The house was quiet.

The team reconvened in the living room. Bush gazed at the collection of Old West Americana in the room. "Did we just break into Clint Eastwood's house?"

Lincoln ignored him. "We'll sweep the outbuildings in twos. Washington, you're with me. Stay sharp. Meet out back if all's clear."

Roosevelt and Bush headed for the rear. Lincoln jerked

his head at Washington, who followed. They walked towards the building furthest from the house, guns at the ready. It was empty apart from the usual assorted tools, shovels, a pickaxe and a post-hole digger. Nowhere for a concealed man to hide.

The team emerged into the rear yard. A low constant rumble caught their attention. At the same time, Lincoln's phone vibrated against his hip. "Vehicle approaching. One visible tango inside. You want me to drop him?"

"No, I need to quiz him first. Stay where you are and keep your eyes open. Don't want any other surprises."

"Roger that."

Washington angled his head, clearly recognising the sound. "Incoming traffic. Sounds big, Hummer or the like."

Lincoln nodded, flicked his hand at Bush then at the side of the house. Bush jogged back to the large window he'd opened earlier.

"Let's give this guy a warm welcome home." Lincoln led the way back into the house. They took up positions in the living room, in triangular formation. The sound of the Hummer came closer, then faded as the vehicle pulled up. Lincoln allowed himself a quick inspection of their visitor through the front window. A short, dark-skinned man clambered down from the Hummer. He stood, considering the team's SUV, then scanned the elevation where Kennedy was positioned. *This guy's no civilian.* The man rolled his neck, then calmly finished the Snickers bar he'd been eating. As he approached the front door, Lincoln moved to intercept him.

Definitely not a civilian. Lincoln was impressed with the impassive expression on the man's face, considering that he was looking up the barrel of the Calico.

"You Jehovah's Witnesses are getting really pushy."

Lincoln scowled. "Sit down. I've got some questions to ask you."

"Do I win a prize if I get them right?" asked the man, showing his small white teeth in a smile.

"You get one of these if you don't." Lincoln pressed the Calico into the man's forehead.

25

"The Doc still breathing?" asked Danny as he and Clay walked back to the pickup.

"Yeah, he'll need to self-medicate for a few days, though." Clay knocked his knuckles against his forehead.

"Maybe he can write himself a prescription."

"I'm not sure he'll be writing anything for a while. The fool tried to grab my gun. His fingers bend both ways now. That, and I hog-tied him with a garden hose."

"Well my wee chit-chat proved very informative. Turns out Clinton just loves to talk."

"Would the fact that you were pressing his broken ribs into his lungs have any bearing on the matter?" asked Clay.

"Maybe, but I prefer to think it was my shiny disposition and winning personality."

"He's going to be mad when he's able to breathe again."

"I figured. That's why I tied him to the table." Danny tapped on the side window of the pickup. Andrea's face appeared from beneath the blanket. She flicked the locks to open. As both brothers clambered into the vehicle, she sat upright and pushed the blanket back behind the seat. "What happened?"

"We know more than we did half an hour ago."

"We know that the doctor's head wasn't as hard as a door," offered Clay with a smile.

"And?"

"Let's get down the road a way and I'll tell you."

Clay slipped the pickup into drive and steered them south.

An hour later they were sat in a roadside diner that promised "the best meatloaf sandwich in America". Clay put that to the test by eating a double portion. Andrea opted for tuna salad on rye with a side order of fries. She noticed that Danny ate his with one eye on their surroundings, a sweep every ten seconds.

"So what did the guy in the house say?" asked Andrea, her voice just above a whisper.

Danny took a long slug of coffee. "They're working for a PMC group called TSI... Trident Solutions International. The company operates out of London."

"PMC?" asked Andrea.

"Private military contractors. The squad that's on our tail is a six-man unit. The men who killed your brother were a separate four-man team. Clinton's team—his real name is Martin Fletcher, by the way—said that they were assigned last-minute when the first team dropped off the grid."

Andrea gave a tight-lipped scowl, thinking of the fight at the Winnebago. Dropping off the grid was one way of putting it. The smell of smoke and death seemed fresh in her nose for a long second. "So these PMCs? What are they, some kind of secret agents?"

"No, nothing so glamorous. Most are just ex-forces looking to make a better living. But these guys are a little different. PMCs are usually used as additional resources by the regular armed forces in a conflict area. Some are hired out as private protection, bodyguards, to visiting VIPs and the like. It's unusual to have a PMC unit with a termination order. That kind of mission is usually handled by government units."

"Who would have sent a team like that after me?" she asked.

"Fletcher didn't have that information. He received the assignment through his team leader, who just got the search and destroy details."

"So what were his orders, exactly?" Andrea's voice caught in her throat, and Clay rested a large brown hand on hers for a moment.

Danny looked at her with a new intensity. "The brief is to recover the package that you are supposed to be carrying at all costs and you are to be terminated with extreme prejudice. Anyone you've had contact with is also subject to termination."

"Fuck."

"He didn't know who's bankrolling the mission. Operators at his level just go and do. Take it on trust that what they're doing is necessary."

"How do you know he was telling you the truth?" asked Andrea.

"Because he wanted to live. I had the guy in an arm-lock with my knee in his broken ribs. He was singing like the lead in a gospel brunch. These are blue-collar killers; they look after themselves first and foremost. There's no vow of silence, no cyanide pills, no *omèrta*."

"Okay, so he's telling the truth. What now?"

"We need to go to an Internet café. I want to do some research on these guys. Then we'll find a motel outside of town."

Andrea rubbed her face with both hands. "How common are these PMCs?"

Clay grunted. "You've probably seen them on television a hundred times and never knew it. There are more private contractors than regular soldiers in the Gulf. A hundred-billion-dollar industry. Danny here should know."

Danny nodded. "I work for a private company myself from time to time. A lot of ex-forces people do. I contract with Odin Corp, based in Paris. And no, before you ask I've never been sent to kill a woman carrying a mystery package."

"Is that how you got all those scars?" She looked at him with new eyes, her impression of him again in flux.

"I've just come back from a term in Iran. A lot of stuff happening over there at the moment."

"And?" She hoped he would elaborate.

After a long pause he continued. "I was on patrol in a town called Dezful. Our convoy was ambushed and the Humvee I was in was taken out by an RPG. The rear of the vehicle took the worst of the hit. Two guys in the back were killed instantly. I was in the front passenger seat. Me and the driver, Mickey Wells, survived but with second- and third-degree burns. Wells got the third degrees. I escaped with seconds. Not something I'd ever like to try again."

"So have you heard anything about this company, Trident?" she asked.

"No, but there are so many companies out there now. Honestly Andrea, I can't stress how big the industry has grown. The biggest of them, Blackwater, has its own planes, ships, supposedly even its own submarines. These guys are being brought in to train our own regular troops."

"A couple of my old buddies from my Ranger days are Blackwater now. They're good guys." Clay didn't meet Andrea's gaze. "Most of them are decent men just doing the job as best they can."

"But private armies? That can only lead to big trouble down the road." A cold chill crawled like a spider across her back.

Danny gave a slight shrug. "They're already everywhere, people just don't realise it. After Hurricane Katrina there were hundreds of PMCs, especially Blackwater troops, in New Orleans. They were there to control the crowds and stop looting. The public thought they were National Guard but they weren't."

Andrea pushed away her plate. The brothers did the same and they rose, Clay leaving a sizeable tip. They returned to the truck and had only been driving for five minutes when they found what they were looking for: a small Internet café sandwiched between an ice-cream parlour and a bookstore.

Clay parked opposite. "You two go and do your research thing. I'll watch the street from the bookstore."

As Andrea and Danny made for the café, Clay called over his shoulder, "Get me some take-out."

"But you've just eaten," said Andrea.

Danny shook his head. "That was just a starter."

Danny moved to the counter and paid for two coffees, two apple Danishes and an hour's worth of browser time. Andrea took a seat at a computer.

She launched Google and typed *Trident Solutions International* into the search bar. The top hit led to the corporate website that detailed the company's worldwide security operations, both in the private and public sectors. The main graphic on the homepage refreshed every five seconds: men wearing full combat gear in desert terrain, then others in suits protecting a motorcade. Danny leaned over, peering at the screen. He snorted. Similarly unimpressed, Andrea clicked on the "contact us" link at the bottom of the page. An email address was listed. She ignored it. She could hardly send them a message saying, *Who paid you to kill me?*

There was also a postal address for the headquarters, somewhere in the English city of Cambridge. She hit the print icon. Seconds later a colour sheet was ejected out of the shared printer near the main counter. Danny collected it from the tray.

Danny pointed to the "about us" icon. "Click that."

The next page gave vague details about the company. Nothing of any practical value. No names and no faces. It was little more than a courtesy display to the outside world.

Andrea sighed. "I guess we shouldn't be surprised."

Danny shook his head. "They work in conflict zones and corporate security. Anonymity is a requirement."

"It was worth a shot," said Andrea. "I'm sending an email to my parents. Just to let them know I'm still alive. I won't say where I am."

The look on Danny's face almost stopped her, but not quite. "They need to know I'm still breathing. That I'll call them when it's safe. Don't worry, I won't start Tweeting that I'm on the run from hired killers." She typed so fast her fingers seemed to barely touch the keyboard.

"I'm impressed. I usually favour the one-finger-on-each-hand jabbing technique. Come on, it's time to get moving." Danny moved to the door but Andrea held up her hand. "We forgot Clay's take-out. I'll get it."

She returned to the counter and ordered a sixteen-ounce coffee and a box of mixed pastries. As she dug into her pocket for money she found the small padded envelope given to her at the Lakeview reception desk. She paid for her order, then ripped the perforated strip from the top of the envelope. Inside were a folded sheet of paper and a USB flash drive.

Danny appeared at her side. "What you got there?"

"The receptionist at the hotel gave it to me. I'd forgotten about it with everything else going on." As Andrea read the handwritten note, her stomach turned. She felt sick.

"Who's it from?"

"An investigative reporter from the *Herald*. One of my best friends."

She read it again.

Andrea,
I didn't know who else to send this to. No one at the office knows about this. I think I've made a big mistake. I was given this video file by a man who I think— although I can't prove it—was trying to blackmail a government minister. I suppose he thought he could

use me as protection. The man was found dead in Hyde Park yesterday. I thought he was just a chancer, one of those conspiracy loons that you hear about. But the video looks real. It's horrible. There is a copy of it on the USB drive, along with another video. I think I know who the man is.

If anything happens to me, make sure this gets out there. I haven't gone public with it yet as I can't verify its authenticity or identify the man in the video. But I will.

I noticed a car following me this morning. I'm scared I've stumbled onto something big. I'm sorry to involve you but I need to know that there is a copy somewhere, out of the country. Just in case.

If all of this turns out to be nothing, I'll buy you the best meal of your life.

Jeremy

Andrea turned the portable flash drive over and over in her hand. Then a sudden thought sent her almost running back to the computer. She typed "Jeremy Seeber" into Google. She ignored the first five results for an artist who specialised in driftwood animal sculptures. The sixth result made bile rise in her throat.

British journalist in double sex suicide shock! The link was to a British tabloid website, the story told in sensationalist style. Jeremy Seeber and his wife of eight years had been found dead at their Kensington home. Their cleaner had discovered the bodies in the main bedroom. The police had been summoned but had ruled out foul play. A preliminary pathologist's report stated that both Seebers had died as the result of autoerotic asphyxiation.

Andrea skimmed the rest of the article, but there was no other real information, just the predictable lurid description of what the practice involved: a ligature around the neck; restricted blood flow to the brain; feelings of euphoria.

"They killed Jeremy and Tess."

Danny took her arm. "Come on. We need to watch that video."

26

Tansen Tibrikot sat bound to a kitchen chair, his hands tied behind his back with electrical cord. He tilted his head in an attempt to divert a stream of blood that trickled into his eye. Two of his four captors were in his living room. One of them had turned on the television, was watching the rolling news station he and Danny had watched together a few short hours earlier. The leader, a man they addressed as "Lincoln", stood in front of Tansen, arms crossed.

"Linc," said the man watching the television.

Lincoln turned. "What is it, Washington?"

"Check it out."

Tansen craned his head. It was familiar footage of the burned-out Winnebago, bodies under sheets. Then another shot of a different stretch of road. And two more bodies. So all four of the dead operatives had been found. How long before the Gunn brothers were linked to the carnage? He twisted against the cord that cut into his wrists.

"Four bodies, plus a cop, all on the 375. That tallies with past data points for the last team's satellite phone. They definitely never made it this far."

Lincoln cocked his head. "But the sat-phone did. That confirms that the target must have it. Probably doesn't realise it's active even when powered off. Good to know. But I don't want to be playing catch-up, tracking them. We need to know their plans. Where they're going."

Beside Lincoln, the man called "Bush" was rubbing his knuckles. He turned to Lincoln, who gave him a nod. He rolled his fingers before snapping another punch into Tansen's face.

"Tansen, I want the names of the men helping Andrea Chambers. I want to know where they are headed. I want to know whether they have passed on the intel to a third party." Lincoln's voice held no animosity. Bush pulled his arm back. Another punch. He drew a black-bladed knife from his belt. "Let me start peeling this Chink motherfucker and he'll be talkin' soon enough."

Lincoln held up a finger. "We'll get to that. I'll ask again, one last time, who are the men with Chambers?"

Tansen allowed his head to sag, then answered after careful consideration. "They're called John Wayne and Richard Widmark. I hear they're hoping to cause a spot of trouble at some place called the Alamo." Tansen gave Bush the widest grin he could muster. Bush stepped in close and delivered three brain-numbing slaps to Tansen's left ear. The open-handed blows were savage and hurt more than the punches.

Tansen closed his eyes involuntarily as Bush held the tip of his knife a quarter-inch away from his right orbit. Then he reopened both eyes and stared directly at Bush.

Bush grinned. "Now that's more like it. I think Charlie Chan here wants to cause me harm."

The other men in the room laughed. All except Lincoln, who studied the prisoner intently.

Bush spoke again. "Look Kwai Chang, I really don't care how long this takes. I want you to play the tough guy. Let's see how much of a samurai you are when I cut off your balls and put them on that God-awful table over there."

Tansen silently recited a prayer to the Hindu Lord Ganesh. Then he raised his head. "Look you ignorant shit. I'm not Chinese. I'm not Japanese. I'm Nepalese. Do you even know where that is? NEPAL! Home to eight of the world's tallest mountains." He paused to shake blood from his face. "I'll tell you nothing about the men you are seeking, only that they are far better men than the ones who pursue them."

Bush slapped him hard again, then bent down so their faces were level. "I don't give a shit if you're from Middle Earth. You will talk. I promise you that."

Tansen shifted his gaze to the picture of Raj. She smiled back at him. He allowed himself a brief genuine smile, then addressed Lincoln, ignoring Bush entirely. "No. I will be dying today, but I will not be talking."

"You Gurkhas are stubborn little bastards aren't you?" Lincoln said matter-of-factly. He replaced his Calico in its hip sling, then nodded at Bush.

Bush rolled his neck. He was going to enjoy this. Then he stabbed down savagely into the muscle of Tansen's right leg. The resulting scream was more a roar of animal rage than pain.

Washington levelled his weapon. "If this fucker starts to turn green I'm outta here."

"I'll bet this against the Hulk any day." Roosevelt shouldered his Saiga assault shotgun.

Bush looked down at the two inches of blade that protruded from his prisoner's lower thigh. He looked theatrically around the room, then strode over to a side table and picked up a bronze statuette of a Native American on horseback. He weighed it in his hands, then nodded, seemingly satisfied. "Do you have 'knock-knock' jokes in the high and mighty kingdom of Nepal?"

Tansen said nothing.

"Knock knock!" Bush brought the statuette down in two sharp taps on the hilt of the knife. The blade sunk in deeper. Tansen ground his teeth but stayed silent.

Roosevelt joined in. "Who's there?"

"Bette."

"Bette who?"

"Bet this fucker is talking within two minutes." The two men laughed.

Bush was enjoying the interrogation. It had been years since he'd been let off the leash. Few assignments required the questioning of subjects and if they did, the government had their own specialists for the job. He knew from experience that a tortured man would say anything in order to survive, if only for a few extra minutes. The information was usually useless. But getting it was fun. Another two taps drove the knife in to the hilt. "Knock knock."

This time Washington answered. "Who's there?"

"Dan."

"Dan who?"

"Dancin's out! I can't feel my legs!" Bush grabbed the

handle of the combat knife and ripped it free. Another defiant roar.

Lincoln spoke again, his voice calm. "Who are the men with Chambers? How are they linked to the package?"

Tansen gave him a look that was half fury, half contempt. "By Ganesh, remover of obstacles, and Kali, goddess of time and death, I will see you all dead—in this life or the next!"

Bush smirked. He'd heard it all before. Another few minutes and the noodle-eater would be singing. He allowed a couple of drops of blood to fall from the tip of the Teflon-coated blade. He swung the knife like a pendulum in front of Tansen's face, making soft tick-tock sounds with his tongue. "Ready for some more? Good."

Lincoln's voice was as slow as melting ice. "The names of the men?"

Bush counted to three, then stabbed the blade deep into Tansen's right thigh muscle, careful to avoid the femoral artery. He didn't want him bleeding out.

"Now you're ready for some more." He raised the statuette. "Knock knock."

Lincoln's cell phone vibrated in his pocket. He answered after glancing at the display, raising a hand to Bush to wait. "Kennedy? Go ahead." A brief pause. "Negative. Let him come." He ended the call. "We've got a police cruiser heading our way. ETA three minutes." He turned to Tansen. "Anything you'd like to share?"

Tansen swallowed. "It'll be Jimmy Walsh, the sheriff. It won't be police business. He comes by regular." For the first time, Tansen's voice broke. "Don't you hurt him."

Lincoln's expression didn't change. He turned to

Roosevelt and motioned towards the bathroom. "Take him in there and keep him quiet."

Roosevelt moved behind the chair, tipped it onto its rear legs and dragged Tansen away.

"Let's have some music," said Lincoln.

Bush nodded and picked up the television remote. He found a music channel playing James Brown's "Living in America" and cranked up the volume.

"Open the door an inch or two."

Bush took up a position to the left of the door. He peered through the gap, and saw a man in a sheriff's uniform climb out of the cruiser and make his way towards the entrance. He braced.

"Afternoon buddy, it's Jimm—"

The greeting was cut mid-sentence as Bush pressed the barrel of his Kel-Tec PMR-30 to the man's temple, then pulled the sheriff's service weapon from its holster.

"Did you call in your location?" Bush asked.

The sheriff shook his head.

"Good." Bush reversed his PMR-30 and slammed the stock of the gun into the nape of the man's neck. Walsh went down onto all fours with a grunt. Another blow sent him fully to the ground.

"Hard-headed old goat, aintcha," said Bush as Walsh tried to climb his way back up the furniture. "Stay down." Another hit laid the man flat.

"Cuff him and tie his feet." Lincoln nodded to the bathroom. "And bring *him* back out. We need to finish this quick."

27

They stopped off at a shopping mall on the outskirts of Vegas. Clay purchased a basic laptop from a Walmart, and another half-hour drive south found them at the Aces High Motel. Danny affected a Texan accent as he paid for the room in cash.

"Do you have a credit card?" asked the young man behind the check-in desk.

"I'd rather not. I'm here with my—" Danny made a show of thinking about his next word "—secretary. My wife goes through my statements. You know how it is."

The clerk, whose T-shirt declared *Chet Rocks!*, nodded as if he indeed knew how it was.

Danny straightened an imaginary tie, giving Chet a conspiring wink. "We're stopping off to go through some sales figures."

Chet smiled knowingly, and handed Danny a key. "Enjoy your sales figures."

Danny made double finger pistols. "You know I will."

Danny left the reception building and made his way back outside, to where the motel rooms were housed in bungalows around a central parking lot. He walked to the door of room 25, turned the key in the lock, and with a hand on the butt of his pistol, entered.

The room proved to be a clone of every other motel he'd ever seen. A queen-sized bed and a small bedside cabinet with a telephone perched on top. A television with a finger-smudged screen faced the bed, and a small circular table with two chairs sat in the corner furthest from the door. The room smelled of old food, stale smoke and pine disinfectant. The bathroom was a simple three-piece in white porcelain. A nest of old hair sat in the shower trap.

"Clear."

Clay shouldered past him to get to the bathroom, dumping the duffle bag of looted weaponry on the bed. "Gotta go."

Danny and Andrea shared a look of brief amusement. "Doesn't do to get in the way of a charging Texan," said Danny.

Andrea moved to the table. She unpacked the laptop, letting the plastic packaging fall to the floor. She turned the main unit upside down, snapped the oddly shaped battery into the rear and after turning it back to its proper position, opened the screen. She handed Danny the power cord without looking at him.

Danny smiled. He remembered learning to field strip his rifle in his days with the Green Jackets. First with eyes open, trying each time to perform the actions faster without error. Then with eyes closed, feeling the components of the weapon with dexterity and purpose. Andrea had assembled the laptop with the same determination. He unwrapped the power cord from its twist tie and poly bag and handed it back to her.

She plugged the cord in the wall and then into the laptop. "It'll take a little while for the battery to take enough charge so we can power up."

Clay emerged from the bathroom. He winked at his brother. "Well, that's lightened the load a bit."

"Too much information," said Andrea under her breath.

"I'll go down the street and pick up some food and drinks." Danny slipped his pistol into his waistband and moved to the door.

"See if they've got any Cheetos," said Clay.

Andrea glanced up from the USB flash drive she was inspecting. "Toothbrush and paste?"

Danny made his way back to the grocery store he'd spotted on the way to the motel. As he picked up various items from the aisles, his attention was drawn to the wall-mounted television behind the cashier's desk. It was set to mute but the news report images were unmistakable.

The screen was filled with Clay's burned out RV. CSIs in dark jackets with the famous three letters blocked in bright yellow moved amidst the carnage. The ground was covered with yellow evidence markers. Officer Ryback's picture sat in the top left of the screen as a suited detective gave his professional "no comment at this time" routine. Another scene, more CSIs, two more sheet-covered bodies. The police had connected two of the crime scenes, found all four hitmen. There were no shots of the rental Jeep that Andrea had described, so it appeared that her brother and his partner hadn't been found yet. That was good—the police wouldn't be looking for her. A new image flashed up along with a BREAKING NEWS banner and Danny stopped in his tracks. His brother's driver's licence photograph, then a shot of Clay in his Rangers uniform.

Danny paid for the supplies. The cashier was an elderly Asian woman dressed in an old-fashioned floral jumpsuit. He nodded at the television. "Helluva thing. I don't know what this country is coming to."

The old woman gave him a smile and nodded. Danny pointed to the screen. "You ever seen anything like it?"

The woman gave him a blank stare. *"Rambo 3?"*

Danny didn't know what else to say.

Andrea looked up in alarm when the motel room door opened, then was instantly relieved to see Danny, a grocery bag under his arm. Clay sat next to her on the end of the bed, and he nodded at his brother before pointing at the news show on the television.

"I know." Danny set down the bag of groceries on the table. "That means we have to assume the second team will know soon enough, too."

"They've got my driver's licence. Traced the plates from the RV, no doubt. I don't know how they got a hold of my old service picture so quick though."

Andrea's voice was flat. "Google. You just search on Google Images. Has the picture ever been used on the news or a social networking site?"

"Well I'm not on Facebook, if that's what you mean." Clay paused. "I was on the news when Diana was killed.

They showed a few pictures of us. I think they may have used my service portrait then."

"That'll be it. Once it's out there, it's out there for ever." Andrea rubbed the USB drive between her thumb and forefinger like a lucky coin. "Still no mention of Greg or Bruce."

"No." Danny had nothing else to offer.

Andrea moved to the laptop and powered it up. The brothers began to spread the food out on the nearest bed.

"Cheetos!" Clay sounded like he'd won a prize.

"I got some subs and fruit as well." Danny unwrapped a ham salad sub, a full twelve inches long. He tore it in two halves and worked his way through the first. "Andrea. Food."

She looked at the Scotsman. "I don't feel much like eating. Too nervous at what's on this drive."

"You should eat now, while we have time. Don't know when our next meal might be."

Clay agreed, touting his family-sized bag of snacks by way of encouragement. "Damn right."

"A wise man once told me, when you're in the middle of it, eat when you can, sleep when you can and shit when you can. 'Cos there may be no time later."

Clay held up a finger thoughtfully. "Sun Tzu, *The Art of War*?"

"Jason Statham, Art of Being a Mean Mother-trucker."

"Deep."

"Indeed."

Andrea smiled despite the knots in her stomach. She picked an apple and a can of Sprite from the assortment. It wasn't diet but given the situation she decided to risk it. They shared the moment, three friends eating their chosen food group. The silence made her think of Greg. The late night snack-attacks. Junk food and beer, talking about their day, their hopes and dreams, jokes, opinions… The mouthful of apple proved hard to swallow. A long pull on the soda helped.

She wiped her mouth and moved to the table. "Laptop's ready." She took a seat in front of the screen, Danny and Clay standing either side. She inserted the flash drive into the USB port. Two mp4 video icons appeared.

She clicked on the first.

The grainy picture showed what looked like a basement, with no visible windows or doors. The camera panned slowly to the left. A tall pole with a single wire-protected bulb illuminated the area. By the convergence of two pools of light, she assumed there was a second lighting pole out of shot to the right. The video footage was clearly old. A date in the corner of the screen stated 03-07-94, the numerals white blocks; this must have been filmed on an old VHS camcorder.

The light shifted, illuminating one side of the room, the wall made of stark grey breeze blocks stained with patches of damp. A low ceiling with evenly spaced wooden beams was visible, a series of thick chains hanging motionless from the beams. Voices drifted in from off camera. The words were muffled and coarse and the resulting laugh was tinny in quality but clear. The light shifted again, as if someone off screen were dragging the crude lighting pole forward into a more advantageous position. The camera pivoted again. The bright arc now cast its glare over a scene that made Andrea grit her teeth with dread.

A young woman was secured to a bare metal bedstead. She appeared to be in her early twenties, slightly plump, and she would have been pretty if her face had not been contorted with fear. Her dark-brown hair was in disarray, and sweat beaded her face. She was naked apart from a stained pair of once white panties. Her wrists were bound with fencing wire, wound four or five times then twisted into an unbreakable spiral. Her arms were tethered above her head. Her ankles were likewise bound, her legs stretched out at angles to each corner of the metal frame. A red stained cloth cut into her face, acting as a gag. The lower half of her face was slightly distorted as the rag stretched her mouth into an unnatural shape. Dark rings had formed below her eyes where her mascara had run. Her upper lip was darkened with dried blood.

"I don't think I can watch this." Andrea's voice seemed small and distant.

Clay put a hand on her shoulder. "This is probably what got your friend and his wife killed. And whoever ordered their deaths also hired the kill squads to deal with you. You *need* to watch." His words made sense but that didn't make them any easier for her to hear.

The image momentarily changed to a blurred white as a man stepped into view. The camera refocused gradually as he walked slowly towards the tethered woman. Her screams were dulled by the restrictive gag but her eyes were stark and bloodshot with terror. The camera zoomed in on them; clearly the camera operator wanted to capture her fear.

Clay spoke. "At least two men. One to operate the camera and the one on screen."

The man moved to the top of the bed. He bent and said something in the woman's ear. The words were too low for the camera's audio to pick up. Whatever was said sent her into a desperate convulsion. The skin at her wrists and ankles appeared stretched to tearing point as she sought to free herself. The man patted her head, patronising, as an adult would calm an overexcited child.

The man took one of the dangling chains that hung from the ceiling beams in his hands. He pulled down and the top of the bed rose slowly from the floor. The small block and tackle unit squeaked as he worked the action. The man moved with a leisurely pace. He was in no hurry. The woman's head turned away from the camera as she and the bed were pulled inch by inch into an upright position.

The man turned to the camera, hands on hips, posing. He gave a casual wave to his future viewers. He wore only trousers and boots. His upper body was bare. His arms, shoulders and back told of an athlete. His were not the oversized muscles of a body-builder. His physique was more akin to that of a seasoned oarsman or professional boxer. Toned, tight and precise.

But the effect of his flat stomach and taut muscles was offset by the mask that covered his face.

"Jesus Christ…" Andrea's voice trailed off. She felt the Gunn brothers tense either side of her. The temperature in the room seemed to have dropped several degrees.

The masked face smiled directly into the camera. A lecherous, sick and deadly smile. It was an anthropomorphic combination of animal and human qualities covering the man's entire head, with only his piercing blue eyes and lower jaw exposed. Gnarled horns curled like those of a ram, the "skin" of the mask etched with folds and wrinkles, each one overlapping and blending with the next. The colouring was a mottled green/grey around the eyes and brow while below it resembled a port wine stain. The nose was wide and cruel, somehow simian and lupine at once. Random needle teeth dotted the upper jaw.

The masked man pursed his lips and blew a kiss, then moved towards his prisoner. He was clearly enjoying her terror. The man behind the camera began to sing. His voice was low and slightly out of tune. "I faaaaall to pieces…"

The masked man turned, his mouth twisting in irritation.

"Each time I see you again…"

The resulting hiss from between clenched teeth silenced the song.

The masked man turned back to the woman and produced a wide-bladed butcher's knife from behind his back. He angled the blade so that it reflected bright spots from the pole-mounted lights. The woman's eyes bulged as he loomed closer, exaggerating each small movement for maximum effect. Then in contrast to his slow theatrical posturing, he executed three rapid slashes with the butcher's knife, catching her just above the top of her underwear. The soft skin of her stomach split. She arched her body backwards into the wire springs of the near vertical bed frame, making them creak in protest.

The masked man plunged his hand deep into the crimson gash that gaped in the woman's lower abdomen. He withdrew his hand, a bloodied coil of intestine stretching far from the wound. There was a joyful laugh from behind the camera.

28

"Any *more* visitors due?" Lincoln's tone was weary. Tansen shook his head. Lincoln pointed to the picture of Raj. "That your wife?"

"Yes."

"She coming back any time soon?"

"No. She's dead."

"She will be if she shows up here unannounced," Bush smirked.

Tansen craned his neck to see where Jimmy lay on the floor. The sheriff was coming round. Blood had formed a viscous covering over his upper lip. A crimson bubble formed at his nose as he strained to control his breathing.

Bush hefted his combat knife, cutting the air with an audible zip. He then handed it to one of the other men.

"Here, Roosevelt. Enjoy."

Roosevelt moved close to Tansen, and whispered in a mock conspiratorial manner. "I wonder if Deputy Dawg here is up to hearing many knock-knocks?"

"He doesn't know anything. He couldn't give you

answers if he wanted to." Tansen spoke through gritted teeth, ignoring the taste of copper in his mouth.

"I know he can't tell me what I want to know, but I'm wondering how long you can keep your mouth shut once I start cutting off his fingers." Roosevelt took a single threatening step towards the sheriff.

Sheriff Walsh, known to many in Castillo as simply Jimmy, spat out bloody saliva that covered the toes of Roosevelt's Gore-Tex boots. "Tell them nothing. They're going to kill us anyway."

There was silence. Lincoln broke the moment by a single word to Roosevelt. "Proceed."

"Tell you what, seeing as you've been a sport with my buddy's jokes, I'm going to give you a two-for-one special."

The knife bit deep into Tansen's deltoid muscle, jarring against the bones in his shoulder. The pain was so severe that the Gurkha felt his consciousness momentarily desert him as the blade withdrew. He snapped back to full awareness as Jimmy filled the room with his own howls of pain. Roosevelt left the knife protruding from Walsh's arm. "How many knock-knocks has the old boy got in him?"

Tansen considered his next words carefully. "The men helping the girl are regular Joes. They caught your guys off guard and got lucky. The bigger of the two caught a bullet and is in a poor state. He'll be needing medical treatment pretty damn quick or he'll be finished."

"And?" Lincoln prompted.

"The other guy is an ex-con. He can pick your pocket with the best of them but he's no threat."

Bush rubbed his jaw. "He's full of shit. The smaller guy

has training. He's good with hand-to-hand and firearms."

Roosevelt made a show of looking disappointed. Then he kicked the hilt of the knife. Walsh writhed and began to hyperventilate, trying desperately to draw oxygen into his strained lungs. Tansen struggled against his bindings. "Help him! He has angina for Christ's sake!" The men looked on impassively. Walsh managed only one word before his ragged intakes of breath ceased.

"No!"

Tansen Tibrikot watched the last spark of life drain from his friend's rheumy eyes. A tear traced a path down Walsh's face before mingling with the congealing blood around his mouth. Insurmountable rage built in Tansen's core. The wash of adrenalin that coursed through his body numbed the pain in his injured limbs. Before that moment he had quietly accepted the inevitability of his death; it was his last moments of life that he now chose to spend differently. In one huge desperate burst of energy he rammed down with his legs. Bracing his chest, arms and back, he drove himself upright. The frame of the chair fractured into a loose tangle of wood and wire. With his arms and legs effectively hobbled, he jumped forward and clamped his teeth down on the only target that presented itself.

Roosevelt was bending to retrieve the knife from the dead sheriff's body when Tansen's jaws closed over his nose and a portion of his upper lip. Caught off balance, he toppled over the corpse with the prisoner on top of him. He tried to push the man away but the suffocating grip on his face held fast.

They sprawled and thrashed, faces locked together, one man grabbing wildly at the other. Tansen's fingers scrabbled at the pouches on Roosevelt's belt. Something popped loose.

Bush drew his pistol but as he was about to put a bullet into the prisoner he received an unexpected boot in the knee. The pistol bucked in his hand and the round punched a hole into the sheriff's back.

Roosevelt rolled on top of the Gurkha and began to punch at his throat, effectively blocking the remaining Presidents from taking a shot. Tansen managed to free one of his hands and brought it to his quarry's neck in a savage motion. Roosevelt fell back, his nose all but ripped from his face. A long sliver of wood from the back of the chair now protruded from his throat just below his left ear.

Washington and Lincoln both had their weapons levelled and ready but it was Bush, from a closer position, that fired first. The bullet punched deep into Tansen's chest, catching him high in the right pectoral. Another round smashed through his clavicle, the collarbone no match for the parabellum round.

As Bush centred on the Gurkha's face, a cylindrical object rolled towards him. He screamed out a single word. "Grenade!"

The blast shattered the windows into a thousand flying shards of glass. Bodies were flung back. Lincoln and Washington had both launched themselves behind the couch, which provided meagre cover but did save their lives. Bush had made a desperate dive, skidding on his stomach into the kitchen. The blast had propelled him head first into the corner of a kitchen unit.

Lincoln struggled to his feet, the ringing in his ears hardly bearable. He pulled a triangle of glass from his scalp. He looked around the room for his Calico, then realised he was still holding it. The room smelled of fire and brimstone and death.

Lincoln walked over to the remains of Roosevelt. Strips of blackened flesh flapped where his face had been. The Gurkha was gone.

Washington joined his team leader.

"Shit."

29

Clay rose as Andrea peered around the motel bathroom door.

"I can't watch any more." She ran a hand through her hair. "I've heard of snuff films… but I thought they were just urban legends. This is murder."

Clay nodded. "This is some serious business." He looked at Danny. "I know someone that can help us disappear while we decide what to do. It's time to get out of town."

"Disappear? Where are we going?" asked Andrea.

"I know a guy in the Keys who can help us. He runs a private charter company out of Florida. He's got a few small jets and twin props. He used to run guns and weed back in the day. But he's mellowed."

Danny frowned slightly. "Do I know him?"

"No, but he's a good friend. He'll get us out of here and off the radar in no time. We can watch the sunset in Key West while we figure this all out. I'll call him now."

Clay walked out of the hotel room, pulling his Motorola from his pocket and dialling a number. Three minutes later he was back. Andrea was still looking green. "It's sorted, but we've got an hour to kill before we head to the airport. Care to take a walk? Danny-boy can watch the rest of the video."

Clay held the door open for her, then shared a brief look with his brother. He knew better than most that Danny could detach himself from horrors on the screen. Almost like the way a mortician would view a mangled corpse, an unpleasant but necessary part of the job. Although they shared the urge for justice, the younger Gunn could hold the vendetta spirit far longer than any Sicilian could dream of. Many Texans were known for their supposedly stubborn ways, yet Clay felt Danny was capable of wrath of almost biblical proportions when suitably aggrieved. The glower in his eyes and the thrust of his jaw was a look that he'd only witnessed on a couple of previous occasions. Neither of which had ended well for the target of his brother's anger.

Andrea heard the video begin playing again as soon as Clay closed the door to the motel room.

Outside, she took a long slow breath. She shuddered, trying to rid her mind of the terrible images she'd just seen. The Nevada sun burned above and she felt its searing effect immediately.

"Can we go and get a drink somewhere?"

"A *drink* drink?" asked Clay, tipping an imaginary glass.

"Yes, a real drink. I could do with one right about now."

"Damn, woman. I'm liking you more and more. I noticed a bar two blocks over."

The walk helped steady Andrea's nerves, but there was a part of her that was sure she'd never be able to feel completely safe again. Especially after what she'd just seen. Clay seemed to read her thoughts, and when he slipped his arm around her shoulders there was no sexual charge to the act. It felt like a big brother looking out for his sister. Andrea let her arm snake around his waist as he pulled her close. They walked the rest of the way without speaking.

The bar had a central door flanked by two plate-glass windows. Neon signs in flickering red and blue told potential customers that both Bud and Miller were served, like there were many bars that didn't offer those American staples. Above the door, a curved sign declared that Ronnie's Bar had been open since 1985. In Vegas that just about qualified as an historical site.

The barman looked up as they seated themselves at the long counter. He was no more than thirty with black hair that hung in floppy curtains over his forehead. He flashed a pleasant smile and poured two beers as requested. They drank them quickly, without speaking. Clay ordered another round and scanned the room. There were only three other customers. A man in a fluorescent vest sat at the other end of the bar, his face and forearms deeply tanned from outdoor labour. The other two patrons looked to be a couple. The man was short and overweight. He looked like he spent a lot of time in places like Ronnie's. The woman with him was much better looking. She gave Clay a quick appraisal and Andrea an envious half smile.

"I still can't believe it. Shit like this doesn't happen to nobodies like me." Andrea took a long pull on her beer.

"Two things: shit like this does happen, and you're not a nobody."

"I'm screwed. My brother murdered in front of me. My friends murdered in London. I'm on the run with you two to God knows where, and now we've got footage of some maniac slaughtering a girl in a Fritzl basement."

Clay turned in his seat and held her gaze. "Look Andrea, I won't pretend this is an easy fix. It isn't. We need to keep moving and stay off the radar as much as possible. If it helps any, I've never seen a situation that Danny and I couldn't turn around and use against the bad guys."

"And that's another thing; how does Danny know how to do the things you say he can do? And more importantly *why* does he?"

"I'll answer the how first. He knows how to do what he does because he's a tenacious little shit who was born in the wrong century. He believes in a code of honour. You know he was a soldier, but that's not it. He learned to shoot and fight in the army but most of what he does comes from in here." Clay tapped his head then his chest, over the heart. "There's something inside him that won't let him back down. He's intense, but even if he wasn't my brother he'd still be my best friend."

"So is he some kind of vigilante?"

"Not in the way you mean. He doesn't cruise Gotham City looking for criminals or any of that crap. But he will do everything in his power to put right what he thinks is wrong. Men like him are called 'fixers'."

"And he fixes the bad guys, right?"

Clay raised his glass in salute. "He fixes them good."

"So why does he do it?"

"He's just got something inside him that won't let him sit

by. He sometimes gets paid for jobs but most of the stuff he's done is out of his own warped sense of justice."

Andrea grinned. "I'm glad he's on our side."

"So am I." Clay looked deep into her eyes, holding her gaze. "So am I." He drained his beer. "Come on, time to go."

The flirtatious woman made a show of smiling provocatively at Clay as they stood to leave. Her male companion turned angrily. After seeing the Texan he turned back to his drink without challenge.

"I bet you get that a lot," said Andrea, blinking as they stepped out of the bar into the sunshine.

"Get what?"

"The look that the Lycra princess in there was giving you."

Clay shrugged. "I do okay, I guess. A lot of the girls are put off by these." He ran his fingers over the scars on his face.

"Their loss if they can't see past a few war wounds." Andrea scowled at the imaginary females in question.

"I'm used to it now. They see someone as big as me with a scarred face and they think 'desperado'."

"They're hardly disfiguring. If your hair was a bit longer you would hardly see the one on your forehead."

Clay gave another dismissive shrug.

"How did you get that one?" Andrea ran a finger down the narrow white line that began at Clay's right eye and continued down to the corner of his mouth.

"I was working as a bouncer at a bar in Austin. I went to put a guy out for getting too fresh with the ladies. He was only a little guy but he had a straight razor hidden up his sleeve. My fault for not paying attention." Clay shook his head in self-admonishment. "Never made that mistake again."

* * *

Danny opened the motel room door upon hearing two sharp taps near the base, then positioned himself behind the door. One look at Clay and Andrea, and he put down the pistol he'd been holding.

The screen of the laptop was showing the Windows logo. Andrea gave the screen a sideways glance. "Horrible."

Danny nodded. "It is. But remember, there are two mp4s on the drive—the other one is quite different. Your reporter friend, he did most of the work for us. I think we can use this."

He tapped the touch-pad and the screen displayed two videos paused side by side. The left-hand one was clearly a still from the torture video. The masked man was turned, with most of his back to the camera. A puckered semi-circular scar was clearly visible. It looked at first glance like a shark bite. The curving scar ran from the base of his shoulder blade to the waist of his trousers.

"Quite distinctive," said Danny. He then pointed to the right-hand still. A handsome man with thick dark brown hair and a strong chin. He was dressed in expensive board shorts and was surrounded by smiling children in swimsuits and sportswear. The man had his back turned and was looking over his shoulder in a candid pose.

"Look." Danny pointed to the faded scar on the man's back. "Pretty sure that this is the same guy maybe fifteen years on. Just to be sure, look at the moles at the top of his arm." Danny pointed out the three blemishes that formed an isosceles triangle on the subject's right deltoid muscle.

Clay squinted at the screen. The two pictures displayed

the same scar, the same geometry of moles. "Fucker, they *are* the same."

"Now all we have to do is put a name to this guy."

"Any ideas how?" asked Andrea. She stared at the unmasked face. "He looks vaguely familiar."

"Well, your reporter friend—"

Andrea looked pale. "Jeremy. His name was Jeremy Seeber."

Danny nodded. "Jeremy thought the man is or was a government minister. That must mean he's British. I was just about to start googling the details from the second video."

"Which are?" asked Andrea. She sat on the end of the bed and stared with contempt at the smiling face on screen.

"It's a local BBC News report on a charity event—a London school raising money for a new swimming and sports centre. The guy with the scar was one of the celebrities enlisted to help with the fundraiser. The fact that he's a politician means it will have been well publicised. I've never met one that didn't like mugging it for the camera."

"Doesn't it say who he is?"

"No. He's just in the background, no interview, no specific reference to him on the voiceover."

"Damn."

Clay laughed. "You said it."

"So once we find out his name, we send the video files to CNN, right?" said Andrea. "Once he's exposed, he's finished and this will all be over."

Danny tilted his head. "Let's find out what we can on this guy; then we'll figure out what to do and how best to handle it."

"What's to think about? We need to expose him quickly. I want my life back." Andrea felt a flare of anger.

Danny sat back, looking her full in the face. "Guys like this are protected. If we make any mistakes we could be on the run for the rest of our days."

"Protected, how?"

Danny pointed to the masked man, frozen on screen. "Look, this guy has killed before and probably after this film. That obviously wasn't his first murder. Serial killers build up to that level of intricacy, usually over years. And you don't stay undetected and have a political career by leaving things to chance. This guy will have power and connections. The fact that he could initiate a hit against you proves he's powerful. He, or someone close to him, initiated and funded the Trident teams that have been after you. They're well-trained men. They cost a lot of money."

"I hate them." Andrea clenched her fists.

"They're not on my Christmas card list either." Clay had produced yet another bag of Cheetos. An orange handful hovered between the bag and his mouth. "But don't forget, those mercenaries really believe that you have stolen intel. That you're an enemy of the state. They've received that mission brief from their controller at HQ. So that means either the company knowingly accepted a false brief or someone in the intelligence services created the false info trail and used it to sell the story."

Exasperated, Andrea ran her fingers through her hair. "So we go straight to the nearest news network and show them the video. The media loves to bring down stars and politicians, they'd snap this up in a moment, surely?"

Clay and Danny shared a glance, then Clay shook his head. "I get where you're coming from, but your friend worked for a big newspaper, didn't he?"

"The *Herald*."

"Right. He knew what he had, would know better than most what would happen if the video came out. And they got to him anyway. I don't think you'd be safe even after it hit the news." Clay laid a hand on Andrea's shoulder. "Depending on who this guy is and who he's linked to, you'd still be a target. Even if the man in the video was put on trial, there's still a chance that the contract would remain active. He wouldn't want you around to testify or fill in any of the blanks. And there are two men on that tape—don't forget the one behind the camera. We have no way of identifying him, so we should concentrate on the guy in the mask, but we really don't know how far this thing goes, or how many people are involved."

"What am I supposed to do?" Andrea's voice was full of a desperate fury. "Run for ever? Lie down and die? Turn myself in and hope for the fucking best?"

Danny rose from his chair and wrapped his arms around her in a comforting embrace. "Easy girl. Clay isn't saying we're beaten. We just need to think this through very carefully. One wrong move and these operatives will have us. Let me look into this guy some more, then we'll decide together how best to proceed."

Andrea rose and rubbed the tears from her eyes. Tears of anger and frustration. "I want to see that smiling psychopath pay. Do it."

Danny seated himself in front of the laptop again and

logged on to the motel's Wi-Fi, then loaded a search engine. He started by entering the name of the school in the news clip: Newtown Central Academy in Brentwood Hill, one of the newer London developments. Clearly the fundraiser had worked: the new sports centre included a swimming pool, a gym, and a set of four all-weather playing fields complete with the latest incarnation of AstroTurf and halogen floodlights.

Danny smiled to himself. When he was a kid you felt lucky if you had a decent-quality football to kick around the streets. The new generation didn't realise how good they had it.

The school website gave no real information on the fundraiser. He clicked the back button and selected another of the search results. This took him to a feature on the school by a magazine called *Greener Living*. His heart rate quickened when he saw the gallery of photographs. He clicked through scores of images of the day's celebrities, recognising a female sprinter who had been the star of the previous Olympics. A couple of football players and a local boxing champion also made an appearance.

Then he saw the smiling man. He was posing with the school swimming team, twenty or so children smiling into the camera around him. Danny's eyes flew to the description line beneath the photograph. His mouth twitched into a tight smile.

"His name is Stewart Strathclyde."

Clay and Andrea were on their feet in a moment, each peering over one of his shoulders.

Strathclyde was not hard to find. Alongside the predictable Facebook profile and Twitter feed, there was an official .gov website, the bio page detailing his humble beginnings in the coastal town of Margate, his education at the University of Cambridge. Danny sneered. "Funny, there's no mention of torture or murder in his list of achievements."

"So who is he, exactly?" Andrea asked.

"Apparently he is currently serving as Junior Minister for Environmental Affairs."

"What the hell does that mean?" asked Clay. He had never been impressed by the pomp of British politicians, finding them every bit as insincere as their American equivalents, just with plummier accents.

"It says that he 'promotes health and well being in communities both urban and rural'." Danny's voice dripped with sarcasm.

"So now we know who he is. What do we do next?" asked Andrea. She stared at the image of Strathclyde, suited and smiling.

30

Topcat roused himself from a light sleep. His neck felt stiff despite the overpriced memory foam pillow his doctor had recommended. Rubbing his eyes, he lifted his tablet from the bedside cabinet, loaded a news app, then set it down again. No developments since the coverage of the Apostles' bodies being found in the desert. He had more confidence in the Presidents. They would put this to rest.

His mouth was dry and he headed to the en-suite bathroom for a glass of water. He stopped and turned as the satellite phone rang. It was Matthew's number.

A voice he did not recognise—cold and angry. "Are you the man in charge?"

"Who is this?" But Thomas Carter felt he knew the answer already. "Are you the one who killed my men?"

"If you're the one that sent them, then yes."

"Who are you?"

"A concerned citizen. Listen up. I did end it for your men, but it was self-defence. They came out of nowhere and started shooting like bullets were on special offer. You're targeting a civilian woman under incorrect intelligence. Now, you either *know* it's a false flag operation, or your mission brief was compromised so you'd do somebody else's dirty work."

"The intel was sound. And I'll tell you something for nothing: you're a dead man walking." Carter felt his face flush red at the audacity of the caller. *Who does this cockroach think he is?*

"Cut the crap. The flash drive that your men were after doesn't contain any knock lists, nuclear secrets or diagrams of spy satellites—any of the crap you were probably told. What it *does* have is a snuff film showing a Member of Parliament murdering a young woman. Now that you know that, you've got one chance: call off your teams or I'll kill every last one of them, then I'll come for you. I'll cut your fuckin' heart out."

Carter gritted his teeth, furious. But not too furious to ignore the Scottish accent and the equal measure of venom and intelligence in the words. "The intel was sound. The mission is justified and you're the one who will be spilling his guts when my boys get hold of you."

"Stewart Strathclyde, Junior Minister for Environmental Affairs."

"What?"

"You heard. That's the man on the video. So forget the bullshit about government secrets. Drop the mission or I'll drop you."

Carter was about to respond when the call was terminated. He sat back on the bed, his mouth drier than ever. Forgoing the water, he hurried downstairs to the living room, opened the drinks cabinet and poured himself a large brandy. He swirled the dark amber liquid around the glass then took a long gulp. He went over the call again in his head. Why would the caller give him a story like that? What had that bastard Banks got him into?

What about this Stewart Strathclyde? *Minister for Environmental Affairs*, he'd said.

It would be tricky to locate Banks at this hour. Carter sat at his computer and loaded a search engine.

Clearly Strathclyde was fast becoming one of those annoying celebrity politicians, as concerned with grinning into the camera as his policy statements. Carter had no love for hierarchy, unless he was at the top. He stared intently at a picture of Strathclyde, tall and darkly handsome, dressed impeccably in a tailored Savile Row suit and shaking hands with an African bishop. Could this man be a killer? Doubtful. But why would the man on the phone bother with such a ruse if there was no truth to it? All he had needed to do was issue his threats of retribution. The mystery Scot had already proved capable of dealing death when provoked.

Know your enemy better than you know yourself and you will never lose a battle. He knew he was paraphrasing to himself but believed in the old adage.

Why would the man feed him that story?

31

Danny growled at the handset as he ended the call. He tossed the satellite phone onto the motel bed.

Andrea felt a spark of hope. "Did he listen?"

"He listened but I don't think he'll call them off."

"But—"

"PMCs pride themselves on getting the job done." He picked up two backpacks. "Come on, I'll start loading up the truck. We need to get to the airport." Andrea watched him leave, his face grim.

"But first..." Clay moved to the bed. Andrea watched as the Texan picked up the satellite phone, opened the rear cover and exposed the battery unit. A sharp tap against the heel of his hand and the angular battery tumbled free. He tossed all three components into the trash bin.

"Why did you do that?"

"It's served its purpose. And it could be used to track us. We shouldn't have taken it at all."

"How do you know it hasn't been? If the power was off..."

"Guess we'll find out. And soon we'll be in the air."

He unzipped the duffle bag of weaponry and ejected a magazine from one of the MP5Ks. *Weapons taken from men who are trying to kill me.* Seemingly satisfied, he slapped it back into place. Andrea watched as he worked with each weapon, checking each magazine methodically, working the slides on the pistols. She rose and took Tansen's Taurus in its holster from the bag and secured it to her belt, then faced herself in the wall-mounted mirror. Drawing the revolver she crouched and aimed at her reflection. "A week ago I wouldn't have known which way up to hold this thing. I can't believe how much your life can change in the space of one day."

"At least you're still here to change."

She pivoted, keeping her weight low, arms locked to her line of sight the way Tansen had taught her.

Clay's scarred face was impassive. "If you end up in a situation where you have to shoot that thing, don't hesitate. Just shoot. And never point it at anyone you don't want to kill."

Andrea searched her soul for a moment then answered what she felt was truthfully. "A couple of days ago I couldn't have dreamt of taking a life. But after what they did to Greg and Bruce, tried to do to us… I think I could pull the trigger."

"Damned right. If it comes down to you and him, put four centre mass then one in the head when he's down."

"What does it feel like after?"

"Well, I've only had to kill a few men, but I sleep easy at night. I took down some in Mogadishu. A couple more since. It's like us Gunn brothers always say: 'I never killed anyone who didn't need killin'.'"

She clenched her teeth, visualised the bullet striking the smiling face of Stewart Strathclyde. He was the cause of all her suffering, all this death. At that moment she was sure she could do it: four in the chest, then one in the head to be sure.

"I'm sure you'll be fine if the time comes. But with a little bit of luck, it won't. We'll disappear for a while, go off the grid; Key West is perfect for it. From there we can skip down into Mexico if we need to. Mojitos and margaritas, shiny."

Andrea holstered her pistol, somehow comforted by its presence. She smiled. "I could go for a couple of rounds with you, for sure."

"A lady after my own heart. Well, I'm buying and they have some great bars down in the Keys. Those Conchs really know how to mix it up."

"Conchs?"

"People in the Keys call themselves *Conchs*. There are two main species of Conch: freshwater Conchs and saltwater Conchs. Saltwater Conchs were born in the Keys, and freshwater Conchs were born elsewhere but have lived there a long time."

"Wow. I feel educated."

"What can I tell you, I'm a man of many diverse talents."

"No doubt."

Clay packed the firearms back into the duffle bag and hefted it onto his shoulder. "Come on. Time to get the hell out of Dodge."

Andrea followed him to the truck, where Danny was waiting.

* * *

The journey to the airport was uneventful but Danny was on edge. He phoned Tansen but the call went unanswered. A moment of unease prickled at the nape of his neck but he dismissed it. Tansen would be out in the hills somewhere, most likely on the back of a horse or reading one of his beloved Louis L'Amour novels.

Clay pulled up to a blue hangar that stood on the perimeter of the airport. A painted logo on its corrugated wall identified it as belonging to UNCO SKY SERVICES. "The pilot is meeting us there. You guys wait here."

He parked the pickup and walked to the hangar entrance, rapping on the wall. A few flakes of paint drifted to the ground where his knuckles had made contact. After a short wait, a man dressed in dark-red overalls poked his head around the door and spoke to Clay. The man glanced furtively at the pickup then motioned for Clay to step inside.

Andrea shifted in her seat. "What's going on?"

"Just give him a minute."

"You sure this is a good plan? Flying to the other side of America?"

"Would you rather hang around Vegas and wait for those guys to get lucky? Clay's right. We fly to Key West, then lie low until we figure how to put an end to this."

Andrea chewed her lip, glancing around as if expecting to see the kill squad appear from behind a parked car.

Danny turned in his seat and pushed her shoulder lightly. "Easy." He was rewarded with a small smile. He turned back to the hangar entrance. Clay appeared with the man in overalls, nodding agreement. Then he strode towards the pickup. Danny smiled to himself. Clay walked like a tiger.

Long loose limbs that held very little tension. His casual gait gave some the impression that he was a stereotypical bumpkin, and to many, that equated to big and stupid. Many had learned the hard way that he was indeed the former and definitely not the latter. Danny rolled down his window as Clay approached. His brother leant on the sill.

"Pilot's just refuelling and then we'll be on our way. We can move our stuff into the hangar."

Andrea felt the tension in her shoulders ease. She and Danny collected the bags and followed Clay into the hangar. She had never been inside one before and was struck by the overpowering smell of oil and fuel and the array of high-tech equipment along the walls. A red box on wheels stood as large as a wardrobe unit with two computer screens, several coloured cables and a length of corrugated tubing hooked onto its sides. She had no idea what the purpose of the unit was. It looked very expensive so she gave it a wide berth. A small Cessna 162 sat with its engine compartment open. Andrea had flown over London in a similar model some years earlier; a birthday gift from her colleagues at a newspaper she had worked for. With space for only the pilot plus one passenger she knew that they weren't heading to Florida in that plane.

The man Clay had talked to waved them over to an enclosed waiting area, formed by two large Plexiglas screens fixed into one corner of the hangar. There was a semi-circular couch alongside a water cooler and a vending machine, which occupied the space nearest the door.

"Make yourselves comfortable. We'll have you on your way real soon." The man was thin, gaunt even, but looked kindly. A couple of days' worth of grey stubble framed his narrow face.

Clay stretched out on the couch. "Thanks, Gerry."

Gerry tipped a non-existent hat and flashed a wink and a smile at Andrea. The gold tooth he sported didn't sit well with the rest of his face. She returned the smile politely but busied herself pretending to look for something in her backpack.

When Gerry had left the room Danny leaned over and nudged her. "You know if you sleep with him you get air miles."

"If I slept with him I'd probably get a dose of the clap."

Gerry strolled over to the main hangar door, which was now fully open. This afforded a limited view of the rest of the airport and adjacent runways. He was met at the door by another mechanic, this one wearing a grey uniform. The logo on the back told he was in the employ of Flyway Air Services.

"Who's that?" asked Andrea.

"Company next door I think," said Clay.

Andrea felt uneasy as the man from Flyway followed Gerry into the hangar, glanced at the three of them in the waiting room then said something she couldn't hear. Gerry handed him a small plastic box that looked like something you would keep fishing tackle in. The man glanced through the window again, his eyes locked on her. Gerry was nodding.

"I think the grease monkey likes you."

Andrea frowned at the Texan. "I feel icky."

"You journalists are so articulate."

Andrea poked out her tongue in way of response. When

she looked up again both mechanics were heading back out into the sunlight.

A gleaming white aircraft rolled slowly into view. The noise from its slowing engines filled the hangar. Clay stood. "I think our ride has arrived."

32

The noise from the twin jet engines was enough to make Edith Bell turn away and pull down the ear protectors she wore perched on her head like a novelty party hat. Her ebony skin was slick with sweat, partly due to the humidity and partly physical exertion. When not working alongside her husband of twenty-one years, Edith tried to fit in regular weights sessions. She'd come late to the world of competitive fitness but now her arms and shoulders were honed to near perfection, a fact that had helped her win the Miss Fitness Florida title two years in a row.

She held a hand low over her eyes and watched the Hawker 400 slow and taxi towards the hangar in which she stood. A face that still made her tingle inside smiled down from the pilot's window. The mirrored aviator glasses hid some of his face but not his wide grin. She'd met Garnett Bell in a bar while on vacation with her sister in Cancun. She had been a different woman back then. Plump and in need of some serious corrective dental work. Yet Garnett had seen past all that and had taken an instant shine to the shy twenty-something from South Carolina. She had been initially wary of him, thinking his attention some sort of ploy to rob her. Yet Garnett had met her for dinner and drinks five nights in a row. They quickly discovered many shared interests: books, black-and-white films, jazz music and strawberry margaritas. They'd spent the last night of her vacation in his hotel room. It had been her first real time with a man. The drunken fumblings of her native South Carolina's boys didn't rank in the same league as the skilled and patient Garnett.

With the vacation over, she and her sister returned home. Never expecting to see him again, she was dumbfounded when he turned up on her front doorstep three weeks later with a bottle of vintage Bollinger and that same winning smile. They had moved first to Fort Lauderdale then later further south to Key West, both locations serving as depots for his growing private jet hire business. Their wedding in Antigua surpassed her teenage fantasies. Garnett had turned out every bit her prince. Yet he referred to himself as a "diamond in the rough". For Edith, this underlying roughness made him even more lovable.

Edith had accepted his criminal lifestyle with an open-mindedness that surprised even her. Maybe it was his brutal honesty. He had never tried to sugar-coat his business dealings. He had flown marijuana into the States along with guns, counterfeit currency and illegal immigrants because it paid handsomely.

The engine noise had abated to a bearable level so she slipped the ear protectors off and gave Garnett a wave as he appeared at the door hatch. Still lean and muscular, he cut an imposing figure despite heading to the wrong side of fifty. Flecks of grey now peppered his short, cropped hair. Garnett was eleven years older than Edith yet they looked good together.

"There was a call for you. That big guy from Texas—Clay. He wanted to charter a ride from Vegas. Seemed to be very keen to get here." Edith planted a kiss on her husband as he drew close. "Sam Whittaker just did that drop-off in Reno, so I told him to swing by. Figured you wouldn't mind."

"Damn, woman, you got a licence for that?" Garnett smacked her playfully on the ass. She knew her tight Lycra exercise trousers displayed her legs and buttocks to perfection.

Edith posed theatrically for a moment, flexing into a classic muscle spread. "You don't need a licence for a force of nature."

The co-pilot emerged from the Hawker jet. "Would you two get a room? You give normal-shaped folks an inferiority complex."

Garnett grinned back at him. "Jealousy is so unbecoming on you, Pete."

Peter Latham hoisted his considerable stomach with both hands then let it drop with a resounding wobble. "I'm working on a six-pack. Well, a six-pack of Coors, anyway."

"See you tomorrow, Pete." Garnett waved him away. Despite Pete's constant self-deprecating humour, he was a fine pilot and a friend of many years. He'd never missed a day of work in the sixteen years that he'd flown for Garnett's firm.

"You say Clay called, huh? Haven't heard from him in a while. Wonder why he wants to get here so bad?"

Edith paused. "He said it was urgent." She had only

met Clay a couple of times but remembered him well. His old-fashioned manners and hulking appearance gave him a semi-melancholy air. Garnett was a big man in his own right but next to Clay he looked almost diminutive. While Edith had fashioned her body into shape with long sessions in the gym, she could tell that Clay's Conan-the-Barbarian stature was due as much to genetics as lifting weights.

"Well I guess we'll find out when Sam brings them in. Actually, screw that, I'll find out now." Garnett walked towards the office space built inside the spacious hangar. He greeted George and Hector Ramirez as they passed, two cousins who worked as ground crew and performed maintenance on Garnett's small fleet of aircraft.

"Fill her up and check under the hood, right?" George quipped as they passed. Garnett gave him the thumbs-up. The cousins looked suspiciously like Cheech Marin but they certainly knew their way around the twin Pratt & Whitney engines of the plane.

In the office, Garnett radioed Sam Whittaker. Ten minutes later he walked over to where George and Hector were busy performing a series of checks on the air-intake valves of the Hawker's starboard engine. "Hey guys, I need to be back in the air tomorrow or the day after. That okay?"

Hector nodded down from the stepped platform on which he was perched. "No problem boss. This bird will be ready to fly when you are."

Edith had changed her clothes and returned from the hangar's locker room. She now wore a simple yellow dress that contrasted perfectly with her dark skin. "You find out what's going on?"

"Seems they are in a bad place and need to disappear for a while." After a long and understanding look had passed between them, he added, "Been there an' done that."

33

"How the hell did this happen?" asked Lincoln, as much to himself as his team.

Washington spat out a blood-coated chip of glass. "He must have snagged the grenade from Roosevelt's vest while they were fighting."

"I figured that part out. What I meant was how the hell did a bound prisoner just nearly end us?" Lincoln tried not to show his inner fury. "He can't have gone far. He's losing blood. Bush pegged him with two to the chest. Let's get on it."

"What about Roose?" asked Washington.

Lincoln wanted nothing more than to lift his friend in his arms and transport him home. Organise a funeral service with full honours as befitted a warrior. They'd been comrades-in-arms for over a decade. Roosevelt had survived blistering warfare in Angola and dozens of missions since. *Where's the justice in the world when a man like Roosevelt dies in an oriental shitkicker's living room?* "We'll come back for him once we've got the dead man walking."

Lincoln's cell phone rang. He plucked it from his

pocket. Kennedy's voice seemed a million miles away. "Hey what's going on down there? Looked like a frag went off, you all okay?"

"No. Roosevelt is gone. The Gurkha is loose. Scope up. Did he go out of the back?"

"Negative, Linc. No one left the building, at least in my line of sight. Roosevelt's really dead? You want me down there?"

"No stay in position. If we get any more visitors just cap them. I don't care if it's SWAT or Jehovah's Witnesses."

"Roger that."

As Lincoln ended the call, Washington helped Bush back to his feet. A deep purple bruise had begun to swell beneath Bush's left eye, courtesy of the collision with the kitchen unit. With reverence they placed a towel over the face of their dead companion.

Lincoln scanned the ruined living room. A single picture frame remained unbroken. It held a badge of rank—three chevrons adorned with crossed kukri knives. A small plaque below declared "Havildar Tibrikot". So the fucker was a sergeant. Lincoln sneered, and turned to his men. "Find him."

"He can't have gone out the front or Kennedy would have spotted him from the ridge. He's still in the house or hiding out back somewhere," Washington said.

Lincoln nodded. "You two clear the rooms and start out back." Washington and Bush moved through the door that led to the bedrooms, weapons raised and ready, hyper-alert for any sign of danger.

Lincoln crouched, the smell of cordite and burned flesh strong in his nose. *Where would I go? Out the back and run for it? Injured… wouldn't get far. Hide in the house? But where? Hide in the outbuildings? Maybe.*

He made sure the tubular magazine was still secure on the top of his weapon then followed his men out into the rear yard. Bush and Washington were twenty yards ahead. Lincoln called to them, "Five minutes and we're gone."

Both men replied with curt nods, but Lincoln knew that they wouldn't be happy leaving without exacting bloody retribution. "Check the outbuildings. I want this fucker split open and left for coyote feed in five minutes."

Bush gave him an amen to that and they moved off. But two hundred and sixty seconds later they were back, faces grim. "Not a trace of this asshole. The guy's a ghost. Disappeared into the bedrock."

Lincoln could not afford to spend any more time on the fugitive. They needed to regroup and get back on the trail of the woman. She was the real target. He huffed air out of his nose in annoyance. "Let's get Roo in the van. We need to move on. We'll come back for the coolie another day."

They hoisted Roosevelt's corpse into the luggage space at the rear of the vehicle and covered the body with jackets and a thermal foil blanket from the van's breakdown kit.

"What about the cop?" asked Washington.

"Leave him. Not our concern." Lincoln activated his cell phone and rang Kennedy, still on his sniper's perch. "We're moving out. We'll pick you up in two."

As they stood at the tailgate of the SUV, Lincoln squinted at Washington, the sun an unforgiving glare behind him. "Get back on the laptop and see if the sat-phone has pinged any new data, now we know the target is carrying it. We need to get back on their asses pronto. This was a waste of fucking time."

A couple of taps on the touch-pad and the tracker program sprang to life. Like images from a time-lapse camera, red dots began appearing on screen. They traced a winding path from the ranch house back through Castillo and on to Las Vegas. A large cluster of the dots centred on an area east of the main strip.

Washington's voice was thick with tension. "There're multiple readings coming back from Spring Valley. They went after Clinton."

Lincoln felt a vein throbbing in his temple. "Are they still there?"

"No they've moved south-east, right to the outskirts of town. The phone has pinged for a couple of hours from this point."

"Can you zoom in on that?"

Washington clicked on the icon of the magnifying glass. The page blurred then cleared to show an enhanced view of south Las Vegas.

"Where is that?"

"Give me a second." Washington tapped on the legend panel on the screen and a series of tiny pinheads appeared on the map. "It's a motel—the Aces High. It's out in no man's land. They've been there for over two hours."

"They still there?" Lincoln's hand crept to his Calico pistol as if he could fire off a few shots via the computer screen. Washington studied the most recent entry. "As of seven minutes ago, yes."

Lincoln checked his email. Nothing from any of his

contacts. Hopefully that meant the target hadn't taken a plane, train or automobile out of the state yet. They might be able to catch up.

Bush joined them at the vehicle. "We shipping out?"

Lincoln nodded in the affirmative. "Call the doc's house. Make sure Clinton's okay."

Bush pulled out his cell phone, rang a number and put it on speaker. After thirty seconds of ringing he ended the call. "No answer, Linc."

"Shit. We have to presume he's out of the game for the time being. We'll confirm later. Right now we go full speed after these fuckers. I want that woman hog-tied by suppertime."

"Give me a minute. A place this isolated… no mains gas supply…" Bush trotted back towards the house. Lincoln watched as he opened a small shed under the kitchen window, revealing three gas cylinders. Two stood unconnected, while one was hooked up, clearly serving as the main supply to the house via a hose and regulator. Bush let out a grunt of satisfaction and dragged the two free canisters into the house. Through the kitchen window Lincoln could see him turning on all four gas rings on the cooker, igniting only one.

Washington, who was bent over his laptop, gave a snort of triumph. "We've got an identity on one of the men who are likely with the target."

Lincoln leaned in to look at the screen. There was a rolling news clip showing a photograph of a large man in military uniform. "Clay Gunn. Ex-Ranger. See what you can find out about him. We were right to think these guys were trained."

As he rejoined Lincoln and Washington, Bush gave his leader a wink. "Better vamoose. I've set the house to barbecue."

Lincoln, normally less inclined to wanton destruction than some of his team, glanced at the makeshift shroud covering Roosevelt's corpse. "Right."

Bush mounted his Harley and Lincoln took the wheel of the SUV, Washington riding shotgun. He drove back towards the main road, pulling over to pick up Kennedy. A sudden explosion made the sniper pause, his hand resting on the handle of the vehicle's door. Lincoln turned in his seat.

The ranch house was almost obscured by a mushroom cloud of black smoke. Then debris began to fall—a rain of wood fragments, glass shards and roofing tiles. The front wall toppled slowly at first, then crashed to the ground like a boxer who had walked into a heavy right hand.

Bush, steering the Harley alongside the SUV like a police escort, pumped his fist.

Tansen Tibrikot, bleeding profusely from more wounds than he had hands to cover, leaned heavily against the door of the concealed panic room beneath his bedroom.

Once a cellar, he had converted it into a bunker. It had not been out of fear; it was a novelty, little more than a nod to the action movies he liked so much. Like so many of what he considered his "Americanisms", the panic room was there because he *could* have one.

The bedrock provided natural protection from the elements and potential home invasion. The half-inch reinforced steel door, hidden from view by the full-length mirror in the master bedroom, could only be opened from the inside once occupied. A small video monitor linked to multiple mini cameras in each of the rooms. The panic room was twelve feet square, with wire racks holding bottled water and food supplies, enough for two weeks.

Wincing, Tansen pulled a medical kit from a rack and fixed a large self-adhesive gauze pad across his right shoulder and pectoral. One round was a through and through, just above the collarbone. The other… he could feel the blood spreading even as the gauze did its best to absorb the steady flow.

Tansen had watched the video monitor as the men searched for him, moving like actors in a silent film. Their faces were grim as they removed their dead companion. Several minutes later, one of them returned, dragging two gas canisters. He had no time to act, to think, before the picture on the viewing screen turned to snow. Even through the thickness of the door, the noise of the explosion made him clap his hands to his ears. He closed his eyes, his emotions a swirling mix of sadness, shock and anger.

They had blown up his house. He had nothing left. His antique books, his Americana. The pictures of his beautiful Raj. His friend, Jimmy. All gone.

He sat down heavily. A debilitating weariness spread through his body. He inspected his blood-soaked clothes. He tried to stand again, reaching for the lock of the panic-room door. But his legs would not obey him.

As darkness clouded his senses, Tansen Tibrikot wondered how long it would be before his body was discovered in his little hole in the ground. His eyes closed and he felt himself slide slowly sideways.

34

Stewart Strathclyde watched his assistant leave his plush office, her hips swaying just enough to be provocative, his eyes drawn to the curves of her body for just a second longer than he cared for. He knew he had to be careful when dipping into the hired help. He didn't intend ever to fall foul of the "Clinton syndrome". No, better to give that little blonde Miss a miss.

But he was not completely immune. He knew that Sonia Birkett-Brown had tried the modelling game while at university. He'd found the pictures. She was nice to look at but probably more trouble than she was worth. She might be the kind to kiss and tell to get her face in the papers. And while he could live with being labelled a womaniser, he certainly did not want any reporters digging into his carefully screened love affairs. He'd barely escaped some murky facts being exposed during the phone-hacking debacle that had done for some of his colleagues but he'd been saved by his then low position in the political pecking order. No one cared about an unknown MP when there were real celebrities to write about.

He leant back in his five-thousand-pound leather chair. Not that he would ever have been so careless as to discuss his extra-*extra*-curricular activities over the telephone. He had learned the hard way not to record any more of his "acts" on film. It was only due to his close relationship with an agent within the ranks of the CHSS that the situation was being dealt with. The press was right. Those with connections really did run the country. He had met Charles Banks at university, and the two men had discovered certain shared proclivities. Now they had a friendship based on mutual assured destruction. Strathclyde was not surprised that Banks had chosen a career that allowed him to indulge his inclinations.

That someone had stumbled across one of only three videos he had ever recorded was an unfortunate event. He'd thought all the copies had been destroyed years ago. His cameraman had some tough questions to answer. But he knew he shouldn't have been surprised. The desire to show off one's handiwork—even if that was only capturing someone else's artistry on film—was too much temptation for some. At least he had always worn his homemade mask. Not one frame of film existed where his face was identifiable. He'd always been vigilant about that; almost as vigilant as in the selection of his victims. But yes, he'd have to talk to his cameraman.

Runaways were best. The homeless in London were everywhere yet virtually invisible to the general public. No one of worth missed them when they disappeared. Even if a bleeding-heart liberal at one of those rat-infested hostels reported them missing, the police did not have the time, resources, or inclination to do anything about it.

But the fact that the watcher had not only somehow

identified Strathclyde but also had the audacity to try blackmail had ironically worked in his favour. The blackmailer had shown his hand, given Strathclyde a lead. The man was a known sex offender. Banks and two other officers from the newly formed Coalition and Homeland Security Service had intercepted him on the southern perimeter of Hyde Park. A quick jab with a Taser and his inert body was bundled into the back of a waiting van. Just one more unmarked white vehicle among thousands.

It had taken less than an hour to extract every morsel of information that the man had to give. In fact he'd begun blabbering and pleading even before Banks had inserted the first needle. Strathclyde had been rather disappointed. He had jumped at the chance to sit in on the interview. The rest of the time had been spent vigorously asking the same questions over and over again to ascertain that the answers given were consistent. During the last hour of his life, the man, Gerald Clocker, begged and cried. Pathetic.

It had become clear that Clocker had worked alone. He had acquired the original VHS from a fellow deviant in an underground swap several years previously, but it had not been to his taste. Re-watching it, he had identified Strathclyde from his scar. That damn scar. Strathclyde rubbed at his lower back, feeling the puckered skin through his shirt. He had fallen onto a fire grate as a child, damn near impaled himself.

Clocker had not been a natural blackmailer. His only backup plan was to send a digital copy of the video on a flash drive to a reporter. Just one. Clocker's body was found in Hyde Park the next day. As he was a known sex offender, the investigating officers didn't exactly break their backs to find his killers. Nor did they pay much attention to a report by one of Clocker's neighbours that three men had entered the murdered man's property only hours after his death, leaving an hour later with several bulging trash bags. *Bags full of every scrap of technology the CHSS men could find, from VHS to iPad, just in case.* Strathclyde smiled. He'd enjoyed watching those bags burn.

The reporter, Seeber, had proved a little more problematic. The man was clean, not a low-life like Clocker. The background checks by CHSS had uncovered very little: a couple of parking tickets and a caution while at university for the possession of cannabis. The Seebers' interrogation had called for a more subtle approach.

Strathclyde had not been present at the event. It was a pity. He would have enjoyed watching another take the lead for a change. Especially with the man's wife. But it would have been too risky. He had had to satisfy himself with the verbal report from Banks. There had been no need for much actual violence, just the threat of torture against Seeber's wife. Seeber had kept Clocker's original USB—the CHSS men had located it in the man's home office and delivered it to Strathclyde that night for a date with the microwave—and had made one copy. He had sent the copy to a fellow journalist at her hotel in Nevada. A journalist called Andrea Chambers.

Andrea Chambers. Strathclyde sat up in his chair, pulled his computer keyboard close, and performed the same Internet search he had done at least a dozen times since first hearing that name. The woman was a nobody, a two-bit hack. He couldn't imagine why Seeber had placed so much faith in her. He checked her Twitter feed. No activity for days. Was that a good sign? He scrolled through past Tweets. Irrelevant drivel about UFOs, for God's sake.

Perhaps he would have a chance to meet Andrea Chambers face to face. Unlike the Seebers. Strathclyde let Banks's report run through his mind. So little colour. But he could imagine... The three-man team moving the couple to the bedroom. First the wife, the makeshift noose cutting off any muffled attempts to scream for help. The nylon stockings strong enough to support her weight as they were fastened to the stout rail in the walk-in wardrobe. Seeber being carried in, seeing the lifeless body of his wife, beginning to kick and fight with a desperate fury, until his cries were cut short by the slashing edge of a stiffened hand across his throat. Strathclyde could almost see the man's eyes bulging as he fought for one last breath, the noose fashioned from the belt of his own dressing gown tightening around his neck.

His chosen PMC unit, Trident Solutions International, had been recently used to remove an outspoken political activist in South Africa, although according to their official brief, they had only been providing personal security. Banks had been quick to clarify that the British government had not ordered that particular hit. But they had utilised TSI on *other* occasions, and the operatives could be trusted to terminate as required. While the agents of CHSS operated only on British soil, TSI had no such restriction. Their boundaries were dictated only by their fee. And Strathclyde knew even more about TSI than Banks had suspected. His own brother, Jensen, was a specialist operator for TSI, under a carefully assumed identity, of course. Stewart could not allow it to get out that he, bright-eyed boy of the Establishment, had a sibling in such a controversial outfit. Stewart envied Jensen the freedom to indulge the family proclivities in his official capacity.

With the woman out of the country and out of the reach of the CHSS, Banks had provided a name at TSI—Topcat—and a code: 004751. Private termination contract, unofficially government-sanctioned, using Banks's name. A call to an unlisted number and the name and location of the target was given, and a terrorist dossier created. Strathclyde was rather proud of that. And the code had meant he had not had to give his name. After all, why would a junior environment minister be dealing with terrorism?

Unconsciously, Strathclyde palmed his mobile phone as if willing an update from Banks to materialise. One more loose end to be tied off. Thoughts of opening up Andrea Chambers with a blade made him tingle momentarily. He checked his watch. Time enough to indulge such daydreams later. He rose, ran a hand through his thick hair—perfectly trimmed for £100 every six weeks—and straightened his tie.

Bianca Sage met him at the door to his outer office, drawing an envious appraisal from Sonia. And no wonder; his fiancée was stunning. Their journey in an unmarked government saloon car was a short one, and they were soon outside one of the most famous addresses in the country.

The flash of the reporters' cameras didn't faze him one bit. Although a relatively new face in politics, he was an old hand at masking his true emotions. Strathclyde never let his public face falter. *Never reveal the beast.* Hours of self-examination in the mirror had allowed him to cultivate a genial look in his eyes; this lent him a boy-next-door appeal that was beginning to pay dividends. People *liked* Stewart

Strathclyde. He was charming and witty and had a talent for building instant rapport. The perfect politician.

Holding the car door open for her, Strathclyde admired how Bianca was able to work it perfectly for the cameras. As they walked from the car to the door of No. 10 Downing Street, she looked back over her shoulder as if responding to the cries of the photographers. She gave a mix of sexy, smart and respectable all in one look. The tabloids loved the new couple. It was Cool Britannia all over again. He made sure to look intent, a man with purpose, his leather portmanteau clutched in his hand as if it contained the nuclear launch codes for the free world. In reality it contained nothing more controversial than projected agricultural yields. But image was everything. If you projected gravitas the public—and eventually your employers—would believe the spin.

He gave a final nod and a smile to the small gathering of paparazzi and a peck on the cheek to Bianca. He turned to watch as she took her time returning to the car. She exposed just enough leg as she slid into the back seat to be tantalising then spoke a single word to the driver. Strathclyde couldn't hear the word but he knew what it would be. "Harrods."

Inside No. 10, Strathclyde was led into one of the smaller rooms at the rear of the building. There were to be no tea and scones with the Prime Minister this evening, only a monthly handover to the assistants to the Deputy PM. Yet Stewart was well aware that the PM liked him. The very fact that he was allowed into the Downing Street spotlight testified to that. Stewart was young, handsome and carried himself with the grace and confidence of an athlete. The PM was desperate to make his party look as trendy and relevant as possible to today's voters, and Strathclyde knew he was a valuable asset.

One of the house secretaries appeared in the doorway. "We're running about twenty minutes behind schedule but the Deputy PM asked if you would wait. He'll be seeing you in person."

"That's absolutely fine," replied Strathclyde. He smoothed out the small crease in the left leg of his trousers.

"Can I bring you a tea or coffee while you wait?"

He glanced at the woman's cleavage, which was perfectly displayed by the deep cut of her Donna Karan dress. "That would be very kind of you Celia. Tea, please." He made a point of knowing the names of all the service staff he regularly encountered. A little thing like remembering and using someone's name could garner a favour when required further on down the road.

"Make yourself comfortable. I'll be back ASAP." She emphasised the final consonant of the abbreviation with a playful widening of her eyes.

Strathclyde smiled. As he sat alone, he again found himself holding his mobile phone. He wondered silently if the woman was dead yet.

35

Lincoln spat. The trail had gone cold. The time wasted at the Gurkha's ranch house had cost them dearly. A good man dead and no workable information to show for it. The transponder in the last team's sat-phone had brought them to a fleabag motel but their quarry was long gone. Their room—the number of which had been extracted from the desk clerk with a single whispered threat—was empty, with only stale smells and discarded food wrappers as evidence it had been occupied.

Bush was kneeling next to a trash bin in a corner of the motel room. He dug around and pulled out several pieces of plastic and metal. The remains of the satellite phone. He turned to Lincoln. "They must have got wise to the signal. That or they're just damn destructive."

Lincoln remained in the doorway. The sat-phone was now an official dead end. He was snapped out of his brooding calculations by the vibration of his cell phone. A monotone voice droned through the handset. Lincoln clicked then wound his fingers in a tight circle: they were on the move again.

"Don't worry Jake; you'll be rewarded well for this information." Lincoln ended the call. He spat out another glob of spittle. "We just caught a break. One of the grease monkeys over at Flyways spotted our target boarding a private jet bound for Key West. I guess we're going to the sunshine state."

Lincoln hit the speed dial for Topcat. After a brief conversation the flight was authorised. Turning to his team with renewed resolve Lincoln said, "There'll be a plane ready for us within the hour. Saddle up. We're heading back to the airport."

As Washington climbed into the driver's seat, he asked Lincoln, "How did the guy at Flyways know who our target was?"

"I sent out a message to my contacts when we first landed, along with a photograph. You know I like to cover my bases. Guy says he'd just walked over to the hangar next door to his, a place called Unco Services. He borrows tools from the mechanic he's friends with there. Some guy called Gerry. He said the woman gave him the stink eye when he smiled at her. When he checked up later, there was no record of her or the two men she was with on the flight manifest."

"This guy provided information before? You trust him?" asked Washington.

"Yeah. He let me know which plane my ex-wife and her new squeeze had fucked off in."

"Didn't your first wife get mugged and beaten up in Acapulco just after she left you for that car salesman?"

"Yeah, funny how things work out. What are the chances? Still, couldn't have happened to a nicer pair." Lincoln smiled, an expression more commonly sported by mako sharks.

"Isn't that the guy who got his balls kicked so bad he ended up losing one?"

The shark smile never wavered. "Could have been worse; he could have lost both."

The rest of the team had settled in the vehicle, with the exception of Bush, who still straddled the Harley.

"It gives new meaning to 'loco in Acapulco'," offered Washington.

Lincoln pointed to the steering wheel. "Thank you, Levi Stubbs. Now when you're ready, we have a flight to catch."

36

Charles Banks paced up and down in his office, his phone clamped to his ear. After ten rings it went to voicemail. He swore and hit redial. On the third ring the call was answered.

"Strathclyde."

"It's Banks."

"Is it done? Have TSI confirmed?"

"No." Banks rubbed a hand across his forehead. "Things aren't going as smoothly as we might have hoped. I just got a call…"

"It's late, Banks. What's going on?"

"I just got a call from the boss at TSI. He was asking if I knew anything about you."

There was a pause. Then Strathclyde spoke. "How did he come to hear my name?"

Banks remembered Topcat's voice, steely with suspicion. "He didn't give any specifics, just that your name had been flagged in connection with the target. Naturally, I denied all knowledge apart from generalities, confirmed that the operation was government-sanctioned but had nothing to do with you. But I'm concerned that they may go off-brief. Try to interrogate the woman rather than just terminate. And that would be very bad for us."

"No shit."

"How shall we proceed?"

Another pause. "Do nothing. I'm going to handle this."

"How—" The call ended. Banks stared at the phone, then threw it down on his desk. He had no idea how Strathclyde thought he could possibly deal with this situation. Just a pissant minister in a low-profile department.

Fine. Not his problem.

37

The sun had set by the time the Gunns and Andrea landed in Key West, reducing the horizon to a golden vista. The pilot had come in low, giving them a great view of the coast on their descent, pointing out the hundreds of spectators gathered on the island's piers and beaches to bear witness to the natural spectacle. Locals stood shoulder-to-shoulder with day visitors from the cruise ships that stopped by the island to or from the Caribbean.

The twin Pratt & Whitney engines of the Hawker 400 slowed to a complete stop as the light jet was guided into its allotted space.

"All ashore that's coming ashore." The pilot's voice echoed through the plane's sound system.

Danny Gunn paused on the set of steps that had been positioned by the plane. The evening heat and humidity was a stark contrast to the desert climate of Nevada, where the temperature dropped to near freezing at night. Within a minute of leaving the air-conditioned confines of the jet, his clothes were pasted to his body by a layer of perspiration.

Large bushes with long dagger-like leaves poked through every available gap in the airport's chain-link perimeter fence, and there were palm trees in the distance. He had visited Florida several times, and he remembered a taxi driver telling him that the trademark palms were in fact not native, but had been transplanted and carefully cultivated.

Danny pulled his shirt away from his chest and shook it a couple of times, creating a brief but welcome draught. He'd visited Disney World and Miami a few years back but had never ventured down to the Keys. Like most, he had seen the long interconnecting bridges that linked the chain of islands to the mainland but had never traversed them.

Andrea joined him on the steps. "What are you smiling about?"

"Last time I was in Florida I had my picture taken with Donald Duck."

Opening her eyes wide in mock surprise she asked, "What? The real one?"

"I knew that would impress you."

"Somehow I can't imagine you at Disney World."

Danny crossed his fingers and held them in the air. "Hey, Mickey an' me are tight."

Clay appeared behind them. "Looney Tunes are better. More fun, more mischief. Can't beat Bugs and Daffy."

"I'll see your Bugs and Daffy and raise you a Tom and Jerry."

"Tom and Jerry weren't Disney."

"Didn't say they were. Just more violent than Bugs and Daffy."

Clay muscled past them down the steps and strode

towards a tall black man approaching from the service hangar. The two men shook hands and slapped one another on the back.

Andrea leaned in. "Who's that?"

"Must be the guy Clay called to get us here. Garnett, I think he said." By the time Andrea and Danny reached them, Clay and Garnett had finished their elaborate greeting and were laughing at some private joke. Clay made the introductions. Danny noticed that Andrea seemed immediately comfortable in their new acquaintance's presence.

It was a short walk from the jet to the reception area next to the service hangar. While his guests sweated freely, Garnett seemed immune to the cloying heat. He moved with a relaxed grace, never seeming to exert himself even when striding across the asphalt to the large corrugated-iron building.

Most of the doors were shut along the row of surrounding hangars, and there was only a solitary worker to greet Garnett and his party. He was short and portly; Danny immediately thought of Cheech Marin.

"You still here, Hector?" asked Garnett. He turned to his companions. "One of my mechanics."

Hector nodded, a rueful expression on his face.

"You fighting with your Señorita again?"

"I can't do anything right around her lately. She shouts if I try to talk to her and shouts if I leave her to it. I can't win. So it's easier to stick around here sometimes. Don't worry, I'll lock up when I leave." He ambled off, shaking his head. Danny and Clay exchanged knowing looks as they followed Garnett into the hangar.

"You know any good hotels that we can crash at?" asked Danny.

Garnett looked back over his shoulder, his eyebrows raised. He dropped into a parody of street slang. "Fuck dat. Y'all be crashin' at my crib."

Danny smiled but kept his tone serious. "We don't want to bring any shit to your door."

"Not a problem, man. I've never been one to sit on the sidelines. There's a nasty rumour that I'm a legitimate businessman these days. Can't have too much of that kind of trash talk going around."

"The kind of guys we're running from use semi-automatics, not switch-blades."

"It wouldn't be the first time I've dodged bullets." The humour was gone from Garnett's voice. He looked Danny full in the face, their eyes locked. A moment of understanding passed between them. Then Garnett turned on his heel and pointed to the office that stood in a corner of the hangar. "I just need to drop off some paperwork, then we'll be on our way."

Andrea watched the exchange, the unspoken words she was sure were there. She took off her backpack and sat on it. Once again the feeling of events spiralling out of her control overtook her. Violence. Murder. She'd just crossed a continent, for God's sake, with men she hardly knew but had no choice but to trust. When would this be over? She'd often thought of her life—a single woman, struggling to make a decent living in a dying industry—as dull and likely to remain so. Now a large part of her wanted nothing more than to be safe at home. Yet she was also thrilled at the Gunn brothers' company. *If this had happened in London, who would have helped me? Anyone? Or would I be dead already?*

Danny squatted beside her. "You okay?"

"Just catching my breath. I feel tired all of a sudden."

"We'll get some proper sleep soon. And we're safer out here in the Keys. We have time to figure out what we're doing next."

"I was thinking on the flight over..." Andrea paused, trying to gather her thoughts. "I know it's connected to the mainland by bridges, but Key West is an island. Doesn't that mean we could be trapped here as well? What if they box us in?"

Danny smiled. "A fair point, but you don't need to worry. No one knows we're here. Our names weren't listed on the flight log. *If*—and it's a big if—Trident tracks us here, roads aren't our only way out. We've got planes, trains and automobiles. And boats."

"I guess you know more about this than most."

"Like Clay says—this ain't my first rodeo." Danny turned his head at the sound of footsteps. Garnett was walking back towards them.

"Ready to go?"

Danny nodded, then stood and held out his hand to Andrea. She took it and he pulled her to her feet. "Don't worry, we're way off the grid. They'll have to be bloody psychics to follow our trail."

Clay—who was using the duffle bag of looted weaponry as a makeshift pillow—grunted his agreement, then pulled himself upright and swung the bag and his backpack over his shoulders as if they weighed nothing.

Garnett led them out of the hangar and round the side of the building to a large, dark SUV that sat in a covered parking space. The corrugated roof had kept off the worst of the day's sun but the vehicle's interior was still hot enough to toast bread. Andrea slid into one of the rear seats, while Clay took shotgun. Garnett fired up the engine, which growled with a satisfactory rumble.

"What kind of car is this?"

Garnett turned and grinned at her. "Infiniti QX80."

"Impressive."

She *was* impressed. She was still getting used to the sheer size of the average American automobile. This one felt bigger than her London flat. And the contours of the seat seemed made to measure. She couldn't remember when she'd felt so comfortable. Not for a few days, that was for sure.

Danny silently slid next to her. Shadows rippled over his face as he settled into the seat, reminding her of the stripes of a tiger. He turned to face her and the momentary optical illusion was broken.

"You okay there?"

Andrea managed half a smile. "You keep asking me that."

He shrugged. "I don't mean to smother you. Anyway…" He looked down at her hand that had crept into his, almost without her realising. He returned her gentle squeeze.

"I know, and I appreciate it. I'm just not used to someone looking out for me twenty-four-seven."

She moved her hand back into her lap, breaking the moment. Feeling a little self-conscious she added, "I live alone back in London. I don't have a steady boyfriend and I don't exactly live the high life on my earnings. The truth is, I spend a lot of time on my own, mostly trying to drum up work from whatever magazines are paying out to freelancers, who are getting fewer and fewer in this economy."

Danny nodded as if he, too, understood the intricacies of freelance journalism. After a couple of seconds he asked, "Why don't you work as a regular writer? You know, something permanent?"

"I did at one point, quite a few years back now. I worked for *Time Out* for a while and also a magazine called *Holiday*. Do you remember the TV show?"

"I think so."

"Well the magazine was a tie-in to the show. It was a sweet deal for a while. Good pay and all expenses were covered. But it didn't last. Nothing good does."

"Ain't that the truth." Danny was silent for a moment, and Andrea wondered if he was thinking about the army. She still didn't know why he had left.

"Enough about me, tell me a little more about you," she said.

Danny smiled. "Nice way to change subjects. But I'm not big on talking about myself."

"I don't need your inside-leg measurements, just tell me something. Clay said you were a Green Jacket back in your army days. Tell me about that."

Danny straightened up in his seat, an unconscious action yet it conveyed an obvious pride that she had not seen in him before. "The Green Jackets are one of the best regiments in the world. More Victoria Cross medals than any other British unit. The count was fifty-six when I left."

"Why did you leave?" she asked but Danny continued as if he'd not heard her question.

"They're now officially known as 'the Rifles' but they'll always be Green Jackets to anyone who matters." He rubbed his chin ruefully. "We were shock troops, marauders, rough necks; but better lads you'll never meet. Mind, some of them could cause trouble in an empty house."

"Fascinating, but you still haven't told me anything about *you*," Andrea admonished him. Getting information out of Danny was like trying to get a loan out of her bank manager.

Clay turned in his seat, a mischievous look on his weathered face. "Forget it, honey, talking to him is too much like hard work. I'll tell you what you need to know."

Danny tried to look stern. "You better tend to your own knittin' there, Yankee."

Clay grinned at his brother's attempt at a Texas accent. Then he fixed Andrea with a serious expression. "Did he tell you that he's named after Daniel Boone, the old frontiersman? You know, the guy with the coonskin cap?"

Danny closed his eyes in mock annoyance. "Did I tell you that Clay got his name because he was born in Clay County, Texas? Lucky you weren't born in Dildo, Newfoundland. Imagine that on the first day of a new school: here's my little Daniel and my big Dildo."

Clay burst into laughter, and Andrea joined in, deep stomach-aching guffaws. Again she found herself feeling conflicted. Laughing like a loon while death trailed behind her like an angry bloodhound. *But surely it's better to laugh*, she thought.

38

"Brightwell."

"It's me, Stewart."

"I didn't recognise the number."

"Burner. Are you still in Atlanta?"

"Yes, why?"

"I need you to do some clean-up, the matter we discussed a couple of days ago."

"I thought that was being handled?"

"It was, but questions are being asked. Banks thinks they'll be asking very specific questions."

"I see. You want me to make sure I'm the one to ask those questions."

"Yes. And I want to watch."

39

As they traced their way through the narrow network of tree-lined streets Andrea was intrigued by the uniformity of the pastel-coloured houses that flanked either side of the road. They all shared a common look, the porches, window shutters and verandas all decorated with fretwork.

"Why do all of the houses have metal roofs?" Andrea asked Garnett.

"Well spotted."

"I can be observant when I want to be."

"Many moons ago we had a big fire on the island, terrible, really. It got so bad that the flames were leaping from roof to roof. So after that a law was passed that every roof has to be made of metal. Makes them fireproof."

Clay held up a finger. "But the rest of the house is still made from wood."

"Yes."

"Then wouldn't the fire still spread anyway?"

"I didn't make the law, just telling our guest about it, that's all."

"Makes sense, I suppose. The powers that be have to be seen to be doing something to make the public feel safer," offered Andrea.

"And all of the properties on Key West have to be maintained and restored to their original style," Garnett added. "No mock Tudors getting erected around here."

Garnett looked over his shoulder at Danny. "Shit, I forgot you were back there, sittin' all quiet like."

"I'm still here, all right. I'm just listening and taking in the sights while I can."

Andrea looked back at the gingerbread houses. "Well I like it. It's lovely down here."

"Lovely," said Garnett in a posh English accent. "That's such a British word."

"Gee, but don't they look swell. Cuter than a spring posy," replied Andrea in a voice that belonged to a sitcom from the sixties.

Garnett elbowed Clay's arm. "I love this girl—she's wild."

Danny smiled absently at the banter. Andrea followed his gaze to the ramshackle wall that formed the perimeter of a large manor house. She pointed. "What's that?"

"That's the Hemingway House," said Garnett.

"Looks like a six-year-old built that wall with Lego and Silly Putty."

"The story is that good old Ernest and his drinking buddies built that one afternoon while under the effect of one too many whiskeys." Garnett tipped an imaginary drink back.

"I could believe that. There isn't a single straight line in the whole wall. It looks ready to fall down," said Danny.

"Nah, it's pretty solid—and the drinking story is probably just that. It's survived a couple of hurricanes and some idiot drove a motorbike into it going full tilt a year or so back. And it's still standing."

"Maybe looks can be deceiving after all."

Clay turned and winked at his brother. "You know that's true. There are times when you look halfway intelligent."

"Is it much further to your house?" asked Danny.

"Just two blocks over. Why?" replied Garnett.

"Because when we get there, I'm going to have to kick his arse."

Clay shook his head. "I don't recognise that one. Gandhi?"

"Moe from the Three Stooges…"

"Ah, wise words." Clay gave his best "Nyuck, nyuck," then playfully speared two fingers towards Danny's eyes. Danny caught the opened fingers on the edge of his raised hand in true Stooges style.

"How the hell did a beauty like you get caught up with these two reprobates?" asked Garnett.

"Some girls have all the luck, I suppose."

"Ain't that the truth. Wait till you meet my wife, Edith—she knows all about that."

The house sat at the opposite end of the island from the airfield but was still a relatively short journey. Lights shone from every window of the pastel pink dwelling, which had stylised fish fretted into its woodwork.

They got out of the car and headed towards the house. Andrea looked down. "Are these yours?" she said, pointing at the three small chickens that were busy picking in the dirt.

Garnett shook his head. "They don't belong to anyone. Those are the original free-range birds, livin' free and wild. They're all over Key West, help keep the streets clean. They're nature's garbage collectors. To tell the truth, I hardly notice them any more."

"Wild chickens in the middle of a town—that's weird. They'd get stolen and eaten in most places I've ever been to."

Garnett shrugged as he opened the front door to his house. "If you think our chickens are weird wait till you see our cats."

"Cats?"

Garnett led them into a long hallway that effectively divided the house in two. "It's another Hemingway story, I'm afraid. There are over sixty cats around here all descended from Ernest's cat Snowball."

Andrea raised her eyebrows. "How can you tell?"

"Snowball the cat had thumbs. A lot of her relatives have thumbs and extra toes too."

Andrea laughed despite trying to hold it in. "You must think I came down in the last shower. Cats don't have thumbs. Not even in the Conch Republic."

"Wait and see."

Andrea looked at Danny but he too shrugged. "Don't ask me. But it sounds a little like the stories of wild haggis running around the mountains of Scotland to me."

Garnett shook his head in mock sadness. "Wait and see," he said again. Then in a loud voice, "Hi honey, I'm home."

A dark figure stepped into the doorway at the rear of the hallway. "And it's about time too!"

Edith strode towards them with athletic grace. She wore black Lycra leggings with a cropped top that left her toned mid-section open to view. Although she didn't offer to shake hands, the warm smile that she gave her guests made Andrea feel instantly at ease. "Come on in. Garnett baby, show these folks into the parlour. Can I get you all a drink?"

"Edie makes the best mojito ever. Or we've got beer: Dos Equis, the good stuff."

Clay stepped towards his host. "Beer sounds good to me. Can I help carry them?"

Edith looked at the man taking up most of the hallway. "Sure, come on through to the kitchen."

"We can't thank you enough for your hospitality. I mean that. We would have been more than happy booked into a hotel," said Danny.

"We're glad to have you. It's nice to meet some people who don't smell of jet fuel and cigars. And I might get some decent conversation that doesn't involve air-speeds or cargo weights." She winked at her husband playfully.

"Hush now girl, you know that kind of talk gets you all hot and steamy," Garnett countered.

"Dream on fly-boy. Come on Clay, let's see about those beers."

As Danny entered what Edith had called the parlour, he breathed a small sigh of relief. His gratitude was genuine. He was doubtful that Keys hotels would accept payment in cash only. That would mean swiping a credit card. The Keys had a reputation of being very laid back, yet so many things had changed since 9/11. Every scrap of information could now be logged on some innocuous database, and databases could easily be searched. It was always best to err on the side of caution when dealing with men armed and more than willing to end you. Credit card transactions were easily flagged and traced in a few keystrokes, if you had the right connections. He shuddered to think what information a private military contractor with money to burn could glean. And it was safe to assume that the operatives knew Clay's identity in addition to Andrea's, now that he'd been identified in those news reports in Nevada.

While drinking the delicious golden Mexican beer, conversation remained light and jocular. Clay and Garnett exchanged tales of bravado and reckless behaviour from their younger years, Andrea and Edith smiling and laughing at the recounted idiocy. Danny sat quiet for most of the banter, tuning out the voices as he weighed various options and possible outcomes. He would have preferred to sit outside, alone, but certainly didn't want to appear ungrateful to Garnett and Edith for their hospitality.

After drinking two beers, Edith made her way to the kitchen, promising to return with some "real food like my mama used to make". She politely refused any help from her guests. Twenty minutes later she called them through to the dining area.

The middle of the room was dominated by an oval table, on which was a serving platter laden with homemade cheeseburgers. A large bowl filled with mixed green salad sat next to it, flanked by two smaller bowls, one heaped with potato salad the other with crispy onion rings. After brief encouragement from Edith, food was scooped, ladled and grabbed.

Clay devoured one of the large onion rings with gusto. "These are great. How do you make a simple thing taste so good?"

Edith sat back in her chair. "It's all in the batter. A little bit of beer, a lot of pepper, paprika and a squirt or two of Tabasco sauce."

"Well I'm jealous as hell. You look like a supermodel and cook like a professional chef." It sounded like Andrea was only half joking.

After the food had been eaten, more Dos Equis was served. Andrea and Clay insisted on clearing up. Once the dishes, plates and glasses had been washed and put away Edith thanked her guests then said goodnight. She didn't bother asking Garnett if he was joining her. She was clearly well accustomed to sleeping alone when her husband had business. Garnett kissed her and playfully patted her behind as she left the room.

Garnett leaned back in his chair. "So, time to tell me why you fellas are on the run with this lovely lady. What happened in Vegas that meant you had to make a quick getaway?"

Danny let Clay do the talking. Garnett seemed to take it in his stride, only occasionally interrupting to ask clarifying questions. When Clay had finished he nodded thoughtfully. "So, what's your next move?"

"I've been thinking," said Danny.

"Uh oh…"

Andrea nudged Clay then placed her index finger against her pursed lips. This elicited a wry smile from the Texan.

Danny's next comment made Andrea pale momentarily. "We have to assume that the Trident team or someone like them *will* find us sooner or later. So we need to have a strike-back strategy before that happens. The psycho in the video, Strathclyde, has the most to lose. But also the British government in general would be severely damaged. With all the shit that's come out over the last few years, the last thing that they would want is a scandal of this magnitude."

Garnett looked into the top of his bottle as if some secret was hidden within. "Why don't you just email the video and pictures to every news channel we can think of? Fox News and CNN would kill for something like this. I don't think they would be too bothered about upsetting some pencil-necked pervert in the UK. Once it's out there this asshole would be toast."

"That was my first impulse as well, but we have to be sure that it would be taken seriously. There's so much fake footage floating around on the Internet it may well be treated as a hoax."

Andrea shook her head. "Once they watch it they'll know it's not faked. It's… horrible."

"But so-called torture-porn was really big in the movies for a while. You know, *Hostel* and *Saw*," Danny pointed out. He knew the authenticity of the footage would be called into question, and despite Garnett's opinions on the cut-throat nature of the news networks, they would not launch an attack against a foreign politician without conferring with their British contacts first.

"Are you one hundred per cent sure that the guy in the video is the same one in the photographs?" asked Garnett.

"Pretty damned sure," Danny replied. "I can show you if you want to see. I'll warn you, though, it's not pleasant viewing."

"Okay."

Andrea handed the laptop to Danny with the proviso: "I don't want to see it again."

"We could go for a walk into the town if you want. The original Sloppy Joe's is only ten minutes away," offered Clay. "Would it be a problem if we came back a bit late?"

Garnett waved them away. "Have at it. Captain Tony's and the Lazy Gecko are worth a visit as well. I'll leave the door unlocked. We'll probably still be up and at it anyway."

Once Andrea and Clay had left the house Danny powered up the laptop, inserted the flash drive into one of the USB ports and activated the media player. He double clicked the video file icon.

Garnett's expression betrayed nothing as he watched the man in the mask slowly taunt then eviscerate the captive woman. Only after the whole film had played through did he speak. "So how did you identify the man? The only part of his face you can see clearly are those damned eyes."

Danny moved the progress button back to approximately halfway through the footage. After less than ten seconds he hit pause. "See those three moles on his right shoulder and the scar down his back? Well, now look at this."

Garnett curled his upper lip in disgust as Danny loaded the publicity pictures taken at the school fundraiser. "How the hell did that maggot get himself alongside a swim team?"

"He's a politician." The ire in Danny's voice matched the deep-set loathing he felt for predators such as Strathclyde.

Garnett nodded in understanding. "That fucker needs the electric chair."

"I couldn't agree more. Unfortunately the death penalty doesn't apply in the UK."

"Oh, Christ, I just had a thought. If this was filmed back in the nineties, how many more poor women has he done this to? He could have done this dozens of times."

"I know. And there's no indication that he's ever been linked to any crime let alone something as rotten as this." Danny stared again at the twin images on the screen. The contrast between the blood-flecked demon mask and the smiling politician defied belief. Yet he knew them to be one and the same. He tapped his fingertips against his forehead as he pondered what to do next. It wasn't as simple as going back to England and putting a bullet between the man's eyes. Sure, it would achieve the desired result but he had no wish to spend the rest of his days eating prison food. Also, the more immediate problem of the hit team required some thought. Danny had no way of knowing the reach and connections of the PMC outfit.

Garnett broke the silence. "I'd appreciate it if Edith didn't see any of this. She's a tough enough gal but this would freak her out."

"Of course," replied Danny. "I still feel awkward us being in your home. We should have booked into a cheap hotel. The last thing I want is to bring any danger to your front door."

Garnett dismissed him with a wave of his hand. "Clay and me go back quite a-ways. He fronted me a lot of dough when no one else would give me a second glance. Without him I could have never gone legit. I'd still be smuggling weed and Cubans for a living."

Danny smiled. "I've done worse."

"No doubt, but you're one of those crazy Highlander types. It's all that running around in a skirt you guys do. No wonder you're always fighting with each other."

"It's called a kilt." Danny furrowed his brow in mock consternation. "And I've never worn one in my life."

Garnett burst into unbridled laughter. "Maybe I'll get myself the full outfit. Can you imagine a black man in a kilt waving one of those big-assed swords around? It'd scare the white folks half to death."

The house was quiet upon Clay and Andrea's return. The others had already turned in for the night. Despite having consumed a half-dozen margaritas in various flavours, Clay was still steady on his feet. Andrea, however, was grateful of the supportive arm that encircled her shoulders.

The tequila cocktails had had a somewhat therapeutic effect. Over the space of the three hours she'd spent in Clay's company she had cried, laughed and talked through her very real fears. She was scared to die. She was scared to go home yet desperately wanted familiar surroundings. She still needed to speak to her parents, to tell them the details of the terrible fate that had befallen Greg and Bruce. She had no way of knowing if her parents had been informed through official channels of their deaths. They would be sick with fear, not knowing if she was dead or alive. Yet Danny had advised against calling home. It hurt to admit it, but he was right. The reach of the PMC was an unknown quantity. Did they have the resources to tap her parents' phone? If so, any information she gave her parents could be used to find her and could put them in danger.

They made their way to their respective rooms.

"Well little lady, I'll see you in the morning."

"Clay, wait. I just want to say… I…" A tear traced a path down her cheek.

The big Texan squeezed her shoulder affectionately. "See you in the morning."

Andrea's room was lit only by the meagre streetlight spilling through the single window. She didn't bother to switch on the lights. She sat on the bed and thought about her parents. How much more could she tell them? There had been no reply to the email she'd sent in the Internet café in Vegas.

Cupping her head in her hands she moved to the top of the bed and closed her eyes.

40

The Calico machine pistol was uncomfortable in the shoulder sling; it was not designed with concealment in mind, yet Lincoln was loath to carry a more compact weapon. What it lacked in comfort it more than made up for in firepower.

He, Bush, Washington and Kennedy disembarked from their plane into the darkness of the Florida night, and clambered into the waiting minivan that Trident had organised for their arrival. Bush huffed noisily that there was no bike for him to use, eventually declaring that he would add it to his ever-growing list of reasons to slice and dice the targets when they finally laid hands on them. The driver of the family-sized Chrysler turned to Lincoln. The man was bald and had a distinctive bullet-shaped head. He introduced himself as Chad Casey.

"Where to?"

Lincoln studied Chad for a few seconds, noticing a ragged scar that looked like it had been made by a barbed-wire necktie. "I'm not really sure. We know the target arrived via private jet a few hours ago. Unfortunately that's where our intel bottoms out. We've got the name of the charter company and the plane's serial number but haven't established their destination in Florida."

Chad grimaced, showing platinum caps on two of his front teeth. "I guess the first thing would be to trace the pilot and crew of the jet. Then we could arrange a little tête-à-tête with them. A flash of green usually loosens the lips of those guys."

Bush brushed his fingers gingerly against the bruised skin around his swollen eye. "If money doesn't work I'll gladly beat it out of anyone we come across."

Chad looked first at Bush then back at Lincoln. He had clearly heard nothing that upset his sensibilities. He pointed to the control office of the airport. "I'll have a word with the operations team first. It's Ps and Qs with these guys though. Let me go in alone and do the talking. I know a couple of the controllers in there, shouldn't take too long."

Lincoln nodded in thanks and agreement. "You're welcome to join the posse if you're free and don't mind getting your hands dirty."

"I've been with TSI for six years. I'm always ready to mix it up when the chance arises." Chad's voice was dry and carried a slight rasp. Lincoln again glanced at the collar of lacerations framing his throat. He wondered if Chad had served in Africa and picked up the grisly souvenir there.

"Welcome to the band, Chad. Once you get back I'll bring you up to speed on the assignment so far."

Chad Casey returned after ten minutes, during which time Bush again grumbled his displeasure at having to ride in "the school bus". As he climbed into the driver's seat, Chad handed Lincoln a slip of paper. After struggling to read the erratic script in the dim light of the car's interior, Lincoln handed it back, defeated. "What does it say?"

Chad rubbed a hand across the back of his neck. "Writing was never my strong suit. It says the plane you asked about is registered to a private company here on the Keys. The guy that owns it is called Garnett Bell. Of course, it doesn't mean he was the pilot of that particular flight but he's a good place to start. If he didn't fly it he'll be able to tell us who did."

"Then we can pick up the targets' trail double time," added Washington. He gave a reassuring nod to Bush, who was fidgeting in his seat, and Kennedy, who was twiddling a single sniper round through his fingers.

"You got an address for this Bell fella?" asked Lincoln.

"Yeah. It's only ten minutes out," Chad confirmed. He pointed two fingers in a vague northerly direction.

"Well let's go and take a look-see." Lincoln adjusted the Calico pistol again.

"We doing it tonight?" asked Washington, glancing at his watch. "We've been up and at it for nearly thirty-six hours now. I don't want these assholes getting the drop on us because we're off our game."

Lincoln considered for a moment. "It's two-thirty eastern time. I say we put our heads down until six then saddle back up. We should be able to catch the pilot in the morning."

"You guys can bunk down at my place and I'll keep an eye on the pilot's house," said Chad. "I'll drop you first and come back out in my own car. I'll leave the company van with you so you can high-tail it if needs be."

"Okay then," agreed Lincoln. "Let's go with that. We'll sleep light and be ready to rock and roll first thing. Here, what's your cell number?" Chad recited his digits and Lincoln dialled. Chad's cell phone rang. "Save my number. Speed dial me if anything occurs that I should know about."

Chad's house was by no means the largest on the street but was well kept. A turtle sat in a small wire enclosure in the front garden, its shell painted in dayglo colours. Chad noticed the curious looks that his pet was receiving. "Say hello to Rastaman. He was here when I moved in."

Bush shook his head. "I've got to ask. Why is he called Rastaman?"

Chad smiled as if the answer was obvious. "His colours. Red, gold and green. Come on in guys, make yourself at home. There's plenty of chow in the kitchen, nothing fancy though. I'll call you if I need you."

Lincoln felt a moment's indecision. Should they keep chasing the trail despite their fatigue or take the respite offered? The grit that seemed to have taken up residence behind his eyelids decided it for him. He wanted to be one hundred per cent for the next and hopefully final stretch of the chase. He was determined to have the target neutralised by the end of play. He nodded at Chad. "Make sure and call if that pilot so much as farts too loud in the night."

Chad grinned, his caps glinting in the glare from the porchlight. "Roger that."

41

Clay, Andrea, Garnett and Edith were eating a breakfast of fruit and cereal when a very hot and sweat-soaked Danny entered the kitchen.

Garnett looked up from his Cheerios. "You're keen, I'll give you that."

"I just needed to shake off the cobwebs. I haven't done much working out of late. My doctor recommended a month of rest and relaxation." Danny pulled at the sweat-stained shirt and shorts Garnett had given him.

"And how's that been workin' out for ya?" Clay guffawed.

"Go have a shower, then I'll fix you some breakfast." Edith pointed towards one of the two bathrooms.

"How far did you run?" asked Garnett.

"About five miles. It's hard work in this heat, even this early in the day." Danny's reason for the morning run was twofold. Firstly to get his fitness back to an acceptable level, and secondly to get a feel for the layout and streets on the island. It was one of the things he did whenever he found himself in a new location. You never knew when you would need to navigate in a hurry. A little prior knowledge could be the difference between survival and running into a literal dead end when under fire. He hoped that would not be an issue here in the Keys. But he followed the old maxim: hope for the best, plan for the worst.

"I noticed you've got a heavy punchbag out on the patio. Do you mind if I use it for five minutes?" He received the thumbs-up from Garnett and nodded his thanks.

Danny stared at the bag with practised intensity. His workout started long before he threw his first punch. He felt his aggression levels build rapidly inside. In his mind, an attacker surged towards him, intent on doing him serious harm. When he felt the moment was right he exploded into the bag. He worked a series of punches first, his arms pumping like pistons, fists driving deep. His body snapped from side to side as he sent punch after punch into the leather. His feet moved in short crab-like steps, circling the bag. He then began to incorporate knees and elbows into his combinations, opening up with punches then crowding close to slam home short-range blows. He stepped out smartly and bent the bag in half with a side stamp kick.

"Shit! And I thought he *punched* hard." Garnett, who had been watching Danny from the kitchen window, turned to Clay. "Did you see that?"

Clay smiled. "I once seen Danny knock a guy clean out with that kick."

"I could believe that no problem," said Garnett shaking

his head in admiration. "I took a few kick-boxing classes in my teens but he's on a whole different level."

Clay nodded. "His moves aren't pretty—he wouldn't win any prizes for form—but he's like a pit bull."

"Reminds me of Dempsey or Marciano. Shit, a rodeo bull would be jealous."

"I remember when this guy sucker-punched a friend of Danny's in a bar, knocked him down just for looking at him the wrong way. So Danny went at him and the guy ran out of the bar and locked himself in his car. If he'd just left it at that it might have been okay, but he started giving Danny the finger. Danny backed up a couple of steps then launched that sidekick of his. He smashed through the side window and knocked the asshole clean out. It was one of those real comedy moments."

Edith raised her eyebrows, a spoonful of chopped fruit halfway to her mouth. "Not for the asshole in the car."

Clay gave her a wink. "*But* the asshole had it coming."

"Danny doesn't suffer fools gladly," Andrea contributed.

Clay smiled again. He could tell these women tales about his brother that would scare the living daylights out of them. Maybe another day.

Danny returned to the kitchen. He pulled at the sweat-stained T-shirt. "I think I'd better have that shower now."

"Before you do, Rocky Balboa wants his sound effects back. Damn it, Danny, you could have made some real money as a boxer."

Danny humbly accepted the compliment from Garnett. "Maybe in my next life."

Clay snorted. "So, what's next? Much as we like playing

house with you, Garnett, we can't impose on your hospitality any longer." He rubbed his chin. They needed a vehicle and he had plenty of money, but what kind of second-hand lot would accept cash only? "Do you know anywhere we can buy a car without leaving a paper trail?"

I can do better than that." Garnett leaned back in his chair. "I have a lock-up garage across town. Paid for off the books, you understand. It's where I keep… sensitive items."

Clay laughed. "I can imagine. Stolen Rembrandts, your bondage gear, that kind of thing, right?"

"Try Cuban cigars for my favourite customers, a couple of illegal fully automatic assault rifles and two vehicles registered to a former—and now dead—friend. One's a Cadillac Escalade, a few years old so it won't draw any attention. You can have it."

Clay rose and put a hand on Garnett's shoulder. He felt rather moved at his old friend's generosity. "I bet you look real pretty in leather."

42

Antonio Urquidez wheeled his father's bicycle the length of the garden and rested the handlebars against the dividing wall. He had been playing quietly with his meagre collection of Star Wars action figures when strange noises had captured his attention. A sharp series of retorts echoed in the morning air. Was Mr Bell beating a carpet? First he tried peering through a small gap in the cinder-block wall that separated his house from the one next door. Mr and Mrs Bell had no children for Antonio to play with, but Mr Bell, who liked to be called Garnett, had shot more than a few hoops with him when his own father had been too busy watching Dr Phil on TV. His father was often too busy but Antonio didn't mind much. Mr Bell was good fun and Pico Vasquez who lived down the block was good to hang with as well.

Balancing carefully upon the aluminium frame of the bike, he peered over the wall. There was a man in Garnett's backyard. The guy, who Antonio had never seen before, was hitting and kicking the big punchbag. The man's hands were a blur. Antonio tried counting the punches but couldn't keep up. Then the man backed up and planted a foot into the leather. The bag folded around his foot, nearly in half.

Antonio had taken some karate classes last summer but this guy looked way more dangerous than Sensei Perry. When Sensei had demonstrated a move he had looked smooth and practised but this guy was way more... savage. He looked like he was trying to kill the bag, not just hit it. Antonio reckoned that if the two met, Sensei Perry would get his ass canned in less than ten seconds.

To his disappointment, the man finished his assault on the bag and began to move through a series of stretches. As he did, the shirt he wore rode up and exposed a large patch of pink mottled scarring, which stood out in stark contrast to his tanned skin. Antonio's friend Pico's sister had a burn scar on her arm that looked a little like it, but this guy's scar was about ten times the size.

The man next door had finished his exertions and went back into Garnett's house. Antonio huffed, disconcerted. Usually nothing ever happened around here. He wished he lived up on the mainland. Orlando would be cool, or even Miami. Pico said all the girls in Miami were dying for it. Antonio wasn't exactly sure what they were dying for, but if Pico said it was so—it was probably true. He climbed down off the frame of the bicycle and went back to his Star Wars action figures. He wondered what Pico was up to this morning. Discarding his toys in an untidy heap he plucked his skateboard from its resting place next to the back door and headed out to find his friend. He wanted to tell him about the dude next door who was faster than Bruce Lee.

* * *

Some three hundred yards away, Chad Casey slouched comfortably in the front seat of his Dodge Challenger. The dark-red paintwork glinted in the early morning sun. He took another long sip from a bottle of Gatorade. The sugar-laden drink was like an elixir that worked wonders in keeping him awake and alert. He then placed a tiny yellow pill under his tongue. Within seconds the wonder-bean kicked in and he felt an almost euphoric rush of warmth spread though his system. He watched a woman emerge from the pilot's house and turn towards the morning sun. A small gym bag swung from her shoulder. He considered calling in for a moment then decided against it. It was the man of the house he was after. The woman was certainly something to look at, though. Her figure was damn near perfect. Nice rack, too. Chad wasn't really into the black thing but he thought he would make an exception on this occasion. Rubbing unconsciously at the ring of scars around his neck, he settled back into the seat as the shapely woman turned the corner and was lost from view.

After ten minutes a young Hispanic boy emerged from the house next door to the pilot's and began to make an attempt at riding a skateboard down the middle of the road towards Chad's parked car. His board skills were pretty dire. Chad gave him no more than half a glance as he passed. Refocusing his attention on the house, he dialled Lincoln's cell phone.

"Any movement at the house?" Lincoln said.

"No. A woman just left. Assume it's his wife or

girlfriend. When you're ready come on over and we'll grill the pilot as planned."

"Okay. I punched the location into your truck's GPS last night so we'll be there in five."

"Cool. Then we can get down to business."

"Saddle up," shouted Lincoln. His team responded accordingly. Firearms were retrieved from their resting places and live rounds racked into chambers. Within a minute the Presidents were in their borrowed minivan and they traced a steady path through the picturesque tree-lined avenues.

Washington glanced at the GPS fixed to the windscreen. Only two more blocks to go. He pushed down on the brake pedal as a group of four teenagers stepped out into the path of the Chrysler minivan. Instinctively he laid a heavy hand onto the horn. The tallest of the teens jumped back, clutching the skateboard to his chest. He gave Washington the finger and added a few choice comments about where he could shove the horn for better effect. The youth made to step towards the vehicle and raised the board as if to slam the hood of the Chrysler. The steely glare that Washington fixed him with soon gave him cause to reconsider. The small gang crossed the road but turned collectively and gave the occupants of the minivan the finger again. Washington smiled ruefully. He turned in his seat to see Bush lowering his window. A glob of phlegm sailed out of the open window and caught the nearest teen full in the face. This brought fresh insults from the gang but the Chrysler cruised onward. In the back seat Kennedy high-fived Bush. "With an aim like that maybe you should take over as the group sniper."

Bush grinned at the compliment. "Little Conch asshole got off easy. Some towns he would have gotten a bullet for pulling that shit."

Washington's attention was called back to business by the Elvis ringtone of Lincoln's phone.

"What? What did you say?" There was a pause. "Fuck. We'll be right there, follow them." Lincoln's voice was hard with excitement. He ended the call and turned to Washington. "Step on it. Casey just saw the pilot leave the house with a woman matching the description of the target and two men, one big like the guy we saw on the news, and a smaller man. Could be the one who took out Clinton. They've been having a fucking sleepover! This makes our job a hell of a lot easier."

Washington hit the gas and the Chrysler responded efficiently; the gingerbread houses became a passing blur. He spotted Chad's Dodge Challenger speeding down the narrow street a couple of hundred feet in front of them. He knew that the pilot's vehicle would be just ahead of Chad's. The phone rang again, and Lincoln put it on speaker. Chad's voice was loud and clear. "I see you behind me. I'll cut over one street and trail you on a parallel course. The pilot is in the dark Infiniti SUV directly in front of me—"

All four men were suddenly thrown forward as Washington slammed on the brakes. A couple in an old Honda Accord had pulled out from the kerb into the path of the Dodge in front. It rear-ended the Honda with a sickening crunch and sent it lurching forward a couple of feet. The Chrysler minivan came to a halt inches from the Dodge's rear bumper.

Lincoln cursed in fury. "You all okay?"

Angry grunts were given in response.

A few moments later the driver of the Honda stumbled from his car and clasped two hands to his neck.

Lincoln exchanged a look with Washington for a second then stepped out of the vehicle. He looked at the front of Chad's Dodge Challenger, taking in the cracked fender. He leaned in at Chad's window. "You okay? Only minor damage, she'll still drive fine."

Chad nodded. "I'm okay. Give that pissant what for."

Lincoln turned to the driver of the Honda. Washington opened his door and stepped out to get a look at the man. He was not impressed. Faded combat trousers, a pale orange T-shirt emblazoned with the *South Park* logo and a badly bleached mop of something that loosely resembled hair.

"Nice driving there, sparky," said Lincoln.

The look in the man's eyes transformed as a thought solidified in his mind. "I hope that guy is insured 'cos I'm sure my neck will take months of medical care to fix... and he'll be paying."

Lincoln nodded in understanding. "Your girlfriend all right in there?"

"No man, she needs a hospital too. This is gonna cost."

"Here, I'll cover it." He nodded at Chad. "He's a friend of mine. Take this for now." The driver looked down at Lincoln's outstretched hand, clearly expecting to see either cash for a quick pay-off or second best, insurance details. What he didn't see was the fist that slammed up under his chin. The man's tousled hair shook as if filled with a rogue electric current then he collapsed in an untidy heap at the side of the car. Washington grinned as Lincoln grabbed the man by the collar and belt and dragged him back to the kerb without ceremony. He then looked in at the woman in the car. Her face told of way too many late nights and way too much tequila. Thick black mascara framed her bloodshot eyes, deep frown lines etched into her weathered features. Her hair looked like it would benefit from a vigorous scrub with half a bottle of shampoo.

"Can you drive?" growled Lincoln.

She nodded, her lips a tight line under wide eyes.

"Then get this pile of shit out of my way right now or you'll get the same as General Accident back there."

It only took the woman a second to scoot over to the driver's seat.

Lincoln walked back to Chad's Dodge. "We'll take point. Follow us." Washington saw Chad give a salute.

By the time Lincoln had gotten back into the minivan, the Honda was back into the parking space it had originally occupied. The man still lay by the kerb. His movements were slow and erratic.

Washington steered around Chad's Dodge and laid his foot heavy on the gas. "Fucking reprobates. That's what's wrong with this country. Too many asswipes like that looking for the pay-off without putting any work in first. Nice shot, by the way."

Lincoln waved his hand in dismissal. "Hardly an achievement knocking that sack of pus on his ass. Now, we're looking for a dark SUV."

In a few minutes Washington saw a dark-blue Infiniti a block and a half ahead. Two cars separated them. Washington scanned ahead for an opportunity to overtake but the streets were narrow and cars were parked on both sides of the road.

Although unnecessary, Lincoln pointed at the SUV. "Turning left."

"Got him," said Washington.

43

Inside Garnett's SUV the air-con was cranked up to the max and provided welcome relief from the steadily rising temperature. Clay and Garnett rode up front, while Danny shared the back seat with Andrea.

Clay turned in his seat. Andrea was looking under the weather, her skin pale. *Poor woman.* He couldn't imagine how messed up she must feel after the past couple of days.

"How you feelin'?"

She smiled weakly. "When I woke up this morning I had no idea where I was. Then I remembered and had to run to the bathroom. I didn't throw up though!" She leant forward to Garnett. "How far to the lock-up?"

"Just ten minutes or so. Just relax back there. You're in safe hands."

Clay was about to make a joke when an ugly-sounding metallic crunch cut through the morning air. He swivelled further in his seat. There, on the street behind them, an old jalopy had been ass-ended by a fine-looking Dodge. Someone had started the day on a crappy note. He watched the driver of the older car emerge into the street holding his neck. From behind the Dodge a man climbed down from a minivan and approached the driver. After a very brief exchange of words the driver was catapulted off his feet. Clay raised an eyebrow. Here was somebody who was certainly sharp with his hands. Ex-military, he was almost sure of that just by the man's bearing. Well-muscled, hair just a little longer than a regulation army buzz cut. Even from the growing distance as the SUV pulled away, Clay could see the ferociousness in the man's face. He watched Buzz Cut jump back into the minivan, the vehicle lurching forward with undisguised urgency. Two cars turned onto the street between the minivan and Garnett's Infiniti.

Clay spoke. "Take the next left."

Garnett looked questioningly at him but from the back seat, Danny, who had also been watching the confrontation, nodded in affirmation of his brother's command. Garnett swung the vehicle around the next corner. One of the two cars between them and the minivan kept on straight ahead and the other made a right turn. The minivan turned left and kept pace with Garnett's vehicle. "Take another left ahead."

When the vehicle mirrored Garnett's sequence exactly Danny cursed from the back seat. "Fuck! We've got a tail. They're here."

Andrea's face blanched. "How?"

Clay didn't bother to respond. *It doesn't matter how, now they're here.* He turned in his seat again. The minivan—a brand-new silver Chrysler—made short work of the distance that separated them and was now close enough for Clay to get a good look at the two faces in the front. Buzz Cut sat in the passenger seat, his face a mask of grim determination. The driver was hunched forward but big enough to be a professional wrestler. The eyes that peered back at Clay belonged more to a shark than a man.

Clay looked over at Garnett, whose jaw was set. "You okay with this?"

"I was chased a few times in my former career… but it's been years." He looked in the rear-view mirror. "And I figure these guys aren't concerned with confiscating booze, cigars or counterfeit dollars." He looked at Clay. "You carrying?"

"Always." Clay responded by tapping the pistol tucked into his waistband. "I'm a Texan, it's the law."

Garnett looked into the back seat. "You two?"

Danny responded with a resounding, "Aye, pistol. Glock 37. But the MP5Ks are back at your place."

Andrea clearly surprised Garnett by producing her revolver. He gave a grim smile. "Okay then. Do we lead them into Mallory and hope they don't attack with all of the tourists around or lead them out into Parker's Yard and take them on?"

"What's Parker's Yard?" asked Clay.

"It's an industrial area over towards the naval base. Mostly lock-ups and storage sheds. It'll be pretty empty this early in the day."

"Parker's it is."

Garnett increased their speed. A soft *whoomph* sounded from the front of the SUV's hood and a small brown tangle of blood and feathers slapped against the windscreen. "Chicken!"

Clay laughed out loud at the unexpected road kill. "Ten points for a cat with thumbs." But the moment of levity was cut short by the Dodge Challenger that had pulled across the junction directly in front of them, effectively blocking the road. Garnett acted on instinct and the SUV slewed right, mounting the sidewalk. The vehicle bucked wildly as he fought to retain control. Clay grabbed for a handhold as the rear fender was ripped off the obstructing car as Garnett swung the SUV left, back into the road.

"Keep going," yelled Clay. Garnett didn't need to be told. Clay turned to see the driver of the Dodge slamming his hand into the steering wheel. *He looks pissed. Was that intentional?* "I don't think that was an accident. They've got two vehicles." Garnett swore. Clay turned and saw that the Dodge was disappearing down a side street, but the minivan was less than fifty feet behind them.

"Hold on," said Garnett as he whipped the Infiniti around a tight corner, sending the rear fishtailing for a few uncertain seconds. The tyres found their traction and the SUV cut a path west down another picturesque street. He leaned hard on the horn as two young women on scooters emerged from a side street directly into their path. Their long hair wafted in cascades in the morning breeze. Both women wore only shorts and bikini tops—no helmets; any spill from their bikes would probably result in grave injuries or death. The nearest woman turned and mouthed a word that was a direct contrast to her prim features. This resulted in another blare of Garnett's horn. The woman sneered, but they reluctantly pulled over close to the kerb, allowing the SUV to speed past. Garnett gave them half a wave in way of apology. He got the *talk to the hand* gesture in return.

* * *

Cheryl Coster looked at her friend, her eyes extra wide for emphasis. "Do you believe that asshole?"

"He was black, he probably, like, totally stole that car anyway," Chantelle opined. She tossed her hair in disgust and pulled back into the road without looking in her mirror. She never saw the Chrysler minivan as it slammed into her rear wheel, sending her cartwheeling off her bike. Her strangled screech was cut short as her nearly naked flesh met the sidewalk. She bounced once, leaving behind several teeth, one of her Gucci sandals and most of the skin from her back. Her face proved no match for a parked Hyundai Getz.

Cheryl watched her friend's fate in what she perceived as slow motion. In her shock she steered her own moped into the hood of another parked car, coming to a very abrupt halt, her ribcage splintered around the handlebars.

Lincoln stared at Washington in anger.

Washington returned his stare. "What? I didn't mean it. She just got in the way. You want me to stop?"

"Keep going." Lincoln's voice was furious, yet only a small portion of the ire he felt was directed at his wheelman. This should have been a relatively simple job. Collateral damage was sometimes unavoidable but dead civilians would bring the cops swarming in from miles around, something that he would rather avoid at all costs. "Just make sure we get them."

Washington's hand shot out, pointing at the rear window of the target vehicle. "That's her. That's the woman."

Lincoln focused on the horrified face under a mop of blonde hair staring back at him through the window. "That's right, bitch, I see you."

44

"Jesus, they just ran those women off the road." Andrea's voice was like fingernails down a blackboard.

Danny nodded and felt something deeper than fury seething deep in his stomach. He would make them pay. Dearly.

Garnett was pushing the SUV as fast as he could without running down any slow-moving pedestrians. "Four blocks to Parker's."

"They're still behind us," said Andrea. Danny saw that she was gripping her revolver like a drowning man would a life preserver.

Garnett powered around another corner, losing one of his wheel trims as he clipped the kerb. The SUV bucked sideways for a second but did not lose any speed. On the kerb, a large Hispanic woman dressed in a bright floral dress shouted and shook her fist angrily at the speeding vehicle.

"There!"

Danny swivelled in his seat to see the entrance of Parker's Yard. A high chain-link fence formed the perimeter and stretched out for hundreds of yards in either direction.

A wide double gate was open and allowed easy entry into the yard. The layout reminded Danny of an army barracks. Two-storey sheds were arranged in long rows, each easily a hundred feet in length. Their walls looked to be constructed from old-style asbestos sheeting, the corrugated-iron roofs painted a dark red. Danny could see at least twenty sheds on each side of the main access road, many with colossal piles of clay-coloured sand against their walls, some higher than their roofs. "Turn off halfway down."

"Left or right?" asked Garnett.

"Right. It looks like there's a bit more room to manoeuvre on that side."

The SUV whipped to the right between two of the sheds. "Slow just a bit."

Garnett slowed the SUV to twenty and without preamble, Danny opened his door and tumbled out onto the ground. Tucking his head, he rolled smoothly and gained his feet in one practised motion. He sprinted back to the corner of a shed. Crouching, he pressed his back against the wall and lifted his pistol. As the pursuing minivan rounded the corner he squeezed the trigger four times in rapid succession. All four rounds punched through the windscreen. Inside the vehicle someone roared in pain. As the minivan sped past, Danny adjusted his aim and sent another three rounds into the target. One of the shots found the rear tyre, which blew out with a satisfying *whoomph*. He then emptied the rest of the clip into the rear window. Glass shattered and the vehicle slewed wildly to one side but continued to follow Garnett's SUV.

Danny ejected the spent clip and slapped a fresh one into the butt of the Glock.

Clay held on as Garnett stamped down on the accelerator and swung the SUV left around the shed. Another tight series of gravel-spitting left turns and they were behind the pursuing vehicle.

"Got them now. I'll ram them," yelled Garnett.

Suddenly the already shattered rear window of the minivan exploded outwards. Two men, each clutching an automatic weapon, glared back at Clay and both weapons opened fire as one. He ducked as a hail of bullets ripped through Garnett's body, shredding his head and chest as if it were made of paper. Clay's roar was that of a wounded bear, beyond fury, beyond conscious thought.

The SUV skidded into the wall of the nearest shed, its hood punching through the thin wall. It came to a shuddering halt as it met one of the reinforced stanchions that formed the shed's internal skeleton.

Clay pulled his Colt Python as the PMCs tumbled out of their minivan and approached the SUV, two men on each side of the vehicle, weapons pressed tight into their shoulders, fingers on triggers. He saw that the driver of the minivan was bleeding heavily, his right arm clutched to his chest. He was big, very nearly as big as Clay. He brandished a sub-machine gun left-handed across his chest, business end still focused on the stationary vehicle. The men approached fast but in strict formation.

Clay wrenched open the SUV's door, knowing that staying inside was sure death. "Out!"

Andrea scooted forward into the front and followed

close on Clay's heels. He raised his Python. He received four muzzles pointed directly at him in way of response. He knew there was no hope of dropping all four before he too was turned to hamburger.

"You want him dead as well, Lincoln?" asked Washington.

Lincoln considered only for a moment. "I want to question these fuckers first, but here's something to keep him occupied." He fired a single shot from his Calico pistol. The lead projectile ripped into the meat of the big man's muscular forearm. The Presidents laughed as the man dropped his hand cannon.

Lincoln nodded at the woman, Andrea Chambers. "You! Get your ass over here."

But she did no such thing. In one fluid motion she pivoted to the side and leapt through the gap in the wall created by the impact of the SUV, into the shed beyond.

Bush darted forward, poking his head through the hole. Two sharp retorts sounded from inside the shed. Bush fell back cursing. A three-inch bloody crease along his chin told how close her bullets had gotten to punching him out permanently. "Bitch shot me!"

"Bush, get after her," ordered Lincoln. "Bring her back alive."

Bush nodded once. He unleashed a hail of bullets through the fragile walls, aiming high. He then kicked a larger hole in the wall and went through it at speed.

"The first man to move gets a bullet in the head." The voice that rang out from behind Lincoln carried a cold lethal edge. "Drop your weapons and lace your fingers behind your heads."

Lincoln turned his head to see a wiry man—the one who had shot Washington, he realised—levelling a Glock at him. He raised his chin. "I know the bleeding fella here is Clay Gunn, saw him on the news looking all shiny in uniform. Who the fuck are you?"

The man didn't reply, narrowing his eyes at the big man. "You okay?"

Clay Gunn held up his damaged arm. "I might not be so good at Texas hold 'em for a while." He locked eyes with Lincoln. "Meet my younger brother, Danny Gunn."

Lincoln kept his Calico trained on Clay but looked over his shoulder at the new arrival. "You're outgunned here, so to speak. You could shoot one of us, maybe two, but one of us will end it for you, that's a guarantee."

"Maybe, maybe not," Danny Gunn answered. Lincoln was surprised at his Scottish accent. It seemed so odd in the circumstances. How the fuck were these two brothers? "But one thing's for sure. You get the first one, right in the back of the head, so even your mother won't recognise you."

Washington took a slow step towards Clay, his submachine gun aimed at his head. "Easy there, Highlander, or the cowboy gets it."

Lincoln grinned without humour. "Looks like we have one of those Mexican stand-offs you hear about."

A woman's scream echoed from inside the shed.

"And it looks like Bush caught up with Chambers." Lincoln spat his next words at Danny Gunn. "Give it up. You tried but you lost."

He saw Clay Gunn's eyes flick to his brother. "We're dead anyway."

The Texan went into Washington low and fast, ramming his shoulder deep into his ribs, driving the sub-machine gun up over his head. Both men went into the ground in a tangle of thrashing limbs. Lincoln rocked back as Danny Gunn put two rounds into his chest. He fell to one side, gasping from the impacts, and squeezed off a devastating burst from the Calico, the bullets ripping through the air where the man's face had been a second earlier. He saw Kennedy open up on full auto, forcing the man to leap behind a large metal dumpster. The heavy trash receptacle bucked and shuddered as the impacts drove it back into the crouching Scotsman.

As Lincoln struggled to his feet, the man dodged out from behind the dumpster and loosed a three-round burst at him, higher this time. *He's trying for headshots. Kevlar is a real bitch.* Lincoln squeezed off another round as a car roared into view.

Lincoln grinned in triumph as Chad Casey tore around the corner in his Dodge Challenger and sent the troublesome Scottish asshole bouncing off the front fender and clean through the wall of the shed behind. A ragged hole displayed a pair of boots, unmoving. Now there was only one of them. Lincoln turned to see Washington still wrestling with Clay Gunn. Washington was no common brawler, even injured. Both men were fighting more or less with one hand each, but Washington twisted inside the Texan's grip and slammed him in the throat with the stiffened edge of his hand. As Gunn reeled back from the severe blow, he received another two shots to the neck for good measure.

"Come on." Lincoln motioned to Kennedy, who had been edging towards the Scot's unmoving feet. Together they joined Washington and hoisted Clay Gunn to his feet, then dragged him to the trunk of the Dodge, Chad giving them a thumbs-up from the driver's seat.

Lincoln pulled back his arm and smashed the stock of his Calico square on Gunn's right temple. Then he and Kennedy pushed the unconscious man into the trunk.

45

The man chasing Andrea was fast on his feet. Every corner she turned he seemed to appear at the far end of her chosen avenue of escape. Her breath was ragged and strained. Her hands trembled. Pausing at the end of a large shelving rack, she waited for him to appear, her revolver at the ready. The racks stretched nearly the full length of the large hangars. The shelves seemed to contain every imaginable spare part for what she presumed were boats, trucks and cars.

Beads of fear-laden sweat trickled down her face. She tried to remember everything Tansen had shown her about shooting. Aim, squeeze the trigger, and don't pull. Breathe. A shape moved off to her left. Pivoting and firing as one, she put two rounds into an oil drum that the man had dislodged from a shelf and sent rolling towards her. She cursed out loud. Then from an unseen vantage point the man fired three shots, one placed either side of her shoulders and the third into the ground at her feet. Her hands began to shake more violently. What chance did she have against this trained soldier?

Another shot creased her right arm. Fuck! He was trying

to disable her. She was sure he could have put that last bullet through her heart if he'd chosen to do so. Frustrated, Andrea sent another two rounds back in return. The next time she squeezed the trigger nothing happened. Empty! She scrabbled in her pockets for the box of ammunition Tansen had given her. Then a dark shape flew through the air at an alarming speed.

Bush watched the bitch empty her chambers into thin air then start to rifle her pockets. *God bless amateurs,* he thought as he leapt from cover and booted the woman full in the stomach. She folded up coughing and spluttering. He kicked her peashooter pistol out of her hand, then wrapped his hand tight into her hair, yanking her to her feet. Finally, the job was underway.

He frog-marched her back into the sunlight and he smiled at what he saw. The big cowboy had been beaten down and was now in the cheapest of seats. The smaller man, the fucking nuisance who had shot at the minivan, was out cold, his hands and feet secured with silver duct tape, and he was being shoved unceremoniously into the back seat of Chad Casey's Dodge.

Bush shoved the woman forward then pulled back on her hair. She nearly went to her knees. He pressed the muzzle of his sub-machine gun into the small of her back. "Look what I found."

"Good job," said Lincoln. He pointed to the flat tyre on the minivan. "Fix that double time."

Bush nodded and thrust the woman towards Lincoln, who leant in close to her face.

"If you don't do exactly as I say, I will douse these two fuckers in gas and make you watch them burn. Understand?"

46

When Danny awoke he feared he was paralysed. The pressure in his head and chest was excruciating. Something akin to a swarm of angry hornets buzzed inside his skull. A painful throbbing pulse racked his frame with every beat of his heart. He tried to sit up but realised something was very wrong. The world was upside down. He tried to shout for Clay but all that emerged was a stream of blood-tinged vomit. He spat the remnants from his mouth and took in his predicament.

He was dangling upside down, his feet encircled by a coil of multi-coloured mountaineering rope. His body traced a lazy arc as he swung from a rafter overhead. His hands were secured behind his back, and the muscles in his shoulder joints were strained almost to dislocation.

"That's ten bucks you owe me." The voice from behind carried a strong American accent. Northern. Maybe New York?

"Shit, man. I thought he was dead for sure. Oh well, now I get to make that so." The owner of the second voice stepped into view. His right arm was bandaged and strapped in a sling across his chest. Danny recognised him as the driver from the minivan. He looked very big and very mean. "Lincoln's got the woman secured upstairs and wants us to make sure that nothing has been passed to any unknown third parties."

The first man laughed as he jabbed Danny in the side of the face. "You know what that means, boy? We get to play twenty questions. Hey, Washington, you want to place another bet? I bet this one's spilling his guts before question five."

"How much?"

"Go fifty bucks?"

"You're on." Washington tilted his head to look deep into Danny's face. "This is my friend, we call him Kennedy. I'm gonna ask a few questions and if you don't give the answers I want he will slice and dice you into filet mignon."

Danny considered head-butting Washington, but he was just out of range. Not stupid, then. He gritted his teeth, pushing his mind into a different mode. He knew what was coming next. The trick to weathering torture was to try to focus on an object and blank out everything else. But it was much easier said than done. He cast his eyes around the sparse room, which was distorted by his perspective. It looked to be a double garage space, probably attached to the side of a house. Then he reconsidered. No, not a garage; there were no doors that he could see other than the one at the top of a short five-step staircase. Upstairs, they'd said: where Andrea was being held. No roller door for a car, just a small window near the ceiling, looking out to ground level. A basement then.

A grime-stained bucket sat in one corner, the kind a child would use to make sandcastles at the beach. A sticker showing the blue-skinned genie from *Aladdin* stared back at him, a wide smile and happy eyes.

Then the pain began.

"Who did you pass the package to?"

Danny stared at the blue cartoon face.

"I think I need to tenderise the meat before we get down to business." Kennedy rolled his shoulders then slammed a punch into Danny's exposed ribs. The punch was well thrown and blasted the air from his lungs. As Danny jack-knifed in pain, Kennedy battered him with another four rapid shots to the gut. White-hot jolts of agony shot through his internal organs.

The genie grinned back at him.

Washington's voice now carried an air of amusement. "Let's try that one again shall we? Who did you pass the package to?"

Danny locked onto the blue cartoon face. He knew that the truth would not serve him here. "Your mother's clap-doctor. Why don't you go ask him for it?"

Kennedy slapped down hard, catching Danny's testicles perfectly. Despite his best efforts, Danny bucked against the explosion of pain.

"Tough guy, huh?" said Washington. "That slope out in the Vegas desert thought he was tough as well. Until we turned his ass into deep-fried wonton."

Danny closed his eyes. Something red and vicious boiled in his head. He hoped it wasn't true. Tansen Tibrikot was one of the bravest men he'd ever known. If they had killed Tansen he would carry that guilt to his grave.

Kennedy punched him again but Danny blanked out the

pain. "Uh oh, I think you struck a nerve. What? Were you and the gook fags for each other? A bit of yin and yang action going on there?"

Washington stepped closer. "My turn. I owe you one for this." He raised his bandaged arm. "Had to pick the bullet out of the bone."

Kennedy grabbed Danny and held him steady as Washington sent punch after punch into his stomach, his left arm working like a piston.

"Let's have this off him." Kennedy ripped Danny's shirt from his back. The seams around the arms ripped into his skin before giving way. "Fuck. Look at that. This boy's been Kentucky-fried already. Now that looks painful."

"Doesn't it just." Washington delivered a vigorous slap to the lattice of pink scar tissue that decorated Danny's flank. Then he did it again for good measure. And again. And again.

It went on for hours.

Clay awoke to the muffled but unmistakable sounds of violence from below. He remembered getting dumped into the trunk of a car, then a seemingly endless drive. The trunk had opened and then something that smelled like distilled camel piss had been sprayed into his face. Then it was lights out.

He was stretched out on the floor of a bathroom. His hands were secured above his head, the ropes that bound him wound around the base of a toilet. He could feel the wooden planking of the floor digging into his bare back. His feet too were bare, roped and fixed to the pipework of the sink. He shook his head; all that was missing was an approaching train, like in a silent film. He wondered where Danny was, hoping he was in a better situation. Then he remembered the sounds from below. He tried not to think about Garnett. His friend riddled with bullets… He would deal with that later.

He looked up to see two men gazing down at him with scorn. He recognised the taller of the two as the guy who'd clocked him with the butt of his pistol—Lincoln they called him. Clay felt the swelling tight on the side of his face.

"If we're gonna have a hoedown, I hope you brought some chips an' dip. I'm quite partial to guacamole."

"No, but I did find this." Lincoln held up a stun gun. "That little woman tried to zap me with it on the ride over here. Can you believe that?"

Clay added that to the growing number of reasons to like Andrea.

"Now, I've had a good long talk with the woman and she assures me that you haven't passed on or sold any intel yet. And I believe her. But I also believe in being thorough, so we're going to have a little conversation anyway. Also, you've got some payback coming for hurting my boys. The woman tells me you're from Texas. So I guess you like barbecue ribs." Lincoln scowled as he pressed the stun gun hard into Clay's torso. Clay bucked and shuddered involuntarily in response to the raw electricity coursing through him. His jaws locked shut, teeth gnashing down. He couldn't breathe. After a three-second hit Lincoln paused and addressed him again.

"The woman also told me that the flash drive contains no government intel but instead some kind of snuff movie. Some tight-assed Brit psycho getting his rocks off. That may well be the case but my orders remain the same. Recover the package and make sure that no one else has had access or opportunity to copy the intel."

Clay looked up from the floor. "You dumb shit. Don't you realise that she's been set up? Most likely by the man in the video. He's sent out a false flag on her so the murder on the film doesn't get out."

"Not my concern." Lincoln's voice was as cold as a winter wind. "I took the pay cheque so I'll deliver the package."

"But the woman is just caught up in something way bigger than she can handle. Wrong place, wrong time." Clay's stomach muscles twitched involuntarily as the after-effects of the stun gun began to wear off.

Lincoln closed his eyes slowly as if he was addressing a naïve schoolchild. He emphasised each of his following words separately. "Not... My... Concern!"

"Fucking retard!" spat Clay. "You had your chance to do the right thing. I guess we'll have to do it the hard way."

Lincoln looked down in genuine amusement. "The hard way? For whom? You're the one trussed up like a pig at a shit-kicker's wedding." This brought a snort of amusement from the other man. Clay recognised him as the operative who had gone after Andrea—Lincoln had called him "Bush". He held a pair of wide-jawed pliers in his fist.

"Hard for you when I get out of here and strangle you with your own intestines."

Bush clacked the pliers open and closed like hedge shears. "Wow, the cowpoke's got a colourful vocabulary. Intestines... you getting that, Linc?"

Lincoln clearly got it. Clay got another shot in the guts with the stun gun. Then he pressed the stun gun tight into Clay's neck. He squeezed down long and hard on the trigger. Clay pulled against his bonds as the waves of paralysing agony swept through every inch of his body. He fought against the blackness that threatened to envelop him. Unconsciousness would provide brief respite from the unwanted shock therapy, but he might never wake up again.

He heard the sound of a zip being undone, then hot liquid on his face. Bush was laughing.

Clay closed his eyes and mouth instinctively, his fury boiling to a new level. When he was sure that the stream was finished he opened his eyes—only to receive another splash of yellow liquid full in the face.

Bush cackled. "Strike two. One more and you're out."

Avoiding his piss-covered head, Lincoln poised the stun gun a couple of inches above Clay's chest. "Last chance. Have you passed or sold any data from the flash drive on to anyone else?"

"There is no intel! Just that murder video. That's what they're trying to cover up. Don't you get it?"

Lincoln pressed the prongs into Clay's chest. "Did you know that a charge from a stun gun like this one administered directly over your heart can send it into cardiac arrest? No? Let's give it a go, shall we? Truth is, we don't need you or the mac-daddy downstairs… so it really doesn't matter how you go out. The girl is to be picked up and shipped off in less than an hour. Think about that as you go to the great rodeo in the sky."

Bush finished adjusting himself and held a hand up. "Wait. I want to try these out. I want to see how many fingers and toes I can squish before Tex here cries like a girl."

Lincoln removed the stun gun and nodded. "Have your fun. But we need to move in thirty."

Bush again gripped the pliers, clearly happy. "Thirty minutes will be more than enough time."

He placed the open jaws over Clay's left pinkie toe. Then he began to exert a slow but steady pressure.

47

"You've definitely got the woman?"

Lincoln's voice was a reassuring purr in Topcat's ear. "Trussed up and ready for shipment. I've sent our man in Key West to the pilot's house to recover the flash drive."

"How far has it spread?"

"There is only one other player that had a chance to view the file, apart from the two men we've got here—the pilot's wife. If she's at home Chad Casey will pick up the data and terminate her at the same time. If not, he'll clip her tonight, just to be sure."

"Who are the two men?"

"Brothers, Danny and Clay Gunn."

"Either of them Scottish?"

"How did you know? Danny, smaller of the two. Why?"

"He called me on the last team's sat-phone."

Thomas Carter nodded to himself. The mission was nearly done. He would be glad when this was over. Ever since the call from that indignant Scotsman an uneasy feeling had taken up residence at the back of his mind.

But he had taken the money so he would see the mission through to the end. "Do it. Call me back when the woman has been loaded." He had already arranged for a specialist to interrogate Andrea Chambers. Marcus Brightwell was a real oddball but he always got the job done, and strangely the man had rung *him*, saying he was available. Yes, strange that, but a gift horse... He was aware that the brief had been only to recover the flash drive and kill the woman. But that phone call had bothered him. What if there was some truth to what the Scot had said? Was the line about government intel a hoax? The man, Danny Gunn, had said the video showed an MP committing a murder. Best to cover his own ass and find out the truth.

Brightwell would take possession of the woman in just over an hour. Then he would know categorically if there were any more risks.

"What about the men with her?" asked Topcat.

"On their way out as we speak."

Topcat ended the call. He sat back in his chair for a moment, then picked up the phone again. Enough waiting, it was time to get to the bottom of this. Time for this minister to answer some questions. If it turned out he'd been used, if some low-level politician had tried to use *his* business to clean up after himself... Well Topcat knew how to clean up, too.

48

Danny was nearing the end of his resilience. Washington had proved remorseless in his assault. When he had finally tired, his second, Kennedy, had stepped back in immediately and begun a new beating. Streams of blood ran down Danny's face. The scar tissue on his side burned with an intensity that almost matched the flames that had caused the original damage.

He sucked in desperately needed gulps of air as both men paused, laughing at some unheard comment. There was a constant drumming in his ears. At first he wasn't sure what the source of the staccato rhythm was, then in a moment of clarity he realised that there was a heavy rain lashing against the room's single small window.

Washington turned to his second. "You ever see the Roman Candle?"

Kennedy shook his head in the negative.

"Aw man, it's nasty." He looked back at Danny. "We're about finished here anyway. Have you got any flares in your kit?"

Kennedy considered a moment. "I think I've got a couple

of red-burners in my bag. Regular road flares. Any good?"

"They'll work a treat." Washington waved his injured arm at the prisoner. "You just hang around there, Batman. Just so you can look forward to the next instalment, we're going upstairs but when I get back I'm gonna stick a flare right up your ass and light it! Cook you from the inside. Something to think about while we're gone."

The men climbed the stairs. Before leaving the basement, Washington flicked the light switch off. "Hope you're not scared of the dark."

The basement door slammed shut, the sound somehow conveying the disdain of the two interrogators. Only a soft glow remained where the single bulb had shone above Danny's dangling form.

Danny began. First he rolled his shoulders in an effort to regain some circulation. Forcing himself to ignore the resulting spears of pain, he folded his left arm tight against his back as if in an arm-lock, then with great care began to move his right arm over his head. He pulled against the rope, hoping desperately that it would prove long enough. He felt his tendons protest to tearing point as he forced his right arm inch by inch over his head. Then with a sudden springing of sinews, both arms passed over his head and dangled in front of him. Bone tired, he forced himself to move.

Slowly at first, he began to swing his body back and forth, like a blood-soaked pendulum, each time gaining a little more momentum. After nearly twenty swings, his hands seized the cross beam to which he was tethered. His vision swam as his body adjusted to the new position. Strange things were happening to his blood pressure and equilibrium. None of which felt good. His hands groped until they found the light bulb. The glass orb was still hot to the touch but not so hot that it stopped him unscrewing it from its fixture.

With a single sharp tap against the wooden joist, the bulb shattered, leaving a triangular sliver of glass held in the circular aluminium base. Danny began to saw frantically at the rope that encircled his ankles. By the time he had severed his bonds his ankles and fingers were lacerated and bleeding profusely from a number of shallow cuts.

He dropped to the floor, landing roughly on his hands and knees. The shock of the impact sent new agony through his battered frame. He looked around the room for a more serviceable weapon than the inch of glass he still clutched in his hand. An old table sat in a corner of the room, an assortment of old newspapers and magazines piled on top. The legs of the table were thick and looked solid. Each one the equivalent of a baseball bat. Danny briefly grinned to himself. It would feel good to swing that bat into the faces of his tormentors. But both of the men had sported pistols on their hips and they certainly knew how to use them. He might get the first man but the second would be sure to drill him a third eye.

He broke the leg free from the table with a sweep of his foot. The table toppled, spilling paper onto the dusty floor. He broke a second leg free from the base. Snatching up the wooden staves, he raced to the top of the short flight of stairs. He tried the handle, turning it slowly. Locked. No surprise there. That would have been too easy. Wedging one end of the table leg tight against the doorknob, he secured the other end into the corner post of the stairs. It took a couple of stamps with his foot to force the wooden spar into place. The result was a brace, fixed at a strong forty-five-degree angle to the door.

Turning, he fixed his eyes on the small window near the ceiling. The portal measured no more than two feet wide and twelve inches high. A constant torrent of water splattered against the glass. He knew how quickly the weather could change in the tropics but even he was surprised by the ferocity of the downpour.

The frame was stiff from age and layers of paint but repeated blows with the heel of his hand pushed the window out a few inches. Danny's muscles ached from a combination of his beating and fatigue, not helped by the fact that he had to support all of his weight on one arm while he levered the window fully open with the table leg. With a squeal of rusted hinges, it sprang free. Immediately, cold water powered through the open gap as if a huge garden hose had been turned on him. Ignoring the pain and the stinging impact of the lashing rain, he wriggled his body through the narrow opening. He stifled a cry as the damaged skin on his flank pulled against the wooden frame.

Outside, he flopped unceremoniously onto the ground, sucking in deep breaths of waterlogged air. Looking around, he quickly realised that he was at the rear of a large two-storey wooden house, complete with the familiar gingerbread fretwork. So the men hadn't taken them far from Parker's Yard. The house was painted a light blue but looked far from idyllic. If Norman Bates had relocated to Florida he would have felt right at home.

Danny pressed himself against the side of the house. He

was free but escape was not an option. Somewhere in that house Clay and Andrea were also being held and had likely suffered similar treatment as him.

Danny backed up a few steps and after a short run, leapt up and caught the decorative veranda that provided a modicum of shade and cover to the back door of the house. His hands—slick with blood and rain—slipped from the ledge. He tumbled to the ground, sending up a spray of brown water. After picking himself up, he leapt again. This time his grip held fast.

A wooden lattice-frame, perhaps two feet wide, extended up from the veranda, framing twin windows, and continued up to the overhang of the tin roof. His hooked fingers and toes sought out the small gaps in the fretwork, and he began to make his way slowly up the outside of the house. Balancing speed and stealth, he edged upwards as quickly as possible. He was near a second-floor window when his hands, tired and wet, slipped. A moment of weightlessness, his breath caught in his throat, then his hands found purchase again. Cold rain and acrid sweat stung his eyes as he pushed upwards. The cramp in his limbs rewarded each movement with a stab of pain. He wasn't sure how much longer he could last. Then he reached the sill of the window.

This was the real danger point. If one or more of the men were in the room he would be shot dead before he could climb through the window. He cautiously looked through the glass and saw the reflection of his swollen mouth twitch into a parody of a smile. The room was unoccupied.

A loud commotion erupted from downstairs, sounds of shouting and what was unmistakably a door being kicked repeatedly. Washington and Kennedy had attempted to return to the basement.

Through the window Danny saw another man rush past the doorway of the room, gun in hand. Danny pushed the window open and climbed inside. He was unarmed, having left the table leg in the garden, unable to scale the house while holding it. Water dripped from every inch of his body as he rested momentarily. He shook his hands in an effort to restore some feeling. He needed to find a new weapon.

The room was sparsely furnished: a single bed in one corner, an old dressing table and a basket of clothes. An ironing board and steam iron stood in mute expectation next to the basket. The bed was neatly made, sheets tucked tightly into the mattress. Tight enough to bounce a penny off. Military style. The house was old and smelled of stale sweat, farts, beer and cigarettes. Man smells. He had been in a few of these himself. Crash pads for men between assignments but too far from home to return. Flop houses where wine, women and song could be enjoyed. A lot of the PMCs Danny had known were frugal characters, preferring to stash their money away rather than spend it on decent hotel rooms between jobs. Houses like this one provided free lodging for a couple of nights, courtesy of the company.

From below came the sound of a door crashing open. They had got into the basement.

Danny knew that the curse of "slippery motherfucker" that echoed through the house was directed at him. With no other weapons in view, he hefted the steam iron. The electrical cord was wound tight around the concave base of the implement. Useless at more than arm's length, the iron was a poor weapon, no match for the assortment of firepower carried by his captors. But it was a little better than bare hands and harsh words.

He heard a man's laugh; it had a cruel quality. The sound carried from the right, on the same floor. Furtively, he crept onto a landing. There were four doors on this level. One, closed, faced the door he had just emerged from at the top of the staircase; another two were further down the hallway. A small chest of drawers sat against the short span of banister that connected the staircase to the landing. Old oak, yellowed with age, complete with small brass decorative handles. The item of quality furniture looked out of place in the crash pad. One of the doors down the hallway was ajar. Muffled sounds of pain and that distinctive rattling laugh issued from it.

Danny ran towards the sound, his feet silent on the threadbare carpet. Damp footprints betrayed his passage but that didn't worry him. He barrelled into a bathroom and took in a desperate scene.

49

Clay had once been kicked by a rampaging bull at a rodeo. The angry creature had cracked his right shin before rounding on him and doing its best to gore him with its horns. Only the valiant rodeo clowns had saved him from more serious injury that day. It had taken months to walk again without a limp. The pain that now shot through his lower legs far eclipsed that agony.

The man with the pliers, Bush, loomed over him, a look of disgust and annoyance on his face. The man glanced at his watch. The grunts of pain emitted by his captive through clenched teeth were clearly not meeting his expectations. Dropping the pliers into the sink he drew a knife from the small of his back. "Well, this has been fun but I really got to go."

Clay watched the man reverse a Teflon-coated blade, point down, its razor edge glinting with menace. He looked over Bush's shoulder. "I've just one thing left to say. He's behind you."

Bush smiled and moved the blade towards Clay's exposed throat. Clay leaned back. One deep slash was all it would take. A shadow fell across Clay's face.

Danny brought an iron down into Bush's skull. The tapered point of the implement crashed through the arch of his cranium. Clay could imagine the shards of bone pushing deep into Bush's brain. The weight of the blow sent the man sprawling on top of Clay.

Either through mental fortitude or just plain rattlesnake meanness, Bush slashed back at his attacker with the blade in his dying moments. Another devastating blow to the back of his head stopped any further attacks. A tremor passed through the whole of Bush's body, then he lay silent, his dead eyes staring accusingly at Clay, who smiled at him. "Told you he was behind you."

Scooping up the knife from where it lay on the floor, Danny severed the ropes that held his brother. Taking in the sad state of his feet he asked, "Can you walk?"

"I think so, but the quickstep is gonna have to wait a while." Clay flexed his feet, curling his toes back and forth. They looked as bad as they felt. Dark blue and purple bruises gave them the appearance of mini-Bratwurst, but not as attractive. Two toes on his left foot were crooked at angles that spoke of dislocation. Danny crouched and, after exchanging a look with Clay, pulled sharply on the swollen digits to set them straight. Clay grunted an acknowledgement of this new pain, then used the side of the bath to lever himself upright.

After stripping Bush's corpse of weapons, Danny turned back to Clay. "Is Andrea still in the house?"

Clay shrugged. "I woke up hog-tied in here. I haven't heard her voice so I just don't know."

Danny worked the slide on the pistol he'd taken from

Bush's holster. "Well, we've got two options. We can go down the stairs or out the window." Neither choice was ideal. Clay said nothing. Danny motioned with his chin. "The stairs, then. Stay behind me."

Clay hobbled after his younger brother, resting his weight on his heels as much as he could manage. The pain in his feet was so sharp he was now sure that several of his toes must be broken.

Hugging the wall, Danny rounded the doorway and moved fast and low onto the landing. He peered down the stairs, and saw Andrea's stricken face staring back at him from the bottom step. He could see white all around the blue of her irises. She was handcuffed and gagged, and being dragged backwards by her collar by the man with the big Calico pistol. Lincoln.

Danny sighted with his pistol, hoping for a headshot, but in less than a second both the man and his hostage were out of the front door and in the rain.

For a split second he wasn't sure where the shots were coming from but as Danny stepped onto the stairs numerous rounds ripped through the wooden steps from below. He only avoided the second barrage by throwing himself bodily back onto the landing. Clay stumbled and crashed into the chest of drawers. Battered, bruised and bleeding, the brothers exchanged a glance. A very British phrase sprang to Danny's mind: *Fuck this for a game of soldiers.*

He returned a couple of shots, aiming down through the stairs and hoping for the best. The result was another sustained burst of automatic gunfire from below. Chips of wood exploded like confetti. Then a second barrage erupted, but from a different angle. These bullets tore up the wall above Danny's head. He pointed down the stairs, one finger indicating the shooter below him, then another finger to the one somewhere off to the left.

Clay followed the hand signals. He grabbed the heavy chest of drawers as if they were made of nothing more than balsa wood and heaved them over the banister edge. The resulting crash of breaking wood was immediately followed by an ear-piercing cry of agony.

Kennedy appeared at the foot of the stairs, an M4 carbine blazing in his hands. He corrected his aim. Then he looked down at the knife hilt and three inches of blade that protruded from his stomach. He scowled in defiance and raised the M4 again. Danny's single shot caught him full in the face sending him sprawling backwards. The carbine clattered to the floor.

Danny stalked down the stairs, weapon trained and ready. He made it to the bottom of the stairs without dodging any more bullets. Kennedy was dead. No doubt there. But the second man was still a threat. He saw the other man from the basement, Washington, lying on his front, trying to claw his way to his assault rifle. The chest of drawers had scored a heavy hit and a wide gash on the top of his head was now streaming blood. The piece of furniture lay across his lower back and one arm. Danny stepped heavily onto the man's outstretched hand.

"Where are they taking the woman?"

Washington glared up at Gunn with hate-filled eyes. "Should have killed you when I had the chance."

"Damn right about that." Danny ground his heel into the

bones of Washington's outstretched hand. "One last chance, and know this: I don't walk away halfway through."

"Go fuck yourself."

Danny moved his foot just long enough to put a round through the back of Washington's hand. Flesh proved no match for the kinetic energy of the bullet and a third of his hand and his pinkie finger flew away in a crimson rainbow. Now both arms were incapacitated.

"Again: where are they taking the woman?"

Stifling a scream in defiance, Washington tried to pull his ruined hand back to his chest but Danny kept it pinned to the floor.

"Last chance to share."

Washington spat out a glob of crimson saliva in Danny's direction. It fell short but brought Gunn's attention to a discarded cylindrical object on the floor.

"Well, now, have you ever heard of the Roman Candle?"

Clay had retrieved Kennedy's M4 from the bottom of the stairs and was now covering Danny's rear. Danny heard him let out a short grunt of amusement as he began to haul the injured man's trousers down around his ankles.

Washington divulged Andrea's exact destination—an abandoned estate at the other end of the island—before the road flare had burned halfway down its length. Danny was very familiar with the smell of burning flesh. He didn't hesitate. Not as an act of mercy, but with a keen sense of the need to move, he blew a hole in the back of Washington's skull.

As the brothers stepped out into the neglected garden the torrential rain stung their battered frames. Danny pointed to an SUV parked out front. "Lincoln must have taken Andrea in that minivan they ran us down in. I'll check those two for keys to that car." Clay nodded and kept a vigil at the front door, the M4 ready at a moment's notice. When Danny returned he was dressed in Washington's shirt and boots. He held out a set of keys like a trophy. "Found these in the kitchen."

"You didn't happen to see my boots or shirt in there did you?"

Danny raced up the stairs, ignoring Bush's zombie-like face resting in a gelatinous pool of red. Clay's boots and shirt lay in the bathtub in a loose tangle. Despite the dire events he found reason to smile. He returned to the front door and handed the items over. Clay held up his shirt, which had been cut into three strips; only the collar was intact.

Danny winked. "I hear cloaks are in this year."

"I'd offer it to you as a bandanna but I don't think there's enough material." Clay tossed the ruined shirt aside and struggled into his boots. He grimaced in pain. "If I don't put them on before my feet swell up, I'll be barefoot till Christmas." Danny handed Clay the jacket he had salvaged from Kennedy. It was a very tight fit across the shoulders and the seams stretched in protest. But it served its purpose. Then both men made for the SUV.

Clay left the driving to Danny, preferring to brood silently in the passenger seat. He rested the M4 across his lap, muzzle pointing away from his brother.

"Don't worry, we'll catch up and end it for these fuckers," said Danny. His brother's face reminded him of old Frank Frazetta illustrations of Conan the Barbarian. Clay's hair was plastered to his furrowed brow, scars vivid white lines against his weathered skin, ice-blue eyes seething pits of impending violence. His mouth was a tight line.

"Do you think Crom will hear your prayers?" he said.

Clay smiled for the briefest of moments, despite his anger. "On a night like this? Crom's down here with us."

Danny could just about believe that. He couldn't see more than a few feet in front of the SUV, such was the force of the relentless rain. The fictional Cimmerian deity may well have stepped down from his mountain of power to lash the world with his wrath. As if in affirmation, a jagged sabre of lightning split the sky. Danny allowed himself a moment of jubilation. With this weather all flights and boats out of the Keys would be grounded.

Time to reverse roles. Time for the hunters to become the hunted.

50

Chad Casey cursed the squall that had rolled up from the Caribbean with sudden venom. Being a native Floridian, hailing originally from Jacksonville, he knew that late summer storms could last for an hour or a couple of days. The wipers were doing little to keep his Dodge's windshield clear. For a couple of seconds his mind drifted back twenty years to thoughts of going through the carwash in his father's old Buick. That was before dear old Dad decided to leave his wife and two sons to shack up with a pole dancer from Miami. Candi—with an *i*. A real class act. Still, at least her tattoos were spelled correctly. Chad had dated a dancer himself, Arlene. The tramp stamp she sported, nestled just above the cleft in her buttocks, was a downward-pointing arrow declaring *fock this*.

But Arlene was pushed back into memory-ville as the pilot's wife clambered out of a taxi, a magazine held ineffectually over her head in a futile defence against the rain. The woman trotted up to the front door, fished in her purse until she found her keys, then let herself into the house.

Chad was parked in the same place he had watched the house from earlier. Before he left the warmth of the vehicle he worked the slide on his pistol, chambering a round. He was almost sure the house was empty apart from the woman. The pilot was dead. But he waited another ten minutes just to be sure there were no visitors to disturb his work.

Flicking up the collar of his jacket, he stepped out into the rain.

Edith changed quickly into dry clothes and towelled her hair dry. She had been busy all day. First she had dropped off some corporate leaflets to the printers. Then she had doubled back to the office and worked on the monthly accounts. A late lunch followed by an hour in the gym and she was ready for home. Then the heavens had opened. She often walked between errands, considering it part of her daily cardio but the storm had sent her sprinting for a cab. She was glad to be home.

She tried phoning Garnett. She hadn't heard from him all day. The call went to voicemail. "Where are you, you big lunk? Call me when you get this." Then as an afterthought she added, "If you're all in Sloppy Joe's without me there'll be trouble. Love you. Bye."

She made a sandwich and settled down in front of the television. Suddenly the hunk of bread she'd just bitten off stuck in her throat as she registered the strange man in the doorway. He looked like a typical Conch barfly, loose clothing, summer colours, badly bleached hair. Harmless apart from the pistol that was pointed directly at her chest. An icy spider of dread crawled its way down her spine as she noticed the suppressor fitted to the pistol. She knew instantly that this was one of the men sent after Andrea. Her mind whirled. Garnett had a pistol but it was locked in a drawer upstairs. There was no way past the man. She looked around for some avenue of escape, tears filling her eyes.

The man spoke, his Floridian twang slow and easy. "You try to scream, I'll put a bullet through your throat."

Edith believed him.

"The people that stayed the night—did they use a computer? I need the flash drive they were using."

Edith began to shake her head to explain she didn't know anything about that, but the man's expression stopped her. "We have a laptop," she said.

"Where?"

"It's normally in here."

The man scanned the living room. Edith wondered where the computer was. "Get up. I need to check the bedrooms."

Edith stood on shaky legs but did as she was ordered. In the second bedroom the man found the laptop.

"Where's the flash drive?"

Her voice trembled. "I'm telling you, I don't know!"

Without warning the man punched her hard in the face with his free hand. Her teeth snapped together painfully, her head leading the way to the carpet. Purple spots of pain danced across her diminishing field of vision as she crawled across the floor.

His punch had failed to knock her fully unconscious but a savage kick to the side of the woman's head finished the job.

Chad began to search the room. He had rifled through the bedside cabinets and the dressing table before his phone vibrated in his pocket.

"Casey here."

"It's Lincoln. Chambers says the flash drive is on the top shelf of the cabinet in the bathroom. Go check."

Chad did as he was told. "Got it."

Lincoln gave him directions to the rendezvous point. "I'm meeting a TSI interrogator, handing off the woman. You're to hand over the flash drive. Then we'll go back to the others at the safe house and find out what the hell went down."

"What do you mean?"

"At least one of the Gunns got free—I didn't wait around to see what happened. My men will have dealt with it by now, but they may need help with clean-up."

"The pilot's wife is out cold. You still want her clipped?"

"Quickly and quietly. I'll meet you in thirty." Lincoln's voice held no emotion. Business as usual.

Chad stood over the unconscious form. The woman was a damned beauty. He pulled the trigger. Two bullets to the chest and one in the head.

Before he left the house he picked up the laptop from the bedroom and the sandwich from the living room. He inspected it briefly. There were only a couple of bites missing. Sweet. "To the victor the spoils," he said, to no one in particular.

51

Stewart Strathclyde looked across the restaurant at the woman sitting in a booth. She was with a man, probably her boyfriend.

He had chosen the mid-market pizzeria specifically because it wasn't his usual scene. He didn't want to risk a chance meeting with someone he knew. The times he'd been bothered by some casual acquaintance while dining out were too numerous to count. Civil servants were the worst kind of insects in his opinion. All too ready to kowtow and flash a false smile at one of the privileged crowd among which he could now be counted. And this place had an acceptable menu.

He ordered a large glass of Peroni and a salad and considered the couple. It was a real case of beauty and the geek. The young man was trying hard to work the hipster look, in a fitted waistcoat, red trousers and ironic black-rimmed glasses, but his large Adam's apple and pitiful beard ruined the effect. He was wearing a badge on the waistcoat— no doubt also ironic—with the moronic legend BANG TIDY emblazoned across it. Strathclyde had no idea what it meant and didn't much care. Many years earlier he had raped, tortured and skinned a woman who had been wearing a shirt that declared FRANKIE SAYS. The memory of his repeated taunts, "What does Frankie say now?" as he slowly dissected the girl brought a smile to his lips.

He dismissed the young man as unworthy of further study. But the woman was a different matter. Where the boy was as white as the underside of a fish, the woman was dark and beautiful. Her mocha-coloured skin was flawless and her eyes were dark pools. The honey-blonde curls that framed her face were obviously dyed but that added to rather than detracted from her allure.

Familiar stirrings began deep inside Strathclyde. After all, wasn't that why he was here? First would come the sexual test, breaking down her spirit as much as her body. Then the real fun would begin. Most of his previous guests slipped into a state of near catatonia after repeated rapes. But not for long. That's when the patient work began. The skilful application of the blade brought them shrieking out of their mental hidey-holes.

He watched her lips move as she wasted words on the wannabe hipster. Strathclyde could feel his penis grow in his trousers as his hand clenched involuntarily around the hilt of an imagined knife.

"Is everything all right with your meal, sir?" The waitress smiled, a look of concern on her face.

"Yes." He answered a little more sharply than he intended. "Why?"

"You looked a little… uncomfortable."

"What? Oh yeah, just thinking about work. The stress can get to you if you let it."

She nodded in understanding. "Can I get you another drink?"

"No I'm okay with this one." He waggled the glass of Peroni. As the waitress smiled again and walked away he gave her a quick once-over. Skinny as a rake. Face as plain as woodchip wallpaper. Not worth even considering. Part of the fun was picking the self-assured ones and breaking them.

Strathclyde allowed his focus to settle back upon the mocha-coloured skin of the woman he'd been watching. For reasons that were unfathomable to him she seemed to be genuinely enjoying her time with the hipster. They were finishing up their drinks and desserts. Strathclyde signalled for the waitress to bring his bill. He paid up, leaving a very average tip. He then crossed the street, positioning himself in a shop doorway fifty yards down from the restaurant, near to his vehicle.

After five minutes the couple stepped out into the street, arm in arm. He watched them walk towards him, then stop at a parked car. He was unsurprised when the woman took up position in the driver's seat—clearly she was the grown-up in the relationship. The car was a new-model silver Ford Focus. Nothing remarkable, but a decent enough ride.

Strathclyde climbed into his own car, a Mercedes SL Class convertible. The paintwork was a midnight blue, the interior finishes kid leather. The car was a thing of beauty and Strathclyde held it in much higher regard than most of the people he had ever known. The engine growled as he pulled out of his parking space and followed the Ford.

He allowed the car a lead of fifty or so feet but felt confident that he would not be noticed. He followed for ten minutes, letting a black cab slip in between the two cars. When the Ford pulled over and parked at the kerb, he pulled in on the opposite side of the street. The Ford's interior light turned on, and he could see the woman lean over and kiss the hipster. Strathclyde's upper lip curled involuntarily. He smiled as he imagined her delicate features in a rictus of unendurable pain. That would come later.

The man left the car and after a brief wave to his girlfriend, entered a large house. Strathclyde noticed a gleaming BMW in the driveway. A smaller Fiat Punto sat alongside the bigger car. "Still living with his parents. Fucking loser."

The woman drove another mile or so into a north London suburb, clearly ignorant of the shark in her wake. Eventually she parked outside an upmarket apartment building. Strathclyde watched as she entered through the front door, and was pleased when he saw lights go on in one of the two ground-floor flats. That would make things easier.

He watched the windows of the flat for nearly an hour. Only the woman's silhouette could be seen through the curtains. It was a safe bet she lived alone. He clenched his fists until the knuckles turned white. He would google the address later from an Internet café and get all the information he needed. Then he would arrange a little tête-à-tête.

The display on his phone briefly lit up and emitted a two-tone beep. He opened the text message, smiling as he read the contents.

Finally…

He started the engine and slowly traced his way home. He hummed along to the song playing on the radio. He'd always liked "Killing me Softly" by the Fugees. It was just a short drive home. Less than an hour at this time of day. A couple of clicks on the computer and he would be linked to a camera on the other side of the Atlantic. His only regret was that he would not be able to participate.

The nondescript white van trailed a hundred yards behind the Mercedes.

The man in the front passenger seat read the brief coded message on his smartphone. He nodded to the driver in confirmation. "We've got a green light on this guy."

"What's the brief from Topcat?"

"Confirmation of whether the subject hired a TSI team under false pretences. If so, reason for and others involved. If positive confirmation, the subject is to meet with an unfortunate accident. Top doesn't care which method we use as long as it looks self-inflicted."

"Roger that," replied the driver. "I've got just the thing in my bag of tricks."

The passenger turned to the two men sitting in the back of the van and smiled. They all knew what lay in that little black bag.

52

Danny Gunn glanced again at his older brother. His expression was pained and there was a fine sheen of sweat on his skin. "You okay?"

"Feel like my feet are in boiling water."

"Maybe it's better if I go on alone. I could drop you at a hospital?"

"No," said Clay, an angry edge in his voice. "We can't lose any ground. We may only have one chance to get Andrea back. If we miss it…" He left the sentence unfinished.

"Then you'll need to keep a low profile. You can stay by the car and lay down suppressing fire if we need it."

Clay stared back with a stony expression. "No way I'm going to be left holding the coats, even if I'm hobbling along like a lame octogenarian. I won't slow you down."

"I know that. Just let me do the running around on this one." He received a begrudging nod in way of an answer.

"To be honest, I'm havin' doubts, too. I don't want to risk your and Andrea's lives, I know you're capable of operating on your own. But if I bail now and something bad happens…"

Danny turned the wipers to full speed. Even so, the beating rain reduced visibility to a point barely past the front grille. He was forced to slow the vehicle. The last thing he wanted to do was end up crashing and being delayed even more. He glanced at the SUV's GPS, trying to match road signs with the digital map of the rendezvous location extracted from Washington with the Roman Candle trick. Luckily traffic was sparse.

"You have reached your destination," intoned the GPS. Danny peered through his window. There was a gate built into a chain-link fence, tangled with creeping undergrowth, and beyond, at the end of a long carriage road, stood a dilapidated red-brick mansion. There were newer corrugated-iron buildings off to one side—it looked like an old tobacco estate given a new lease of life. Several of the new-builds had US Navy Jeeps and transport trucks parked in their shadows.

"Looks like the navy boys are repurposing the land as a surplus depot," said Clay.

Danny nodded. The drab government-type buildings to the west stood silent and unlit, and newer construction works were evidenced by the heavy equipment standing near freshly dug foundations: a dump truck and a battered JCB. The backhoe of the excavator looked like a dinosaur sniffing the damp air. "No construction crews."

"You seen the weather?"

"True. Chances are they won't be holding her in one of the navy sheds—too risky. Likely up at that house." Danny pointed to the red-brick mansion, which sat on a wide spur of land that poked out into the ocean, looking over the water. It was three storeys high, the third encircled by a widow's walk. The main entrance was flanked by two sets of marble pillars that stretched up to the first-floor balconies, fronting large windows with ornate storm shutters, folded out and pinned securely to the exterior walls.

"I don't reckon we can drive up to the front door. It's nearly a quarter-mile up that road, little or no cover," said Clay. "Don't appear to be any back roads. If there's one man on that roof with a sniper rifle we'll be dead before we make it halfway."

"And there's a chance that they'll kill Andrea before we can get to her. But she's dead if we don't. Fuck."

Danny reversed the SUV slowly away from the gates, turned and drove back the way they had come.

53

Andrea's face was stiff and swollen from the beating she'd received at Lincoln's hands. Yet he had been methodical and businesslike in his attitude, showing neither compassion nor overt cruelty. The man who now stood before her was a different matter altogether.

The leader of the PMCs and another man she didn't recognise had delivered her to the front doors of a large house and handed her over without ceremony to the waiting party, this man, whom Lincoln had called Brightwell, and five other men, clearly his subordinates. Andrea had been dragged unceremoniously up the stairs to one of the rooms at the rear of the house. The man—tall and thin with blond hair—watched silently as two of his team tied her to an old metal bedframe. He seemed to direct them with only a flick of his skeletal fingers or slight nod of his head.

All of his five-man team were nearly identical, but looked nothing like their leader. All small wiry men with cropped black hair and high cheekbones. Only their eyes moved, the hard faces remaining static. Each man wore an identical uniform, a dark maroon jumpsuit without insignia or rank, and carried a large pistol on their right hip and a combat knife on their left.

The leader drummed his fingers in a wave pattern against his opposite fist as he watched the proceedings. Once his team had left the room, he carefully checked that Andrea's bonds were tight. Suddenly his gaunt face sprang into focus mere inches from her own. The speed and surprise of his sudden movement made her cry out in fright. He reached out and gently placed two fingers against the side of her throat. She could feel her pulse hammering against his cold fingertips. He gave her a thin smile that did not reach his eyes. His breath smelled of copper and garlic and stale tobacco.

She shuddered in response to his touch. His fingertips felt like wet worms on her skin. He stepped back and Andrea looked around the room. The furniture was covered with dustsheets, vague shapes comprised of humps and angles. The bedframe she was tied to was propped against what might have been a wardrobe. She had been tied in the classic spread-eagle position with her limbs stretched out diagonally. The cords that held her to the bedframe bit into her skin as she instinctively pulled at her bonds.

"That's it, girl, fight against it." The man's voice was English, cultured. He did not smile but his fingers drummed continuously against each other as he allowed his gaze to move over Andrea's body. She squirmed under his scrutiny as if being violated. "Always better when they fight."

Andrea forced herself to take deep breaths. Her heart bumped loudly in her chest. She watched the tall man pace back and forth in front of her, his fingers drumming and twitching like some freaky piano player. His face was gaunt, dark circles under his deep-set eyes. He stood as tall as Clay, but while the Texan was big and broad the man in front of her was almost skeletal. His skin was pallid and his blond hair was styled into gelled spiky tufts. He wore black skin-tight Lycra workout gear. It reminded her of the cyclists in the Tour de France.

She felt a sense of defiance rise. "You look like a male model for a fucking pipe-cleaner company."

The tall man's fingers halted their staccato drumming as he glared at her.

"My friends are going to come here and kill you. You and your little minions are all going to die horribly."

The tall man laughed and shook his head. "I like your spirit. It'll be fun breaking you. Your faith in your friends is misplaced, however. They're already dead. There's no one to save you, Miss Chambers. No one at all. You're mine for however long I decide to keep you alive." He added a Shakespearean flourish to his already cultured accent. "There is, I fear, no tomorrow for you, my dear."

The man moved to a camera set upon a tripod in the corner of the room. "Now let's get better acquainted. I'm sure you heard that Neanderthal Lincoln refer to me as 'Brightwell'. And, indeed, I have a British passport in the name of Marcus Brightwell." He paused, and Andrea shrank from the pleasure in his eyes. "But that was a name I took for expediency. My brother understandably didn't want to be associated with my chosen profession. He always was one for outward appearances."

He ran his hand through his blond hair, and smiled at Andrea. "I was born Jensen Strathclyde. I believe you had something that belongs to me." He held up the flash drive, turning the small cartridge around in his fingers. "This is a real blast from the past. Haven't seen this one for ages."

Andrea gritted her teeth as his words hit home. "Strathclyde?"

"Yes, Stewart and I are brothers. I know we look nothing like each other. He takes after my mother's side."

"Different looks, same brand of psychopathic arsehole!"

Raising his hands with an almost camp flourish, he responded, "We are what we are."

"You're dead, soon, that's what *you* are!"

Jensen Strathclyde smiled fully for the first time, showing small but perfectly white teeth, returning his attention to the camera. "These things are so much better, and smaller than they used to be. Do you remember the old camcorders? Some of them were bigger than a shoebox. And clunky to use. Do you remember those big old VHS tapes that went inside?"

Andrea watched him slip a mask over the top half of his face. The mask was an old-style executioner's cap. His eyes and lower jaw stood out in stark contrast to the black material. He tapped the mask and again smiled. "It's surprising what you can find on eBay these days." He pressed the record button on the mounted camera, which was connected to a laptop by a cable. A small red light went on.

"You were the man behind the camera in that old video, weren't you?" Andrea, making the connection. Jensen clapped his hands slowly in mocking response.

A surgical scalpel seemed to appear in his hand; she

hadn't seen him pick it up. He brandished the implement with pride. "Number ten blade. Teflon-coated shaft. The blade makes cutting almost effortless. Now we are going to have some fun. I'm going to ask you some questions and you are going to tell me the truth, the whole truth and nothing but." He laughed. "Not the questions TSI think I'm going to ask, of course. It was a neat trick convincing that fool Carter to give me this assignment. No, I shan't be asking you about Stewart. But I do want to know how many others have seen that film."

"Freak."

Jensen continued as if he had not heard her. "Did you know that both the ancient Egyptians and the Mayans made knives from obsidian? One of the sharpest substances in the natural world. But these last longer, much more hard-wearing."

Andrea involuntarily closed her eyes as he took a step closer. She could feel the heat radiating from his body as he pressed in close without yet physically touching her. The blade hovered an inch from her face. She released a breath she didn't realise she'd been holding as he finally stepped away. The grin from below his mask was full of satisfaction. Anger surged through her as she pulled again at her bindings. "Freak!"

Jensen's hand flicked out like a snake's tongue and the scalpel bit deep into Andrea's eyebrow. Andrea gave out a screech despite clenching her teeth tightly together. She felt a trail of warm blood run down the left side of her face. Abject terror threatened to shut down her senses yet still she remained defiant. "Danny and Clay are going to kill you when they get here and I'll be standing over you when they do."

A patronising smile spread across Jensen Strathclyde's

face. "I think not, my dear. Your two bully boys are probably shark bait by now. Last I heard they were full of holes and squealing like stuck pigs."

"We'll see."

"If I were you, I would be far less concerned with those two and more with what is about to happen to you." Jensen pressed his nose against hers, his voice filled with contempt. "You must have watched the film on the flash drive by now. Have you any idea how long I can keep you alive? I'm going to enjoy opening you up and hearing your screams. My brother was the master back in the day, but now I'm better than him at this. I can peel you like an orange, piece by piece."

Andrea winced as he slipped the blade inside her shirt, the scalpel like ice against her skin. In a few deft motions she was effectively naked from the waist up. Then the blade bit into her skin. Slow and deliberate, he dragged the scalpel across the centre of her sternum. Dark blood trickled in the wake of the blade, the wound opening like a crimson teardrop. The incision was less than two inches long but bled profusely. Her chest began to burn as if it were being attacked by a dozen angry hornets.

Something deep inside Andrea Chambers changed for ever at that moment. A violent creature that she'd never experienced before emerged as if from a cocoon. Fury on a primordial level ripped through her like a tsunami. The scream that sprang from her was not one of fear but of defiance. "NO! I'm going to be the one who kills *you*, you worthless piece of shit!"

Jensen Strathclyde stepped back for a second, clearly pleased at her outburst. He turned and smiled at the camera, holding the pose like a film star. "Are you getting this, brother? Oh, I wish you were here so we could share this one between us like we used to."

Andrea followed his gaze. "Don't tell me, your fucker of a brother is watching us. Tossing himself off, no doubt!"

"Live from our London studios," said Jensen in a mocking American accent.

Andrea strained towards the camera, feeling the tendons in her neck standing out like ropes. "After I kill this motherfucker, I'm going to find you and kill *you* as well!"

The red light on the camera remained steady and in Andrea's mind came to represent Stewart Strathclyde's voyeuristic avatar. He was that red light. A scourge to women everywhere. How many lives had the two Strathclydes taken between them? How many families mourned their lost wives, sisters and daughters? Strathclyde was that light. A light that she was determined to extinguish.

54

Danny slipped over the fence unseen. Rain soaked his clothes in seconds, causing them to cling like a second skin. He ignored the cold, knowing it would counter the heat caused by the adrenalin surging through his body. He stayed close to the western edge of the grounds, running full tilt with his weapon held close to his body. He pushed thoughts of a sniper on the roof from his mind. There was no time for a cautious approach. The harsh reality was that if there was a sniper, he was dead anyway. His feet slipped and skidded in the wet grass but he stayed upright.

He reached the side of the red-brick mansion unhindered. As his breathing slowed he checked the magazine on Kennedy's M4. Twenty-five of the full thirty rounds remained. He thumbed the selector switch to three-round bursts. Every shot would have to count. Eight bursts of fire, then it would be up to him to improvise. He still had five left in the Glock pistol. He would have preferred many more, but he knew that dead men tended to drop their weapons. Crouching low, he passed a window on the side of the house.

Stealing a glance inside, he saw an empty room.

He pressed a hand against the window but it was fastened securely. Despite what most people believed from watching action movies, jumping through a window was not a great way of entering a hostile building. Most of the time you would just bounce off the glass and look really stupid. If you did succeed it was a quick way of severing vital body parts. Danny moved on, lowering his head in an effort to keep the rain from obscuring his vision.

He made his way to the back of the house and found a door. He tested the handle with a slow pressure and the mechanism turned slow and easy. He went through the doorway low and fast, the barrel of the stubby M4 moving in a tight arc. A voice from the past echoed in his mind: "Where the eyes look, the weapon points."

He was in a utility room that led into a wider kitchen area. The left wall was taken up with a rusty washing machine, tumble dryer and a set of racked shelving, on which boxes of ancient detergent and household cleaning materials had been abandoned.

Danny moved into the kitchen. The sound of the rain beating against the windows was a constant annoying rattle. The room was dominated by a large utility island in the centre above which a few dusty pots and pans hung from a rectangular display rail. Danny moved around it, pausing to listen for any telltale sounds from the doorway beyond. He blanked out the timpani of the pounding rain. Nothing. He crept forward as fast as he could without making any noise, keeping his weight balanced and constant, and moved deeper into the interior of the house.

A man stepped through the doorway at the same moment and they collided in a tangle of limbs.

Danny stepped back, his head ringing from the unexpected impact and through sheer instinct fired off a tight three-round burst. The man yelled out as he took one of the rounds through the muscle of his right shoulder. He too dodged backwards, putting the doorframe between him and Danny. Seconds later a hand brandishing an angular Glock snaked around the frame and loosed off a rapid series of six shots. Sparks flew from kitchen counters and cooking pots as several of the bullets ricocheted. Danny winced as one of the bullets tore a tuft of hair from his scalp. Sighting on the hand, he squeezed the trigger on the M4. The pistol, along with an explosion of blood and fingers, was ejected high into the air.

The man's mouth was wide open in a silent scream when Danny stepped through the doorway. He gagged as the barrel of the M4 was inserted deep into his open mouth, the flesh of his tongue and throat sizzling from the heat of the weapon.

"Where's the girl?" Danny's voice was like a blade on a whetstone. The man tried to speak but the bullet that tore the back of his head free from the rest of his body ended that intent in a fraction of a second. "Don't bother, I'll find her myself."

Scowling, Danny moved on. So much for the element of surprise. He had no way of knowing how many enemies were in the house. In way of testimony three more faces appeared at the far end of the entrance hall that was divided by a large central staircase. Each man held a Glock pistol and all three commenced firing at the same time.

Danny scooted sideways using the base of the stairs as

cover. The men spread out in a loose curving line, moving forward constantly. Two of the men kept on firing as the third reloaded his pistol.

Danny knew they would be on him in moments. With a defiant roar he returned fire with the M4. The three men dived for cover of their own as the fearsome carbine spat death in their direction.

Danny risked a glance upwards and saw that the stairs led up to a long landing with a balustrade running its length. Shit, if any shooters were up there then he was a dead man. The landing gave an ideal vantage point. He needed to move. But the three men were disciplined and were keeping him pinned down by their constant rate of fire. The only option he had was to backpedal into the kitchen.

The harsh stutter of the M4 was drowned out by an explosion of wood, masonry and glass as the front of the house seemed to disintegrate.

The three men tumbled away from the carnage, their faces masks of surprise. The scoop bucket of a JCB rose to its full height then smashed down again, obliterating the wall to the left of the front door. Through the dirt-covered window of the mechanical beast, Clay's face was an angry white smear.

The closest of the men raised his pistol, targeting Clay. His shot went high into the doorway as Danny emerged from his cover and sent another volley at the trio. The JCB powered through the rubble, its heavy caterpillar tracks crushing the bricks and mortar easily. Then the cab of the machine was inside the house. Its hydraulic arm rose high, sending out another shower of debris, then again crashed down into the midst of the three men. All three scattered in different directions. The teeth of the scoop shattered the ornately tiled floor.

Inside the cab of the JCB, Clay growled and muttered curses as the three little bastards dodged and sent a hail of bullets into the machine's windshield. The toughened glass held for the first half-dozen shots then hot lead began to get through. A ricochet cut a long furrow down his chest before drilling into the thick muscle of Clay's thigh.

Two of the men were now to his left and were reloading their weapons while the third had scrabbled backwards away from the machine. Clay steered the metal behemoth in the direction of the two to his left. Both men continued their assault, sending shot after shot into the cab. He saw the third shooter send a wild shot in Danny's direction then jump onto an ornate armoire and using this as a platform, vault high onto the side of the staircase, taking the upper ground above Danny. Both men fired simultaneously, and Clay saw Danny stumble as a bullet bit through the flesh of his right hip. His opponent crumpled back onto the stairs gasping for breath. His pistol dropped from his hand and clattered down several steps. He was doing a fair impression of a crab on its back, arms and legs waving in the air. Danny squeezed the trigger of his own weapon but it didn't fire. Empty!

The man on the stairs grinned and ripped a combat knife from the sheath at his waist, launching himself bodily down the stairs before Danny could reload the carbine. Clay gasped, but his attention was then firmly drawn back to the two other men, who had reloaded and resumed their assault on the

JCB. He tried to crush the little fuckers with the bucket of the earthmover but they managed to evade the saurian jaws by continuously dodging back and forth while keeping up a constant rate of fire with their pistols. Then both clambered onto the body of the JCB. Clay managed to dislodge one man at the front of the cab with a desperate jerk of the steering wheel. The machine lurched forward and the man tumbled from view. The second man swung the cab door open, clearly hoping for a clean shot to end the fight. As the JCB pitched to the right he struggled to maintain his balance and clung to the door handle for support.

Clay launched himself out of the cab at the gunman, sweeping the man's Glock up and away with the edge of his hand. Both men bumped painfully over the heavy segmented tracks and landed in a heap amidst the rubble. Clay secured a hold on his opponent's throat and began to squeeze. A noise from behind made him turn his head. The second man had rounded the cab and was rushing at him, a knife held high.

55

Jensen Strathclyde was considering his options. He was sure that the contents of the flash drive had not been posted online. He'd searched the web relentlessly as soon as he'd received the call from Stewart. And even if it made it to YouTube or CNN, it would likely be dismissed as a fake. On the off chance questions were asked, other versions with obvious CGI manipulation would be posted online, discrediting the original. It had worked many times before and was standard practice. And everyone knew that snuff films were an urban legend.

So it came down to business as usual. He had carried out many interrogations on behalf of TSI, some of which had ended in termination, but this time it was different. This time he was going off script; he would have some fun. Stewart had always run the show during their joint exploits, taking the dominant role and only letting Jensen participate after most of the real fun had been had. Jensen had operated the camera on six of their kills but had only taken the lead once. This was his time to shine. Stewart was on the other side of the Atlantic, reduced to the role of voyeur via video-streaming. Sure, he would get to see all the action but this time he would not get to dictate it. And he could see what his brother had learned...

Jensen looked over Andrea's exposed torso. He leaned in close and slowly inhaled. A faint perfume and a slightly acrid aroma combined. It was often said that animals could smell fear. Jensen felt sure he shared that ability. The bitch in front of him reeked of it. He tapped the cold blade of the scalpel against her nipples in an alternating rhythm. He inspected the trails of blood that still trickled from Andrea's brow and chest.

"You ever play 'eeny meeny' as a child?"

"Fuck you."

"Eeny, meeny, miny moe, catch a bitch-whore by the toe."

"You fucking insect. What's wrong? Your mother never loved you? Your father abused you?"

Jensen smiled. "If you think I'm going to lose it and kill you quickly you'd better think again. And forget being rescued. Those two cowboys are already dead."

From below came the unmistakable sound of gunfire. Jensen turned, the blade in his hand momentarily forgotten. Then a deafening crash shook the floor beneath his feet. Jesus, had a bomb gone off?

The woman's lip curled back in a snarl. "Dead already, eh?"

Jensen raced to the bedroom door, the flaps of his executioner's cap bouncing as he ran. He crossed the short landing and peered over the balustrade at the carnage below. A mixture of fear and fury swept through him. The front of the house was in ruins. This was not how it was supposed to be! He turned and stalked back to the woman. It just wasn't fair. This was supposed to be his day, his time to step out from Stewart's shadow.

Andrea's heart beat hard against her ribcage. Dare she hope she might survive after all? She felt a mixture of relief and vindication; Clay and Danny were not only still alive but fighting to rescue her. Strathclyde burst back into the room, swearing. "You're fucking dead, bitch."

Andrea closed her eyes involuntarily as he raised the gleaming blade as if to slash her throat open. But no lethal blow came. She released her breath. The executioner's cap swivelled from side to side in indecision.

"You're my insurance if those fuckers manage to make it past my men." He wrapped his hand through Andrea's hair, wrenching it as he pressed the scalpel against her neck. "You as much as twitch and I'll gut you from arsehole to breakfast time!"

He sliced through the bonds that held her limbs, then used her hair and the blade at her throat to steer her out of the door and onto the landing. Andrea wrapped her now free hands over her exposed breasts as he tightened his grip on her hair. Her hand came away crimson. She tried to turn and drive her knee into his groin but the scalpel at her throat sliced into the underside of her chin as Jensen hissed a warning. Her legs felt like they were being controlled by some external force as she was guided puppet-like to the balustrade that overlooked the entrance hall. Her hands and feet tingled painfully as circulation resumed.

"Want to see your friends die?" Jensen wrenched her hair

to emphasise his question. He forced her forward, pressing his groin tight into her backside and pinning her legs against the railing.

The sight that greeted her was unbelievable. A huge bulldozer had crashed through the front of the house. Bricks, mortar, splintered wood and glass lay everywhere, and a cloud of grey dust hung in the air. Bullets cut the air and sparks flew from repeated shots aimed at the cab of the bulldozer.

One of Jensen's men leapt over the rail midway up the stairs, pointing his pistol at Danny. *Boom!* Both men went down.

"Danny!" Andrea screamed.

Jensen laughed in her ear, then kissed the side of her bloodied face. "One down, one to go!" Despair gripped her heart as Danny staggered. Jesus Christ, could he really be dead?

On the far side of the bulldozer, Clay was on top of one of Jensen's men. Another was on his back, stabbing over and over with a knife.

All is lost.

Jensen was still leaning over her. "Well that was an entertaining interlude. Now, back to business."

As he pulled on her hair, Andrea went with the force and slammed the back of her head into his face. Caught off guard, he stumbled back, loosening his controlling hold. The scalpel dragged across the side of Andrea's jaw, cutting deep as it glanced off the bone. She continued to turn, swiping her fingernails at his eyes. She missed as he staggered back, holding his nose. A kick directed at his groin connected but only her toes made real contact as he dodged. He grabbed at her hair again but she lunged first one way then the other. A wild sweep with the scalpel cut the air where her face had been a second earlier. Lurching after her, Jensen stumbled, going to his knees as he tried another desperate grab for her hair.

Andrea yelped as she tore along the landing at full tilt. She pushed through the first door she found, which opened onto a steep set of wooden stairs leading upwards. With no other choice available to her, she kicked the door closed behind her and raced up the steps. She emerged into a room very much like the one she'd just been dragged from, filled with dustsheet-covered furniture. But there was a window, its glass battered by the relentless rain. As she wrestled with the latch she heard the door to the stairs wrenched open below. He was coming.

There was no time to force the latch. She picked up a small stool and smashed the window out of its frame, then climbed out. She felt like she'd stepped into an industrial carwash, such was the force of the pelting rain. She was on a flat walkway that encircled the uppermost part of the roof, the only barrier between her and open air a set of iron railings. A quick glance over the edge left her in no doubt that a fall from this height would leave her broken on the ground far below. Steadying herself by placing one hand on the railings and the other against the sloping roof tiles, she scooted away from the window.

Jensen Strathclyde held out the scalpel, ready to stab or slash if the woman tried to blindside him. The bitch had got lucky with that head-butt but no way was she going to get him twice. He padded up the stairs light and easy at first, then the crash of breaking glass spurred him into a run. He reached the top of the stairs and entered a room just in time to see the bitch's naked back disappearing through a window.

If she was on the walkway she could get to the fire escape. But there was no way this cow was getting away from him now. He'd catch her on the roof and either drag her back inside or, if needs be, just gut her and call it quits. Jensen ran to the window and poked his head out, then immediately retreated in case the woman had a weapon. But even the quick glance revealed the woman clambering along the widow's walk like some terrified child. He felt himself grow stiff at the thought.

He climbed out into the storm. Out of sheer instinct he grabbed for the railings. The force of the wind and rain was savage, and he found himself struggling to stay on his feet. The sky had turned a battleship grey and the lights from the town in the distance were reduced to indistinct blotches of pale orange. He swore as he saw his target turn a corner and vanish out of sight.

Strathclyde started after her, then paused. He looked up at the sloping roof. If he could get over it he could cut her off as she made her way around the circumference of the house. With his scalpel clenched in his teeth, he began to climb.

56

Danny Gunn raised his empty carbine as the man armed with a combat knife launched himself down the stairs. The blade glanced off the M4 but the man immediately twisted and stabbed at Danny's exposed hands. Dodging the blow by mere inches, Gunn used his weapon as a stave and jabbed the barrel into his opponent's face. The M4's front sights clattered against the man's teeth, rocking his head back, but still he fought on. The man's arms were a blur of motion as he tried to grab the carbine with his free hand and slash with the other. In response Danny swung the M4 like a baseball bat, climbing the stairs one by one. Swing, step, swing, step.

After a few exchanges Danny waited for the man to surge forward. He didn't have to wait for long. His opponent kept up a blistering pace and was not to be underestimated. As he sprang forward with a slash to Danny's throat, the Scotsman used the additional length of his carbine to his advantage, swinging it in a wide horizontal swipe. The man ducked low under the M4 and kept on moving—into Danny's stamp kick. The heel of his boot caught the man just below his nose, smashing nasal bones deep into his skull. The man toppled down the stairs and Danny followed, making sure he stayed down by driving the butt of the M4 repeatedly into his ruined face. Unbelievably the man raised his knife as if to throw it. Danny kicked out one last time, this time driving the man's head back against the edge of the bottom step. Vertebrae crunched and the knife dropped from lifeless fingers.

Clay was fighting for his life, one man beneath him and another coming up fast behind him, knife in hand. The blade tore a ragged line across his shoulders. Clay roared and struck back with an elbow, turning his whole body as he did so. The man on his back forced the blade deeper into Clay's flesh, but the point became wedged against his shoulder blade. The man lost his grip and was sent sprawling as Clay clipped him hard in the face with another elbow jab.

The pain in Clay's broken feet was almost intolerable yet he forced himself forward. He grabbed the first man who was reaching for his fallen Glock and caught him mid-motion, one hand around his throat and the other tightened into a vice around the man's groin. Hoisting his screeching opponent like a power-lifter, Clay raised him above his head and threw him at the second man. Both went down amidst bricks and shattered timber.

Charging forward, Clay caught both men up in one massive sweep of his arms, their backs pressed together. A couple of violent shakes and Clay had them in the classic bear hug wrestling hold. The Texan felt his vision swim momentarily but held on tight, his arms like a steel band around the operatives. One of the two had an arm free but his blows were delivered from an ineffective angle and were little more than backhanded slaps. Clay wrenched with all of his remaining strength. Both men struggled furiously, kicking and thrashing, but inch by inch Clay's arms constricted, crushing their ribcages. He felt bones snap beneath his corded muscles. He stumbled, his back grinding painfully against the tracks of the JCB, but he held on.

Clay felt his legs fold beneath him and all three men slumped to the ground. The two killers slipped from his grasp. One lay dead, pink bubbles trickling slowly from his mouth. The other stared up at the Texan with hate-filled eyes. His hand closed around a ragged spar of wood. Clay slashed the edge of his open hand across the man's throat, crushing his trachea into his spine. Then all three men were silent.

Danny's head snapped up at the sound of a woman's scream. It seemed to be coming from above, but there was no sign of Andrea. He risked a glance over to Clay, who had snatched up the two other men and was shaking them like rag dolls.

Switching from the now empty M4 to the Glock at his waist, he slung the carbine onto his back and raced up the stairs. He paused on the landing. Several doors stood to either side of the main staircase. He was faced with a simple choice: left or right.

The choice was made for him when yet another jumpsuited man stepped out onto the landing A space of ten feet or so separated the two men. Danny brought up his pistol and squeezed the trigger. Twin holes appeared in the wall as with surprising agility the man pivoted the top half of his body then in one continuous motion leapt forward in a combat roll. Danny had never seen anyone move as fast. One second he was standing motionless ten feet away, the next he was coming up under his guard and pushing Danny's weapon towards the ceiling. Danny felt his heels teeter on the edge of the stairs. Rather than go down backwards, he broke the hold and ran down the steps, turning at the bottom, gun raised.

A hand slammed into Danny's throat like a piece of iron. The man was fast! Danny struggled to take a breath as his trachea constricted in response to the tiger mouth strike. But his opponent pressed home the attack with relentless determination. Danny felt the man seize his wrist and twist it to breaking point in an effort to disarm him. Instead of resisting the wristlock, Danny dropped to one knee, his gun hand now above his head, drawing his adversary over his back. As the man was sent tumbling over his shoulder, Danny's pistol spat out another three shots. He scowled as the slide bucked back; the magazine was empty.

The shoulder throw would have at least stunned most men, but Danny's opponent landed not on his back but in a crouch, and again sent a killer blow at his throat. Danny blocked the throat shot with his right elbow and slashed his pistol backhand across the man's face. The open slide of the pistol gouged a deep furrow into his cheek, sending him reeling towards the kitchen area. It was Danny's turn to press the attack as the operative snatched his own Glock from the holster at his hip. Using his empty pistol again as a club, Danny brought the weapon down on the man's hand. The thumb snapped with an audible crack. Without losing any momentum Danny seized the broken hand with a vice-like grip and smashed his empty pistol into the man's upturned face.

Yet the man did not fall, and the barrel of his Glock inched closer to Danny's body as they butted and gouged at each other. With a last effort Danny charged, picking the man up bodily and propelling him backwards, through the doorway where his first opponent lay dead, and into the kitchen beyond.

57

The cold took Andrea's breath away as she clambered along the narrow platform of the widow's walk. She felt herself slip towards the edge of the roof as rain blasted into her face. Her numb hands found the wrought-iron railings and she clung motionless until she felt steady again. Squinting against the downpour she turned in time to see Jensen Strathclyde emerge from the window onto the walkway. She silently wished for a bolt of lightning to fry the bastard. She continued to claw her way along until she turned the corner of the roof and the storm seemed to reach a new level of intensity, the rain slapping into her like a solid wall. Forcing herself forward she inched along at what seemed like a snail's pace. The wounds on her face and chest buzzed with an angry life of their own. Her mind flitted momentarily back to the overlook at Area 51, where this nightmare had begun. It seemed like a lifetime ago. Were Greg and Bruce lying in some mortuary cold room? Had her parents read her email? Did they even know that their son was dead yet?

Her mind snapped back to the present as she spotted

a point thirty feet along the walkway. A pair of curving handrails indicated the top of a fire-escape ladder. Andrea, spurred on by the real chance of flight, renewed her efforts.

Her moment of hope turned to one of horror as Jensen Strathclyde slid down the rain-slicked roof onto the walkway in front of her. He looked like a ghoul, in his bizarre black bodysuit and mask. Only twenty feet or so separated her from the safety of the ladder. The twenty feet might well have been a thousand. He advanced towards her, but, more intent on reaching her than his footing, Strathclyde slipped and clung to the railings for support. Andrea started to backpedal, went round the corner again, and then turned and ran back towards the shattered window. She heard him curse behind her as she threw herself through the window frame, ending up on all fours with a wide sliver of broken glass in her hand. Her legs wobbled as she forced herself upright.

Andrea began to pick her way through the maze of covered furniture when she felt an icy hand grip her neck from behind. She was spun around in a tight circle to see Jensen's leering face above her. He raised the scalpel.

"No escape this time, bitch." He gave a contented sigh, then stabbed down at her unprotected throat.

58

Danny wrapped an arm around his opponent's legs and drove his shoulder deep into his midsection. Powering forward, both men crashed through the kitchen and into the utility room beyond. After bouncing painfully off the top of the washing machine, the man was momentarily airborne, then Danny slammed him down to the floor. As the man reeled from the impact, his head bouncing sharply on the tiles, Danny's kick sent the Glock spinning from his grasp. The gun slid under a shelving unit at the far side of the room. A second kick, this one aimed at the man's face, was partially blocked by his hastily crossed forearms. Without pause the man kicked out in return, his feet striking Danny painfully in the shins. Springing back in order to avoid being upended, Danny snatched up a large bottle of bleach and used it as an impromptu bludgeon to beat the man around the head, landing three solid shots before the man rolled to one side and drew the knife from his belt. He held the knife point-down in his left hand with his injured right close to his chest.

Danny intercepted the first stab with a swipe of the

plastic bottle. The second strike pierced the plastic with a solid thump. As the knife was pulled free Danny squeezed the bottle, sending a stream of bleach at the operative's face. The man ducked to avoid being blinded but liquid saturated his hair and ran over the back of his head, causing him to screw his eyes tight shut as he raked his sleeve across his face. Danny raised the bottle and sent it bouncing off the head of the man, who swore. The language was alien to Danny but the sentiment was all too clear.

Danny aimed another kick at his opponent's groin, and as the knife descended, twisted his leg in a tight arc away from the knife and snapped a roundhouse kick into the side of the man's exposed jaw, sending him crashing into a shelving unit. Cans and bottles were sent flying, rolling around the floor at their feet. The look on the man's face as he righted himself was one of unbridled fury. His skin was burned red from the bleach, and his lips were curled back, exposing his teeth.

"Come on then you little fuck-nut." Danny's challenge sent his opponent into a blind rage. Calculated attacks gave way to wild slashes with the blade, each less considered than the last. Danny let a slash pass over his head and moved closer. As the momentum of the swing caused the man's body to twist, Danny drove him to the floor and clung to him like an alligator wrestler. He repeatedly knocked the knife hand against the side of the washing machine until it dropped. The operative bucked and thrashed, trying desperately to throw Danny off him, his free hand scrabbling under the shelving unit, reaching for his Glock.

Danny snatched up the nearest weapon: an aerosol can of spray starch. He smashed the can into the side of his opponent's face, sending the cap flying, then inverted his grip so the can was upside down. He shook the can vigorously as he depressed the spray button, holding it tight against the man's face, expelling the propellant agent difluoroethane as a freezing liquid rather than a gas.

The effect was devastating. The operative thrashed like a man possessed for long seconds then succumbed to the poisonous effects of the spray, his nasal tissues frozen, his lungs in spasm. He managed to reach out and take hold of Danny's collar but there was no strength left in his grip. A frosted coating of white residue covered the lower half of his face and protruding tongue as he gave a last choking shudder, then lay still. The Glock spat out a final impotent shot as the dead man's fist tightened. The bullet drilled a neat hole in the white enamelled front of the washing machine, the retort deafening in the small room.

Danny continued to press down on the aerosol until it was empty and only then did he climb to his feet with a disgruntled sigh. "You stay there and chill out."

59

Andrea watched as the scalpel stabbed down towards her, almost in slow motion.

Yet the razor edge of the scalpel never reached her exposed neck. Jensen's face contorted as he tried to push Andrea away, but she had one hand wound tight into the fabric of his Lycra bodysuit. The scalpel fell from his grasp. Looking first down in disbelief, he then locked gazes with her. "No…"

Andrea gripped the base of the long shard of glass that she'd snatched up as she'd tumbled through the window. The rest was buried deep in Strathclyde's gut. She twisted it, the edge cutting into her hand. Jensen screamed, a high-pitched and extended wail of agony. Andrea pushed him back against a wardrobe. His legs began to buckle but she pressed him harder.

"From arsehole to breakfast time!"

Andrea spat his earlier threat back in his face as she pulled up on the glass shard with all of her remaining strength. The Lycra of his bodysuit parted as if being unzipped, the glass cutting upward through his entrails. It took a full five seconds for the shard to become wedged under his ribcage. Pink blood frothed at his lips as he offered a pleading, "Stop…"

"It's because of you and your motherfucking brother that *my* brother is dead. See how you like it!" Andrea wrenched her hand to one side and felt the shard splinter deep inside his torso. The glass that remained in her hand was barely the length of her thumb. She let it fall from her lacerated hand.

Taking two steps back, she watched Jensen drop first to his knees, his blood and entrails spilling from the front of his suit, then topple face down. He lay motionless. She cradled her bleeding hand; only now did the pain begin to creep from the cuts on her palm. Staring at the dead body, days of pent-up emotion washed over her like a tidal wave. Deep, racking sobs shook her and tears spilled freely down her face. Then she bent over and vomited.

When the heaving had finally subsided, she looked back at the corpse, and experienced an irrational fear that he would sit up like some monster from a slasher movie. She felt both horror and revulsion that she'd taken a life, which conflicted deeply with the euphoric sense of victory over her would-be murderer. Her legs felt unsteady as her adrenalin levels began to recede. With a deep tremble taking hold of her limbs, she became aware of her semi-naked state. Wrapping a hand over her breasts, she ran down the stairs, through the door and onto the landing that overlooked the entrance hall.

And straight into Danny Gunn.

Danny was battered, bleeding and looked slightly dazed. He was holding a pistol in a preparatory position, but lowered it as soon as their eyes met.

"Andrea!"

She could do little more than give a slow blink in way of response.

Danny covered the distance between them in three loping strides and pulled her close. Their lips pressed tight against each other. The kiss and long embrace were of comfort rather than passion.

"Are they all dead?" she asked.

"I think so, but we'd better get out of here just in case."

"Okay."

Suddenly his eyes darted around urgently. "Where's the guy they delivered you to?"

"Dead." Andrea grimaced. "I killed him."

Danny embraced her again. "Good on you, girl."

"He was another Strathclyde." She took a deep breath and explained the relationship between Stewart and her torturer.

"Two psychos in one family. Shit, that's bad. I bet their parents are proud. And he was the cameraman on the video? Fucking unbelievable."

Andrea wiped a hand along the line of her jaw. The skin was raised and slightly puckered where Jensen's blade had cut her. The wound was raw and painful and the blood that came away on her palm was thick and beginning to coagulate. Her whole body ached.

"Where's Clay?"

Danny released Andrea from his embrace and stared over the balustrade at the hall below. A cold hand gripped his heart as he spotted Clay lying amid the rubble of the ruined portico. He lay face down, arms spread out either side in a crucifix position, on top of the two men he had been fighting.

"Clay!"

Danny tore down the stairs, taking them four at a time. The three bodies were unmoving. The two jumpsuited men were lying twisted into shapes that spoke of death. A wide gash had opened Clay's back along the length of his shoulder blade. Danny felt dread spread through his body at the thought of losing his brother. He pushed the Glock into the waistband of his trousers and crouched by his brother. Clay had fifty pounds on him, and Danny struggled to turn the limp body over. Clay's face was covered with a thick coating of brick dust, darkened in places to a sticky blackness where it had mingled with blood.

Danny pressed two fingers to the side of his brother's throat. The pulse he felt was like a drumbeat against his fingertips. A whisper escaped Danny's lips. "Thank you, God."

Danny began vigorously shaking Clay, who eventually opened his eyes. Cracking a half smile, Clay groaned, "Did I miss the end of the party?"

"'Fraid so, big bro."

Danny helped Clay sit up. The Texan looked around at the carnage. "Sorry I was a bit late. The JCB wouldn't start."

"No problem. You did just fine."

Andrea crouched by Clay's side, hugging him with one arm and covering herself with the other. "Clay."

"Hey, darlin'."

"Hey yourself." She planted a kiss on the side of his face, which elicited a tired wink and a smile. "What are you doing lying down on the job?"

Clay frowned in mock insult, slapping his palm against

the track of the JCB. "I was doing okay but I seem to have banged my head on the side of this jalopy."

"With a head like yours I'm surprised the JCB is still standing." Danny cuffed his brother lightly.

Clay rose on unsteady legs, assisted on both sides by Danny and Andrea. "Are they all dead?"

Andrea effected a fair imitation of Danny's thick Scottish accent. "As disco-dancing dodos!"

All three were still laughing as Lincoln and another man stepped into view, weapons levelled and ready to fire.

60

"Does this shit never end?" groaned Andrea.

Lincoln looked around the entrance hall, a Calico assault pistol pointed at Danny's head. "You really made a mess here."

Danny snorted and cocked his head at the man next to Lincoln. "Who's your friend?"

"Oh, this is Chad. You may remember him. He ran you over."

Danny curled his lip. "So, what now?" He eased away from Clay, slow and steady, as he spoke.

"I came back to end this. I got a call from my boss. The assignment is cancelled." Lincoln stared hard at the trio, his face like stone. Hard and professional.

"Cancelled?" asked Danny.

"Aborted. Terminated. Cancelled."

"So someone finally showed some sense. This was a clusterfuck from the start."

Lincoln gave a nod. "The man that initiated the contract did so without official sanction. He used the company for his own interests."

"Well, that's never happened before." Danny's retort was drier than Sahara sand.

"Seems he was found dead in a London hotel room." Danny heard Andrea give a short gasp. If both Strathclydes were now dead, perhaps her life could now return to some sort of normality. "Seems he died while taking part in some sort of sicko sex game. He was found hanging in the closet with ropes around his neck and genitals. And a lot of electrical burns on his junk."

Danny remembered what had happened to Andrea's friend, Jeremy Seeber. It was not the first nor would it be the last time a sex-game scenario was used to tie off a loose end.

"So Strathclyde's really dead." Danny bent forward slightly, hands on hips and let a gobbet of bloody saliva drip from his mouth to the floor. "So where does that leave us? Are we done?"

"The job is," replied Lincoln coldly. "But I went back to the safe house. Saw what you did to my men. And I also got a hold of Clinton. You remember him? The injured man you beat the living shit out of in Nevada? He sends his regards, as does Chavez."

Clay grunted. "I remember Chavez. That one was me. Bendy fingers, that doc had."

Lincoln ignored him. "I was going to walk away, y'know? A job is only a job, right? But you made it personal."

"I take it personal when people try to torture me to death and kill my friends. Kinda grates on my internal ethos," growled Danny. He looked hard at Lincoln's face. He looked a lot like Clint Eastwood had during his Spaghetti Western years. Craggy but still kind of handsome. He smiled to himself as a line from one of Clint's old movies came to mind.

Lincoln extended the Calico, its unusual top-mounted cylindrical magazine full of promised death. "So I had to come back. Put an end to you for my men."

As Danny bent forward again, letting more crimson-tinged spittle fall to the ground, he growled his own version of Clint's words. "Well, are you fuckers gonna shoot those pistols or whistle 'Dixie'?"

The blur of motion as Danny pulled the Glock from his waistband was as fast as he'd ever moved. Then the room exploded with the sounds of death.

Lincoln pitched backwards as a bullet punched through the centre of his face. His finger squeezed the trigger of the Calico as he fell, shots pounding into the ceiling above. Beside him Chad went down on his knees, both hands coming up to his ruined throat. He tried to speak but only a high-pitched whistle sallied forth. He reached out a hand towards Danny.

Danny shot him again without comment or deliberation.

Danny stripped Lincoln's jacket from his body without ceremony and handed it to Andrea. She turned away while she slipped on the garment.

Danny waved a hand at the storm beyond the ruined portico, which still showed no signs of abating. "Come on, then. We need to get out of here. We've still got a pile of shit ahead of us. Too many bodies around here for my liking." He turned to Clay. "I hope your lawyers are as good as you say they are because we're gonna need them."

"Don't you worry Danny boy. They got O.J. off. We'll be a walk in the park."

61

The next three days passed as a blur for Andrea. Countless faces talked at her relentlessly, despite the protestations of the hospital staff. The nurses were great. The cops were dicks. They asked the same things over and over again. Two agents from the FBI showed up on the second day, spouting jurisdiction over the Florida State Police due to the fact that the crimes had crossed many state lines. The locals were pissed but succumbed to the federal gravitas.

She was kept separate from Clay and Danny, but a lawyer provided by Clay harangued the FBI agents whenever they became too forceful with her. Jacob Silverstein was the first lawyer she'd really talked to. She liked him despite his dubious choice of ties. After the first session he could control the agents with little more than a cough and a raised finger. She was very glad he was on her side.

Andrea told the naked truth. She never dressed it up or shied away from the dreadful details. The tears that she spilled while recounting the events came sporadically, but when they did they came in torrents.

On the fourth day she was allowed to see the Gunn brothers.

That was the day Clay received a long-distance call to his bedside phone. The pretty nurse who had been tending to the Texan handed him the receiver with a bemused look. "There's some angry guy called Tansen on the line. Says that you owe him a new house."

Andrea and Danny sat at his bedside. All three had been stitched, sutured and bandaged. The scars on Andrea's face had caused her the most concern. The slash over her eye and the matching wound across her jaw left her looking like she'd been clawed by an angry dinosaur. Large Steri-Strips also decorated her chest, ribs and leg.

Danny also had a large selection of adhesive gauze pads about his person. When Andrea asked how he was feeling he responded with a shrug. "Not the first time I've been patched up and shipped out. Probably not the last, either."

Andrea raised a hand and touched her jaw with tentative fingers. "I know it did really happen but so much of the last week seems like a bad dream. I keep expecting to wake up back home in my flat."

"If this is a dream, I think you should lay off the cheese before bedtime."

She looked at Danny and tried to smile. "What I really mean is that I can't believe I'm still alive after all that happened. I owe you guys my life. I'll never forget that."

"Aye, it's been quite a ride," said Danny.

"That's the understatement of the year!" replied Andrea. "You've been kicked, punched, tortured, shot and stabbed!"

Danny waved his hand dismissively. "I never got stabbed."

"I did," grunted Clay. "Four times in the back. Still, I kind of liked the little guys that attacked me. You could say I had a bit of a crush on them."

"Oh dear," Andrea shook her head in mock upset. "I fear your jokes haven't improved during your period of medication."

Clay shrugged. "I'm hungry. It's been hours since they last fed me."

"It's been twenty minutes." Andrea pointed to the wall-mounted clock to emphasise her point.

"Would you go to the store for me? I'm starving."

Andrea took the twenty offered by the recumbent Texan. "What do you want?"

"See if they've got any Cheetos."

"How many bags do you want if they have?"

"Just buy them all. I'll be here a while."

62

It was another four weeks before Andrea could return to the UK. Her parents had flown out to Florida, which proved to be a very emotional reunion for all. A second trip to Nevada was necessary but soul-searing. Greg and Bruce were officially identified and so began the legal rigmarole of having their bodies transported back to England for burial. Andrea's father wept inconsolably over his dead son. Years of arguments over Greg's sexuality were swept away by his tears.

Andrea, Clay and Danny attended the funerals of Garnett and Edith Bell with heavy hearts. Clay hobbled to the graveside on crutches, his feet still almost unbearable to walk upon. He had stubbornly refused a wheelchair, saying he needed to stand in tribute to his friends. They had been good people and had died because of their connection to Andrea and the Gunns.

When Andrea did finally return to England, Danny travelled with her on the long flight home. An hour after landing at London Heathrow, they found themselves in one of the airport coffee shops.

"I can't believe it's all really over," said Andrea. Several passers-by gave her sideways glances as they registered the long rows of stitches in her face. She cradled a steaming cup of coffee in both hands as she regarded her friend and protector.

"It is." Danny blinked a slow sign of affirmation. "You can get back to your life once and for all. No more psychos with knives or guns."

"What about you? Are you going to stay in England for a while?"

"A while… maybe," he said noncommittally.

"You can visit me any time you're in London. My flat is near Clapham Junction and I've got a spare bedroom. You can stop as long as you like."

Danny smiled. "Yeah, I'll keep in touch from time to time, but I warn you I'm not much for emailing or calling on the phone."

"Well, the offer stands. You're welcome in my home any time."

They lapsed into a comfortable silence during which she tried, as she had many times before, to gauge what was going on behind those inscrutable eyes of his. Something Greg used to say came to mind: *still waters run deep.*

Andrea looked down at her watch with a sad sigh. "I guess I should be getting back. I have to go and see Mum and Dad about Greg's funeral. Will you come?"

"Of course. It's tomorrow, isn't it?"

"Yes."

"I'll be there."

"Thank you Danny… for everything."

Andrea stood, moved around the table and hugged him

for what seemed like ten minutes. Danny waved as she left the coffee shop and merged with the crowds of travellers.

Danny ordered another large coffee and took his time drinking it. He would see Andrea tomorrow. Taking a deep breath, he moved slightly onto his right hip. The burned skin on his ribs had nearly fully healed but still felt tight and uncomfortable at times.

Yes, he would see her tomorrow, but then what?

He looked up at the departure board, showing flights to cities around the world. His eyes fixed on one and he smiled. He knew where he was going.

Draining his coffee, he went to buy a ticket.

Acknowledgements

As with a lot of fiction, I have at times taken liberties with geographical facts and features. That's just the way it is.

The facts about the Hemingway House on Key West are true, however. A very wonky wall indeed! And it's also true that many of the cats in the Keys have thumbs!

The character of Tansen Tibrikot was inspired by a Gurkha I worked with briefly. The story of the train attack is true. It just happened to a different Gurkha.

A big thanks to the following: Matt Hilton for his continued support, help and advice, and Robert Gray for his info on firearms and all things "shootie". Also a big thank you to Kirstie Long who helped set me on the journey, and to my tireless editor Miranda Jewess.

ABOUT THE AUTHOR

James Hilton has written several short stories that have appeared in anthologies both in print and as e-books. A lifelong martial artist, James has studied various arts and is currently ranked as a 4th Dan Blackbelt in Jujitsu and Kempo Karate. He is a frequent visitor to the USA, being particularly fond of all things Floridian and Caribbean. James lives with his wife, Wendy, in the beautiful but rugged north of England. *Search and Destroy* is his first novel.